THE AUTHOR

JACQUES FERRON was born in Louiseville, Quebec, in 1921. The eldest of five children (including his sisters Madeleine, the writer, and Marcelle, the painter), he took the greater part of the classics course at the Jesuit Collège Jean-de-Brébeuf in Montreal, then studied medicine at Laval University from 1941 until 1945. After a brief spell in the Canadian Army, he practiced as a country physician at Rivière-Madeleine in the Gaspé. In 1948 he returned to Montreal and set up his consulting office on the South Shore, where he lived until his death.

From the moment he returned to Montreal, Ferron began to lead a public life, contributing regularly to medical and literary journals and taking an active part in politics. In 1963 he founded his own party, the Rhinoceros Party, designed for the purpose of satirizing the federal political system.

Playwright and essayist, novelist and short story writer, Ferron remembers, especially in his tales, the multifaceted aspects of his cultural heritage. His tales invest the present with the vitality and richness of a strong Québécois past. His first collection won the Governor General's Award for Fiction in 1962.

Jacques Ferron died in Saint-Lamb

TALES FROM THE UNCERTAIN COUNTRY AND OTHER STORIES

JACQUES FERRON

TRANSLATION AND AFTERWORD BY
BETTY BEDNARSKI

Library and Archives Canada Cataloguing in Publication

Ferron, Jacques, 1921-1985

[Tales. English]
    Tales from the uncertain country and other stories / Jacques Ferron ;
afterword by Betty Bednarski ; translated by Betty Bednarski.

(New Canadian library)
Translation of selections from: Contes du pays incertain, Contes anglais
    et autre and Contes inédits.

ISBN 978-0-7710-9404-0

    I. Bednarski, Betty, 1943- II. Title. III. Series: New Canadian library

PS8511.E76A22 2010   C843'.54   C2010-901471-5

We acknowledge the financial support of the Government of Canada
through the Book Publishing Industry Development Program and that
of the Government of Ontario through the Ontario Media Development
Corporation's Ontario Book Initiative. We further acknowledge the
support of the Canada Council for the Arts and the Ontario Arts
Council for our publishing program.

Typeset in Garamond by M&S, Toronto
Printed and bound in Canada

McClelland & Stewart Ltd.
75 Sherbourne Street
Toronto, Ontario
M5A 2P9
www.mcclelland.com/NCL

1 2 3 4 5   14 13 12 11 10

CONTENTS

TRANSLATOR'S NOTE

Tales from the Uncertain Country and Other Stories is a revised and considerably expanded version of my translation, *Selected Tales of Jacques Ferron*, published by House of Anansi Press in 1984. The thirty-seven stories of the 1984 edition had themselves superseded my original eighteen-story selection, *Tales from the Uncertain Country* (1972), also from Anansi, the first book-length translation of Ferron's work to appear in English. To the 1984 selection, published here with extensive revisions and corrections, have now been added three completely new translations ("Animal Husbandry," "The Rope and the Heifer," "The Witch and the Barleycorn") and a fourth, "Little William," originally published in a translation by Ray Ellenwood, and revised with his permission.

Like those of the two previous editions, all forty-one stories are drawn from among the forty-four that comprise Ferron's now classic *Contes, édition intégrale* (Éditions HMH, 1968), an edition which brought together the author's previous two collections, *Contes du pays incertain* (1962) and *Contes anglais et autres* (1964), along with several other stories grouped under the heading "Contes inédits." The present edition also groups the stories under three main titles: "Tales from the Uncertain Country," "English Tales," "Other Stories." It follows scrupulously the order of the 1968 French edition, with the exception of the two thematically linked stories, "Ulysses" and "The Sirens," which are no longer separated.

Even though less than half of the stories in this revised and expanded edition come from Ferron's *Contes du pays incertain,* in choosing an overall title for the English-language collection I have decided to highlight that one, as I did in 1972. It is Ferron's most famous title, the one most readily associated with his work and it sums up better than any other his literary universe: the social, political and ideological uncertainty of a Quebec caught up in painful transitions and grappling with the ambiguities inherent in its status within the Canadian confederation; the equivocal atmosphere of a literary landscape where nothing is clear-cut, where the seemingly contradictory elements of pathos and humour, blunt down-to-earthness and unrestrained fantasy combine to disconcert and to delight; the tale, heir to the folktale, that fabulous genre of the magical and the commonplace, privileged in Ferron's work as it has been in the culture of Quebec.

It is a joy to see this important work revitalized. I am grateful to the editors of the New Canadian Library for the chance to translate additional stories and to revise and breathe new life into existing ones. I thank the Canada Council and The Banff Centre for their support.

A translator's work is never done, and it is never done alone. I thank editors David Staines and Jenny Bradshaw for their advice and patience during the delicate and time-consuming process of re-crafting these complex stories. I am grateful to Ray Ellenwood for his generosity in sharing his "Little William," to the late Larry Shouldice for coming up with a story title, "Animal Husbandry," that simply could not be improved upon, to Luc Gauvreau for providing invaluable help with the footnotes, and to friends and colleagues too numerous to name for lending me their ears.

– Betty Bednarski

TALES FROM THE
UNCERTAIN COUNTRY

BACK TO VAL-D'OR

One night the husband woke up; his wife was leaning on her elbow looking at him. He asked: "What are you doing?" She replied: "You're handsome, I love you." The next morning, at daybreak, she was sleeping soundly. He shook her, he was hungry. She said: "Go back to sleep; I'll make you lunch."

"And who will go to work?"

"Tomorrow, you can go. Today, stay with me. You're handsome, I love you."

And so he, who was in fact quite ugly, nearly did not go to work. It felt good in the house; his children, awake now, looked at him with their big doe-eyes. He would have liked to take them in his arms and cradle them. But it was fall; he thought of the cost of living; he remembered the other children, three or four, or perhaps five of them, who had died in Abitibi – that hell of a place. And he went off without breakfast.

That evening he hurried home, only to find the house cold. His wife and the children had spent the day in bed, under a pile of blankets. He lit the fire. When the house was warm, the children slid down off the bed. Then the wife got up, joyful. In her hand she held a small bottle of perfume bought several years before, such a delightful extravagance she had kept it unopened. The bottle she uncorked, the perfume she poured – on her husband's head, on her own, on the children's. And all evening long they celebrated. Only the husband held back. But during the night he woke up; his wife was leaning over him, saying: "You're handsome, I love you." Then he gave in.

He did not go to work the next day, nor the days that followed. After a week, having used up his supply of wood, he began to tear down a shed adjoining the house. Whereupon the landlord showed up, furious. However, when he saw what was the matter, he calmed down. The wife was as beautiful as her husband was ugly. He reprimanded her gently. He was a fine talker, this landlord! She wished he would never stop. He told her that man was created to work and other such nonsense. She agreed; everything he said sounded so fine! When he had talked himself dry, he asked her: "Now, will you let your husband work?"

"No," she replied, "I love him too much."

"But this woman is mad," cried the landlord.

The husband was not sure. They sent for priests, doctors, aldermen. All of them had their say. Oh, what fine talkers they were! The wife wished they would never stop, or at least that they would go on talking all night. But when they had finished, she said: "No, I love him too much." They decided she was mad. The husband was not sure.

One evening, snow began to fall. The wife, who ever since their arrival in Montreal had been afraid to go out, terrified by the city, cried: "It's snowing! Come, we'll go to Senneterre."

4

And she dressed in haste.

"But what about the children?" asked the husband.

"They'll wait for us. The Blessed Virgin will look after them. Come, husband, I cannot stay here."

Then he too decided that his wife was mad, and he took the children in his arms. She had gone out to wait for him in the street. He watched her from the window. She ran round and round in front of the door, then stopped, unable to wait any longer.

"We'll go to Malartic," she cried, "we'll go to Val-d'Or!"*

A taxi came by. She got in.

---

* Senneterre, Malartic, Val-d'Or. Place names from the northerly Abitibi region, where many Québécois were encouraged to move in the late nineteenth and early twentieth century after land in the fertile Saint Lawrence River valley had become scarce. Most eked out a miserable existence there, on the land or in the mines, and by the 1950s and 1960s poverty had driven huge numbers back to the south, to urban centres like Montreal. In the context of Ferron's story the three names are poetically suggestive – Senneterre and Val-d'Or, with their evocation of an earthly paradise, ironically so.

SERVITUDE

The first time, Mr. No-Thumb had put his hand on the table; the second time, he'd kept it in his pocket. The first time, the habitant had said to himself, "Here's a hand that's known the axe and the saw, rugged and honest, just the hand to help me now." And he had signed his name on papers, here and there, without bothering to look too hard. The second time, no fraternal hand, but a gold chain, a pompous belly: Mr. No-Thumb, merchant, exporter of seed and hay, was asking him for money. Now money, unfortunately, was the one thing the habitant hadn't got.

"I'll call again next week."

"Call again, by all means, Mr. No-Thumb; you're always welcome."

The next week, the habitant hadn't a cent more. He was in bad shape, that's for sure. And so he stayed out in the barns most of the time, and kept clear of the house. How he loved them now, his animals – his cows, his horses! And his pigs, and his sheep, and the whimpering dog that laughed and cried! If he had his way, he'd cast the barns loose from their moorings, just like that, and they'd all set sail together on the very first flood.

When the merchant came round again, with his pompous belly, and his hand deep in his pocket, it was Armande who said to him, "Won't you sit down, Mr. No-Thumb? My father is out in the barn. I'll make you a cup of tea to drink while you wait."

Mr. No-Thumb – out came the hand now, all four stiff fingers of it – was taken aback. A girl of fourteen, good-natured and pretty, who hadn't appeared on the inventory! Why, that changed everything! He put his hand on the table; he offered it, gave it – his big, rugged hand. The habitant arrived on the scene, saw it, and said, "Mr. No-Thumb, I knew we'd see eye-to-eye in the end."

Mr. No-Thumb took the girl. He kept her four or five years. After which, ennobled by her service, she made a good match.

"Don't worry," he told her, "I shan't forget you."

Was she in any doubt? Here were some names: Angèle, Marie, Laure, Valéda, all former servant-girls, who were set up now in homes throughout the county, and whom he never failed to stop and visit on his way through, in winter, when the men were at the lumber-camps.

"And you know what? I'll come to your wedding."

Mr. No-Thumb kept his word. He was there at Armande's wedding, with his pompous belly, and his hand on the table. It was a great honour for the family. The bridegroom stood next to him, stiff as a taper, burning with gratitude. The women fluttered whenever he looked their way. He was lord of the wedding. As for the habitant, he had stepped aside, no longer certain he was Armande's father. No one noticed he was gone. Sitting in the straw, among his silent animals, he listened to the twang of the strings and the sawing of the bow, but he didn't hear the music. They danced until dawn. Then Mr. No-Thumb closed the four fingers of his hand, put the wedding in his pocket, and left. Everything went flat. The fiddler stopped in the middle of a jig. He was grating on everyone's nerves; it was unbearable. Armande began to cry. A sad little cock on a grey fencepost crowed to the morn.

CADIEU

Ahouse dating from the time of the Indians, built of stone to discourage the fire-brand, which burned all the same, but from within, as the reader of this story shall learn. Ancestral home, property of my father, in it I was born. Passed down from habitant to farm-labourer, of its original estate it had kept only the dilapidated farm buildings, and continued its days in destitution. My father was a big, solitary man, who said neither yes nor no, keeping his teeth clenched; but when he did open up, what a voice! He sang in church on mornings when there was high mass, and this way earned a few cents. During the day he went to work for the habitants, who kept him till nightfall. As he was up early and late to bed, we would go for weeks without seeing him. Sometimes he would be without work; then it was he who did not see us.

Of us children there were five, seven, ten. I was the eldest, the first on the ladder. Father was at the very top. Each year I would go up one rung, and yet could never manage to reach the soles of his shoes. Behind me clung my brothers and sisters, eagerly waiting to grow up. With the exception of the youngest ones, in the yard with the hens and piglets, carefree and happy, much to the distress of our poor mother, who would not rest till they had taken their place on the absurd ladder, till they had joined our pathetic cluster.

The beggars, successors to the Indians, sometimes stopped at the house. "For the love of God," they would say, looking as though they meant it or as though they did not, depending on their technique. We gave them charity – grudgingly, for we were very poor – in order to keep them away, out of some kind of ancestral fear. One of them would appear only after there had been a birth, but he never missed one. His name was Sauvageau*. He would say nothing, just hold out his hand and take, without so much as a thank-you. My father used to say to him: "Here – that's the last time!" He was expressing the earnest desire of his wife. But Sauvageau, fixing him with his beady eye, would shrug his shoulders, and my father would understand that for him it still was, and always would be, the time before the last.

When I was fifteen I managed to find work. Everyone was very glad. My mother even made quite a fuss of me. She was older than I. Of the happy days of her past I hadn't the slightest inkling, knowing only her harassed hours, her moments of impatience. I couldn't understand this young girl look of hers; I wondered what it was she wanted. Finally, when she enquired about my plans, I replied that with my wages I intended to buy myself a fine suit of clothes. With that her coyness ceased.

The fine suit of clothes gave me certain rights on roads and thoroughfares and in public meeting-places of all kinds.

---

* Sauvageau. The surname suggests that this beggar is an Indian (*sauvage*). According to a Quebec legend it is an Indian, not the stork, who brings the new-born baby.

This could have gotten me far, but I made little progress, at best betaking myself on a Saturday evening to the village restaurant, the *cuiquelounche**, where, perched on a stool, straw in mouth, like some beautiful insect, I savoured little sips of soda pop. I didn't gather much through my five-cent proboscis, but it cost me so little that my means increased. Once my suit was paid for I continued to hold on to my wages. Soon I had enough to pay for a more potent drink. I didn't realize it, but word got round, and one fine Saturday Thomette Damour stopped his big black taxi in front of the *cuique-lounche*. "Yahoo!" he howled, "I'm going down to Montmagny. All them as has dry throats, climb aboard with me!"

I came home late, drunk, my wad all gone. This caused quite a stir. The old man growled. So what! his name was Cadieu the same as mine. I lost no sleep over him. The next day, however, I was not so sure of myself. When his wife reminded me that, in the first place, my name was Cadieu the same as his, and that in such circumstances, especially when one's father sang in Latin at Church, it was advisable to curb the yahoo of one's youth, I agreed, I agreed. A month later I still agreed, but I had gotten back some of my nerve. Up comes Thomette and slaps me on the thigh: "Hey, Cadieu, got your wad?" "Wad or no wad, I'll not be drinking any more." But who said anything about drinking? Thomette was simply going to Berthier; he was going to call on his best friend. Really? Well that was different, I'd gladly go along with him. We arrived at Berthier, but the best friend was not home. "He must be at vespers, I'll go and meet him." Whereupon Thomette left me with that devout man's daughter, who asked: "Can I trust you?"

---

* *cuiquelounche*. Ferron's own gallicized spelling of "quick lunch."

"Yes."

And she proceeded to shower on me all manner of unexpected attentions. I began to doubt my own word. In any case I had but one word to give – so let her continue! And continue she did till in the end, villain that I was, I had her all in tears, poor child. Afterwards, I didn't know how to console her. I gave her a dollar, two dollars. She cried and cried. I continued to empty my pockets, and still she cried. It was my last dollar that consoled her. At that moment Thomette returned. I'd lost my wad again and was feeling pretty disillusioned. "Don't tell me you want to take your vows?" I didn't bat an eyelid: "Yes, I want to take my vows."

"That's no joke!"

And Thomette himself was not joking. It was with great respect that he escorted me home. The old man was waiting for me by the side of the road. Thomette said: "Say a prayer for me," and drove off in his big black taxi. I stayed in the dark, beside the old man, who said neither yes nor no, keeping his teeth clenched. "Father, I want to take my vows." The old man took hold of my arm. As we were passing the pigsty he opened the gate and pushed me in. I landed on my back among the pigs. "Start your novitiate in there, good-fer-nothin'!"

The next day my fine suit had lost its sheen. However, I had become a man. I put on my everyday things and left the house, the village, and the county of Bellechasse, strengthened by my calling, seeking another novitiate. I went on foot, left, right, left. "Hey, tourist! Just a minute!" There at my side, haggard, thin, more ragged than ever, appeared Sauvageau, with his sack on his back, making a great effort to keep up with me. It was too much for him, he was soon all out of breath. "Wait, wait!" I kept on going.

"Okay, go on, scram!"

I turned round: he was standing in the middle of the road, his hand on his heart, his mouth open, his lips black. I asked: "Are you sick?" Then he, already out of breath, stopped breathing to fix his beady eye on me, curious to see the man who would ask such a question. Once he'd seen him, he was no better off, and he began to chase his breath again, pumping and pumping till at last he'd caught up with it. This didn't give him back his strength; no sooner would he move than he'd again be overcome by fits of choking. I offered to help him; the town was near, but he showed me a barn; I took him to it. Lying in the hay he seemed more comfortable. Did he still need me? If not, I would be on my way. He motioned to me to stay: "What do you want me to give you?" I needed nothing; besides, what could he, a beggar, give me!

"Children – do you want any? How many? One, two, five, twelve – just say the word and you shall have them."

No, thank you. His beady eye was on me: "None at all?" – "None at all." Then he drew from his pocket a shabby doll and an awl: "Sure?" – "Sure." He pierced the doll. It had not the slightest effect on me; I was too young to understand. "Farewell," I said to him, "I'll pray for you." "You will? And by what right, young fellow?" "I'm going to take my vows." Sauvageau nearly choked with laughter, then: "We'll talk about it some other time." "But I shan't see you again!" "Go on, off with you," he said indulgently. And off I went. At Levis I stopped, perplexed. The river had crossed my plans for going to Quebec. "Take the boat," they told me. That was wisdom itself. But I didn't have a cent; I came up against the ticket collector in his admiral's cap. I was wearing a homespun shirt and felt breeches. My boots smelled more of the barnyard than of mass.

"Well, where's your ticket?"

I went through my pockets; naturally, I didn't have it. And not being in a position to take advantage of my calling, I thought I would die of shame. The passengers behind me, well-dressed city-dwellers, tight-fisted fat-heads all, were beginning, some of them to fidget, others to snigger. However, there was in the group a red-faced fellow, dressed like myself, who was not enjoying the scene. He'd soon had enough. Out of the way, fat-heads! And there he was in front of the admiral: "Here – take your damn tickets!" Then he pushed me onto the boat, not at all pleased. He'd taken my part, but that didn't mean he approved of me: since when did a fellow venture into the big city without a cent to his name? I explained my situation. He calmed down. I'd done right, of course, to leave home. But he couldn't go along with me all the way; his father didn't sing at mass like mine. Personally, as communities went, he preferred lumber camps to the novitiate. "Mind you, I've nothing against your calling." No, of course! Only somehow it happened that I followed him up the Gatineau.

A few months later, Red, the most good-natured of fellows, had become irritable and quarrelsome. Old Jesse Marlowe, our boss, who knew a thing or two, didn't even attempt to reason with him; he sent him to Maniwaki, to a lady whose name was Blanche, an expert at putting a fellow back on his feet again. We were inseparable; so I too went along on the pilgrimage. Once back at the camp, we started work again. Red was cured; he no longer lost his temper. Soon we'd have earned enough to make up for the cost of his treatment. About this time I began to experience a strange sensation. When my fish was full of water it was uncomfortable, I was uneasy. As this happened more and more frequently, I became quite wretched. Red saw how I looked, and, after enquiring as to the reason, said: "Bah! it's only a strain!" A strain that wouldn't loosen its grip, that was draining the very marrow from my bones. After a few days, I was weak, oh, so weak; the axe fell from my hands. Red couldn't understand: at Maniwaki we'd gone with the same girl, the one and only Blanche, the boss's expert. She'd been good for him but bad for me. Why the difference? We consulted old Jesse. "Because of your calling," said he.

And he was not at all pleased. If he'd known he never would have hired me. What was God's was God's, and what was his was his. As fellow bosses you looked out for each other's interests. In any case he wouldn't keep me a minute longer; my place was in a novitiate. That same evening I was on the train for Montreal.

The car was empty. Between stops, the brakeman, his tortured soul imprisoned in his lantern, came and sat down near me, and began to clear his throat. I pretended to be asleep. Once I opened my eye a crack, and before I could close it again, through that little crack he had caught me, started talking and would not let me go. Soon he had me where he wanted me. But just who was I? With French Canadians you can never tell; sometimes it's enough to exchange first and last names and you can call each other cousin.

"Huh?"

"What's your name?"

I blushed, and yet it was not my face that was sick. "My name is Dubois," I replied, "Eugène Dubois."

"Well, well!" exclaimed the brakeman, "I have some Dubois in my family."

"So have I," I said, cutting him short, "but I don't know them, having lost my father and mother when I was only a child. Some charitable folk took me in. Cold and starving, I lay on my little death-bed. They saved my life. Their name: Cadieu. The father is a well-to-do habitant, the mother a perfect saint. The house they live in is the finest in Bellechasse – the farm buildings likewise. In the paved courtyard the children play quietly among sedate hens and bashful pigs. Monsieur Cadieu, seated on the front steps, a new-born baby on each knee, sings hymns. To passers-by, who doff their hats, he replies with a nod of his head."

With this tableau the brakeman could find no fault. He was unable, however, to understand why these Old Testament Cadieus should not have kept me.

"I beg your pardon, they did try; I rejected them, ungrateful, wicked, loose-living, a real swine in a nest of swallows. Their tears were in vain; I went away, blasphemy on my lips, a ten-ounce flask in my right hip-pocket."

Here again the brakeman had no fault to find. He picked up his lantern, bade me a polite good-bye, and left. The train whined as it twisted its way through the night. We arrived at Montreal at daybreak. From the start the doctor was in no doubt as to the nature of my malady; he insisted, however, on examining me; sounded, pawed, sniffed; finally got to my wad; of four hundred dollars took three hundred and eighty; a month's treatment, very cheap. I was lucky. Every day from then on I brought him my malady, a right *h*onourable* one to him, an elephant to me: its trunk he dunked in a mixture of beetroot juice and potash, and in a matter of five minutes I was free to go as I pleased, provided

---

* *h*onourable. In French: *honorée* – almost identical in sound to *gonorrhée* (gonorrhoea).

I walked as little as possible. A month of this, eighty cents a day, charity soup and the flophouses on the Main. I drifted aimlessly around Viger Square.

Sauvageau, the beggar with the black lips, suddenly appeared before me. I was not surprised; nor was he. "And what about your calling?" "I haven't forgotten it." "In that case why not be a novice here?" I could tell by the look in his beady eye that he was not joking.

"But there is only one religion."

"So there is, but you can take it in two ways: the right way, as everyone else does, or the wrong way, as we do here. I'll send you Mithridates. He'll explain. The man knows all things."

The next day an individual came and sat down beside me. Some driveller no doubt. But he said to me in a swift, clear voice: "I know that you are only passing through and that soon you'll have to leave." Then I knew who he was. Keen eyes, heavy lids, a flattened nose, and a lock of faded hair – he looked like an unfrocked clown put to some serious task, a difficult mission, both extravagant and abject. He asked me my name. I blushed. Yet it was not my face that was sick. I gave him my alias.

"Dubois, the name of a registered herd. I prefer the sound of Eugène. As for me, my name is Mithridates – like Mithridates of Pontus. I'm King of the Bridge.* Water is of

---

* King of the Bridge. In French: *le roi du Pont* – meaning both the King of the Bridge and the King of Pontus (Mithridates' kingdom). An untranslatable pun. In the Montreal of Ferron's day, winos gathered near the river, not far from the Jacques Cartier bridge.

no interest to me. I pass over the canal. My drink is *la robine*.*
To live you have to feel yourself die, poison yourself drop by
drop. And all the rest is futile. I should know. I had a former
existence. I bore another name. It was a name I hadn't chosen,
an honourable name of past and future generations. I was
travelling from the flood to the Antichrist, among skeletons
and embryos; it felt like a dream. I jumped from the train in
order to live."

That was his speech. Unable to understand it, I was still
flattered to have heard it. My youth inspired him, I believe.
Besides, he was quite a personage in the Park, a kind of lawyer
whom well-dressed outsiders sometimes came to consult; an
agitator too, who was never still, going from group to group,
leaving a stir behind him; a wino who cared little for his
"wine," intoxicated mainly with words. He had managed to
organize a beggars' fraternity. On this racket his kingdom was
founded. Yet he cared no more for power than he did for the
bottle. He ruled in the same way as he drank, out of respect
for his name and, as he said, to justify the existence of the
Academy. He was terribly futile.

As time went on he became more and more attached
to me; soon he would not leave me. He asked me to tell him
the story of my life; he was fond, he said, of country air. His
whole attitude changed. He began to drink great gulps of
robine. He grew haggard, detached, silent. Then one day, he,
who until now had kept me outside of his kingdom, handed
me the bottle. With the curiosity of a novice, so as not to
offend him, I took a few sips. It was fire. I smiled at him,
my eyes filling with tears. Slowly the trees began to bleed

---

* In Québécois French *la robine* – from the English "rubbing
alcohol" – is the cheap drink of down-and-outs.

chlorophyll. Someone clasped me; I was carried away. After that I heard the sound of water. I can remember nothing more. The next day I woke up beside the canal; a Great Lakes steamer was passing. I went to the doctor to receive my final treatment. The pure air made me dizzy.

When I returned to the park, the beggar with the black lips was waiting for me. He said to me: "You can go now; your novitiate is over."

I kept my alias. This enabled me to do well in business. After five or six years a successful man was I – gloves, hat, the lot. I even had friends in the government. But I still bore the name I had taken in shame. To that of my forbears I longed to return, longed to replant the family tree, to have an umbrella of ancestral skin with micro-filmed tattoos, bleeding heart and fleur-de-lis. First I would have to be recognized by my family. So I returned to Bellechasse. The old man was deaf, but he was still chewing on his hymn. My little sisters had grown up; there were three or four left. My brothers had all gone away. "I'm Monsieur Dubois." "Do come in, Monsieur Dubois." No one had recognized me; they took me for a suitor. The little sisters were sitting demurely, each with a kitten on her lap. The kittens stretched and purred and yawned and showed their little pink jaws. The old mother cat fussed around the chairs. Which one would you like, Monsieur Dubois? I began to feel embarrassed.

"I've come to buy the house."

At this the kittens pricked up their ears: with the house sold they would run free. The deaf man growled. "Monsieur Dubois has a pile of money and friends in the government. If we sell him the house he'll find you a job as night watchman." "Eh?" "A job as night watchman." I got the house for next to nothing, a large house and tall, which, passed down from habitant to farm labourer, had lost its lands and stood in tightened straits by the side of the road. In order to free it I set fire to it. It was a fine spectacle. The whole parish came to watch. I was about to leave when I caught sight of my beggar with the black lips, his hands held out towards the blaze.

"Ah, what a good fire," he was saying, "what a good fire!"

HOW THE OLD MAN DIED

There was a bone askew above his stomach; he wasn't sick, but the bone made him uncomfortable, stabbing him with every breath he took. He would have to stay quiet until the bone reset. After three or four weeks the wretched bone had not moved, the old man was going from bad to worse; they sent for the manipulator, but the manipulator, having felt him, refused to manipulate him, for by shifting the bone, he would have dislocated the nerve of the heart at the same time. The old man was done for. They sent for the priest.

"Old man," said the old woman to her husband, "maybe you're not very sick, but you're so old that you're dying."

"I'm dying?"

"Yes, you're dying; what's to become of me?"

"And what about me?" asked the old man.

"You've got nothing to worry about," replied the old woman. "All you have to do is lie back; the priest will take care of everything. Only you'll have to be polite; you'll fold your hands, look up, and think of the good Lord, if you can;

if you can't, just pretend to. And no funny business, do you understand!"

The old man was having difficulty breathing. He promised to behave. However, the arrival of his boys with their sanctimonious faces upset his resolve. His hands were already folded, he tried to separate them without being noticed, but the old lady had her eye on him; she fastened his wrists with a long rosary. Just then the priest arrived, concluded that there was no hope for the old man, and accordingly made haste to administer the last rites. After that he was at a loss to know what to do; it wasn't yet time to say the prayer for the dying.

"How are you feeling?" he asked the old man.

"Bad, thank you," replied he.

Bad, to be sure, but not bad enough to go under. Now higher, now lower, he was still rising and falling with the swell. The priest, who was inclined to be squeamish, retired to the kitchen, accompanied by the women. The boys, who had stayed with their father, didn't waste a moment: his handcuffs they removed. The old man gave them a wave:

"Hi there, boys!"

"Hi there, Pa," they replied.

Short waves shook the old man. This lasted an hour or more; then after the final wave came the final hour; the old man was at peace at last in his bed; the bone pained him no more; he was healed; he was about to die. The women had returned to his side, smothering little seagull cries in their handkerchiefs. The priest was saying the prayer. It was too good, too good; it was too good to last.

"The pot," cried the dying man.

The priest stopped. The chamber pot was brought, but the old man pushed it away:

"Too late; I'll go on the other side."

And he died.

When they had put him in the coffin, clean-shaven and smartly dressed, he looked very distinguished. The old woman couldn't stop gazing at him, and tearfully she told him:

"Ah, old man, my old man, if only you'd always been like this, sensible, clean, quiet, how I'd have loved you, how happy we'd have been!"

She could talk all she liked, poor woman! The old man was not listening to her: he was in the kitchen laughing with his boys, laughing as much as one dare laugh at a wake.

MÉLIE AND THE BULL

Mélie Caron had only thirteen children. She expected to have more, one a year until she died; but after the thirteenth, Jean-Baptiste Caron, her husband, said to her, "Stop, Mélie!"

So the poor woman stopped, not yet fifty years old. She remained unsatisfied, deprived of her due, all warm and trembling like an animal checked in full career. However, her trouble was not without remedy: did she not have her thirteen children? Thirteen children is not much; but it is a family. Alas! the consolation was shortlived. One by one her children left her. She had fed them too well: full of ardour were the boys, ripe and tender the girls; once fully grown there was no holding them back. In the end Mélie lost them all. She remained alone with her old man.

He, like a prisoner whose sentence is served, now found his freedom. He was no longer to be found at home, but spent most of his time with the other freedmen of the village, old eccentrics of the same breed as himself, parleying and laying down the law, drinking whenever the opportunity arose, and then pissing, drop by drop, the burning fire of his repentance.

Mélie would take advantage of this to offer herself: "Let me help you, old man."

The suggestion was enough to make the waters flow again. Forty years of married life had taught the old man much; he knew that at the slightest sign of weakness his wife would get him into her clutches and not let go till she had mollycoddled him into senility. He remained on his guard.

"Thank you, Mélie. I'm all right now."

Now it came to pass that the old lady, deprived of children and husband, her corpulence notwithstanding, began to feel confined, loath to be restricted to her own company. Humours began to rise to her brain. At first this made her head swim, then she felt unsteady. It was the end of August. Alone in her kitchen, with her fly-swatter in her hand, she listened: not a fly in the house. This silence astounded her. In the absence of flies she was prepared for much worse: for the appearance of snakes, of preposterous frogs, of demons armed with scapularies, against which her fly-swatter would have been useless; prepared for an attack of raving madness. She was on the point of screaming when she heard a moo which saved her. Fleeing her monsters, she rushed out.

Outside, giving shade to the door, there rose a cherry tree, with flashes of sunlight and the redness of cherries moving among its leaves: beyond that there stretched a garden, then, as far as the river, a field. Mélie crossed the garden. The calf in the field saw her; with his tail in the air he came up towards her with faltering little leaps. The fence that separated the field from the garden brought them both to a stop. The old lady leant down; the calf raised a round, wet muzzle: they looked at each other. And suddenly Mélie Caron was moved by a feeling worthy of her heart. This muzzle, this trust had overwhelmed her; tears came to her eyes; had she been able to cry tears of milk, she would have wept buckets to satisfy the appetite of the poor animal.

That evening when Jean-Baptiste Caron came home, she announced to him: "In future I shall look after the calf."

The soup was steaming on the table.

"Fine," said the old man, sitting down. Discussions have never been known to keep soup hot. Better polish it off now and talk later. When he had eaten his fill: "Why look after the calf, Mélie?" he asked.

She replied: "Because I want to."

"Have I by any chance not taken good care of him?"

"Good or bad, you'll not take care of him any more."

"Fine," said the old man, who in actual fact was not particularly concerned about the calf.

He was nevertheless surprised a few days later to see his old lady in the field, sitting under a huge, black umbrella, which protected her from the sun and whose light shade, far from hiding her from view, made her most conspicuous.

"What are you doing there, Mélie?"

"Knitting."

And so she was.

"Perhaps you'd be more comfortable knitting in the house."

"No, old man, I'm more comfortable here." And she added: "Besides, I can't leave him now."

He asked anxiously: "Leave who?"

"Come now, old man, the calf, of course!"

The animal was lying at Mélie's feet. The picture was not lacking in charm. But to Jean-Baptiste it gave not the slightest pleasure.

"Shall I tell you something, Mélie? Shall I?"

She made no objection.

"Well," he said, "you look like an escaped lunatic, and that's a fact."

"Old fool, yourself," she replied.

You cannot reason with a woman when she is in full possession of her faculties, much less when she loses them. Reason attacks front on; such bluntness is a drawback; with the weaker sex you have to use some stratagem, or simply take them from behind.

"If Mélie were twenty years younger," the old man said to himself, "a few little pats on the behind would bring her to her senses."

In fact he could have done with shedding a few years himself: he had long since lost the art of those little pats. So how was he to bring about a recovery? What could he do to stop the old lady's madness becoming the talk of the village?

"It'll be quite simple," thought Jean-Baptiste Caron. "Since she's mad over a calf, I'll sell the calf."

In this way he hoped to cure her. The remedy was simple indeed. He went off at once and made the necessary arrangements with the butcher. The next morning at daybreak along came his man, paunch bulging beneath a white apron. He had donned for the occasion a bowler hat. He took away the calf. Soon afterwards old Mélie, still heavy with sleep, came out of the house suspecting nothing. The cherry tree, branches held high, for it had not yet lowered its panoply, revealed a strangely slender trunk. The sun was coming up. Dazzled, the old lady stopped a moment to blink her eyes, and then set off along the garden path, calling: "Littl'un! Littl'un!"

She reached the fence; there was still no sign of the calf. Again she called him, but with no better luck. Then she made a thorough search: she searched high and she searched low, but, from the garden to the river, the field was empty.

"Ah, mercy me!" she cried.

And back she rushed, the sight of the water having convinced her that the animal had drowned. Is it Christian to put rivers at the bottom of fields? This arrangement of Nature's filled her with indignation. In her haste she bumped into the cherry tree, who, preoccupied himself, had not seen her coming, absorbed as he was in the foliage, distributing his fruit to the birds. The birds flew away, cherries fell to the ground, and the wicked servant was caught in the act at his very roots. Much to his surprise the old lady continued on her way. So he signalled to the birds to come back.

Mélie Caron went back into the house.

"Old man, old man, the most terrible thing has happened."

This most terrible thing roused no interest.

"Can you hear me, old man?"

He could not hear her, and for a very simple reason: he was not there. The old lady ran to his room: she searched high and she searched low, but the bed of Jean-Baptiste Caron was empty.

"Ah, mercy me!"

But at the sight of the chamber-pot she was not alarmed. No old fellow who has trouble pissing is ever swept away by the flood. Besides the pot was empty. However, this incapacity of her husband's for drowning did not altogether lessen the mystery of his disappearance. Mélie Caron remained as in a dream. At first her dream revealed nothing; on the contrary it masked her view; the veil was coloured, for she was dreaming with her eyes open. Suddenly the veil was drawn aside: she saw a knife, and behind the knife, holding it, his paunch bulging beneath a white apron, wearing for the occasion a bowler hat – the butcher.

"I'm dreaming," she said to herself.

With which statement the butcher agreed, closing the curtain. Then old Mother Mélie rushed into the wings, and off to the butcher's she trotted. On her way she passed the church.

"Mother Mélie," said the priest, "you're tripping along like a young girl."

"Yes, yes, *Monsieur le curé,* if you say so – like a young girl. But have you seen my old man?"

"I saw your old man and your calf, one joyful, the other pathetic."

"Oh, the poor dear! Oh, the ruffian! Pray for him, *Monsieur le curé.*"

And the old lady continued on her way. She arrived at the butcher's. The butcher, who had not had time to remove his hat, was surprised to see her again so soon.

"Good day, butcher. Where is my calf?"

"Good day, ma'am. I don't know your calf."

"Oh, don't you now!"

She paused in the doorway just long enough to blink her eyes. The morning was behind her, radiant, making the room in front of her dark. However, she was soon able to distinguish the carcasses hanging there.

"There are many calves here," said the butcher, showing her the carcasses. "Only they all look alike since we undressed them."

"I see one that seems to have kept its coat on."

"Where's that, Mistress Mélie?"

"Here."

And pointing her finger, she touched a very shamefaced Jean-Baptiste.

"That's your old man, Mistress Mélie."

"Cut me off a leg all the same."

"He's very skinny."

"Cut it off, I tell you!"

The butcher refused. The old lady took away his knife.

"Then I'll help myself to that leg."

Whereupon Jean-Baptiste Caron intervened. "Don't act so foolish, Mélie. Your calf's here."

He handed her a rope; the poor dear animal was on the end of it, his eyes startled, his muzzle round and wet.

"Littl'un!"

"We weren't going to hurt him," said Jean-Baptiste Caron, "only cut him."

"A calf develops better that way," volunteered the butcher.

"Quiet, you liars! My calf shall remain entire, as the Lord made him."

Having made sure that he still had all his vital parts, including his little phallus, the old lady set off with him. The priest, who had not yet finished his breviary, was still in front of the church.

"Well, Mother Mélie, I see you've found your calf."

"Yes, *Monsieur le curé,* but I got there just in time: they were about to cut him, the poor dear animal. I stopped their cruelty. You see, *Monsieur le curé,* he still has all his vital parts, including his little pointed phallus."

"So I see, Mother Mélie, so I see."

The old lady continued on her way, pulling her calf behind her. Soon afterwards the old man, Jean-Baptiste, appeared on the scene, looking very dejected indeed.

"It appears," said the priest, "that you're jealous of a calf. Your old lady showed me what you were planning to deprive him of."

"She showed you! Forgive her – she's not herself any more."

"Forgive her for what? I don't take offense at that. Surely you wouldn't expect her to put drawers on her calf?"

The bell for mass began to ring. The priest was obliged to leave the old man. One month later the latter called at the presbytery. He was looking even more dejected; he walked bent double. When he sat down the priest noticed his face: he thought he seemed worried.

"Worried, no. Let's just say I'm weak."

"Well now! You're getting older."

"That may be, but it's not just age; for the last month I've eaten nothing but mash and grass."

"No!"

"Yes, mash and grass."

"The same as a calf?"

"You said it, *Monsieur le curé;* the same as a calf. I like meat, beans and lean pork. This food doesn't suit me at all and Mélie won't listen to me. She says we're all one nation."

"What language do you speak at home?"

"We still speak like people, but only because we don't know how to moo."

The priest began to laugh. "It's just the same with French Canadians; they still speak like people, but only because they don't know English."

Jean-Baptiste Caron nodded his head. "It's quite possible that calf is English," said he; "he's taking my place."

"Your place! You mean you live in the stable?"

"No, *Monsieur le curé,* we don't live in the stable. But the calf is living in the house."

"You don't say," said the priest, "he must be an English calf."

"He must be: he's not at all religious."

The priest rose to his feet. "We must drive him out."

This was also the opinion of Jean-Baptiste Caron.

"But how?"

Jean-Baptiste Caron also wondered how. The priest put a finger to his forehead, and this had the desired effect.

"Return to your house," he said to the old man. "But first pull yourself together and look cheerful. Once home, eat your mash as though you enjoyed it and be loving to the poor dear little animal."

"I won't be able to."

"You will. After a week or two Mélie will think you share her feelings. At the same time, bring other animals into your house."

"You must be joking, *Monsieur le curé!*"

"Cats, dogs, mice, rabbits, even hens. I don't say you should bring in cows or pigs. Just domestic animals. Mélie will grow attached to them and so become less attached to the calf. Then it will be possible to use a stratagem."

Jean-Baptiste Caron: "A stratagem?"

The priest: "You will tell Mélie that you're worried about the calf's future."

"I'll tell her the truth: in six months he'll be a bull. It seems to me that's something to worry about."

"Exactly, this is what we must prevent. After all he's an English calf: mating isn't for him."

"All the same, we're not going to send him to school!"

"No, not to school: to a seminary."

The priest added: "A professional in the family is no disgrace."

"You're right, *Monsieur le curé*; a professional in the family is no disgrace."

At times advice is worth heeding, especially when it comes from one's priest. Jean-Baptiste Caron decided to make use of that offered him. Under the circumstances there was little else for him to do. He therefore declared himself to be in favour of calves, which won him the confidence of the old lady. Then he brought up the subject of education.

"Well now, it's no joke; a professional in the family is a worthwhile and honourable thing."

Mélie Caron knew it was no joke. But completely wrapped up in her calf, she was not particularly concerned about honour or the family; she wondered which of the two, the bull or the professional, would suit her best. Her heart inclined to the one, her reason to the other, and the animal looked at her puzzled. She too was puzzled.

"What are we going to do with you, poor little fellow?" she asked him.

"Moo, moo," replied the calf.

This reply did nothing to solve her dilemma. Then she reflected, not unreasonably, that once educated the animal would express himself more clearly. So she opted for the professional, telling herself that if by chance he did not like this condition he could always go back to being a bull. Without further delay she went to the priest and told him of her decision.

"A good idea, Mother Mélie! And since you want him to be educated, send him to the Quebec Seminary: that's where I studied."

The old lady looked at the priest. "You don't say!"

The priest was forced to climb down a little. "We mustn't exaggerate," he said. "But all the same I do think, with his intelligence, this little fellow could become a lawyer or even a doctor."

The old lady seemed disappointed.

"A doctor, that's no joke!"

The old lady knew it was no joke. She simply said, "Pooh!"

"A lawyer then?"

She preferred the lawyer.

"Then the matter's settled, Mother Mélie; next week they'll come for your little one: a lawyer he shall be."

As had been arranged, one week later to the very day the Father Superior of the Quebec Seminary sent his representative, a great giant of a man, part beadle, part deputy, who arrived with much to-do in a carriage drawn by three horses. The carriage drew up in the courtyard of the presbytery. Immediately the postulant was brought forth.

"*Ali baba perfectus babam,*" cried the representative.

Which is to say that at first sight, without further inspection, he had judged the calf fit to become a lawyer. On hearing these words the animal moved his ears. The priest noticed this.

"Well, well, he understands Latin!"

Mélie Caron did not understand it. She said "Amen," however, with a heavy heart.

This amen had an effect she had not foreseen: the representative rose to his feet and standing up in the carriage pointed his finger at her:

"Thou, *Mélia, repetatus.*"

"Amen," repeated the old lady.

Then the giant of a man leapt from the carriage, seized hold of the calf and carried him off into the church barn.

"He's not as good as the Father Superior of the Quebec Seminary," said the priest, "only being his representative, but you'll see, Mother Mélie, he still knows all about giving an education."

Indeed, no sooner had he entered the barn with the calf than he reappeared, alone, holding in his hands a long object, which he gave to the old lady.

"Thou, *Mélia, repetatus.*"

"Amen," said she.

And the terrible pedagogue went back into the barn.

"But it's my Littl'un's tail!" cried Mélie Caron.

"Yes," replied the priest, "it is your Littl'un's tail. Keep it. He no longer has any use for it."

At that same moment the door of the barn opened, and who should appear but the calf, stiff, in a long black frock-coat, walking like a little man.

"Littl'un!"

He stopped and slowly turned his head toward the old lady. This head did not fit, it was shaky and too high, its features motionless. And he stared at her with vacant eyes.

"Littl'un!" the old lady called again.

He did not even twitch his ears. The old lady did not know what to think. What had they done to her little one in the church barn that he should come out looking so distant? They had cut off his tail, to be sure; they had put clothes on him, true; he was walking on his hind legs like a prime minister, so much the better! In short they had educated him, but did that mean they had to make him blind and deaf? This being the case, education did make the farewell easier.

The seminarian calf, drawing a white handkerchief from his frock-coat, waved it, but distantly, oh so distantly: the fingers holding the handkerchief were already human. Mélie Caron made no attempt to hold him back. He climbed into the carriage beside the representative of the Father Superior of the Quebec Seminary, and there sat upright on his little behind, he who had never used it before. The carriage moved off and soon disappeared from sight.

"Well?" asked the priest.

Well, what? The old lady did not know, so she made no reply.

"Well, yes," the priest began again, "he is gifted, that little fellow! He's not even at the Seminary yet, and all there is left of the calf is its head. Education is for him. A lawyer he shall be, and what a lawyer!"

"What lawyer?" asked the old lady.

"Why, Lawyer Bull! A famous lawyer. Come, come, be proud: he'll be a credit to you."

Mother Mélie was holding the calf's tail in her hands, and it hung there pitifully. Proud? with her head down and her tail, so to speak, between her legs, she did not feel in the least like being proud. "I'm very happy," she said, and very sadly she went off. To see her leave like that worried the priest. The next day after mass, without stopping to have lunch, he went to call on her, and found her in her garden, feeding the hens.

"I was afraid I might find you in bed, Mother Mélie."

"I very nearly did stay in bed, *Monsieur le curé.* When I woke up I had no desire to do anything, only to die. Surely at my age I'm entitled to a rest. Then I heard the clucking of the hens, the barking of the dog, the animals making their morning noise, and I thought of my poor rabbits twitching their noses without a sound. Who else would have looked after all these animals but me? So I got up."

The priest took off his hat while he recovered his breath. His plan had worked, the calf was out of the way, the old lady cured; what more could he ask, under the circumstances? He was satisfied; he remembered then that he was hungry. Mélie

Caron gave him a meal and he ate till he could eat no more. When he rose from the table she was still not satisfied: "Just one more little mouthful, *Monsieur le curé*?"

"So you're not cross with me, Mother Mélie?"

She was cross that he had eaten so little. Apart from that she had nothing against him, considering him to be a good Christian.

"But what about your calf, Mother Mélie?"

She saw no reason why she should be cross about that. Hadn't she parted with her calf so that he could become a lawyer? It had been for his own good; of what importance was the sacrifice she, poor woman, had made?

"Besides," said Mélie Caron, "I'm used to these separations."

She was thinking of her thirteen children, well-fed all of them, full of ardour the boys, ripe and tender the girls, who had left her one by one. And where had they gone? One to Maniwaki, another to the States, a third out West.* As for the rest, she did not know. Besides, Maniwaki, Maniwaki . . . she had never been outside of Sainte-Clothilde de Bellechasse: what could Maniwaki mean to her? Or the States? or Abitibi? or the Farwest? "I lost my children, *Monsieur le curé*; I can part with a calf. Besides I still have my hens, some rabbits, a dog, a cat and some mice, enough to keep me going for some time yet. My supply still hasn't run out."

"You'll die one day, all the same."

"The worms will console me."

"Come, come, Mother Mélie? And what about the good Lord?"

"After, once the worms have eaten their fill."

---

* Ferron writes, mischievously: *Maniouaki*, *Stétes*, and *Farouest*.

The priest thought of his position; there was nothing in the Scriptures to prevent Mélie Caron having her bones cleaned off by worms before going up to join the Almighty. "Very well," he said, taking his hat and preparing to leave. Whereupon Mélie Caron, still not satisfied, asked him if he thought that at the Seminary the little fellow would keep his head.

"His calf's head? Of course not."

"Then how shall I recognize him?"

The priest thought of his position and either because he had forgotten his theology or because the question had not been dealt with, he could think of nothing very Catholic to say in reply. He hesitated, feeling somewhat ill at ease in his cassock.

"Mother Mélie," he said at last, "there exists something which, as a young bull, your little fellow would have worn in all innocence, but which as a lawyer he will have to conceal; it is by that incorruptible root – for education cannot touch it – that you will recognize him."

And doubtless judging he had gone too far, without explaining himself at greater length, he went off, leaving the old lady with her curiosity, naturally, unsatisfied. So when Jean-Baptiste Caron came home she eagerly asked him for an explanation. Jean-Baptiste Caron, who was not inhibited by theology, answered without hesitation: "It's the phallus, pointed in the case of a calf that's become a young bull."

"And in the case of Littl'un?"

"Likewise, since education can't touch it. He'll keep his root even though he's a lawyer, and this way he'll be easy to recognize."

And so, reassured, Mélie went back to her daily routine, and the months passed, the winter months, then spring, and the cherry tree bloomed; then came the summer months, June, July, and the ripe hay was harvested. In August the newspapers announced the famous fair to be held at Quebec in the early fall, and which Jean-Baptiste Caron had been wanting to see for a long time.

"Old girl," said he, "we really should see the Provincial Exhibition before we die."

The old lady burst out laughing. "Have you gone crazy, old man?"

In order that she might judge for herself he handed her a page of the newspaper. On it she found this professional announcement: "Maître Bull, lawyer."

"Anyway," she said, "I've nothing against your crazy idea."

So to Quebec they went, their hearts anxious, their eyes wide. The city, the fair, amusement and pleasure soon lifted the anxiety. Fatigue came more slowly; however, after two or three days, they could hardly keep their eyes open, and were beginning to miss the peace and quiet of Sainte-Clothilde.

"But," said the old lady, "before we go back, there's someone I have to see."

Jean-Baptiste Caron was not in the least surprised.

"Someone you have to see?" he asked.

"Yes, old man! Just because we've never had any fallings out, that's no reason why we shouldn't see a lawyer before we die."

Old Mélie was right: they should see a lawyer. It was unfortunate, however, that the lawyer had to be Maître Bull. Jean-Baptiste Caron could see no good coming of the encounter. It was one thing to recognize a young bull under a gown, but quite another to get the lawyer to agree to the test. At any rate, Mélie should go alone.

"I'm thirsty," said Jean-Baptiste Caron, "I'll wait for you at the Hôtel de la Traverse."

So Mélie went alone. To Maître Bull's office she came. "Come in," cried he, in a beautiful deep voice. She went in and found, in a dusty little office, a young man dressed in black, handsome as an archangel, sad as an orphan, who, after the normal formalities, asked for her name, first name and place of residence: Mélie Caron of Sainte-Clothilde. And the purpose of her visit: whom did she wish to bring action against?

"No one," the old lady answered.

Surprised, he looked at her, and said, with relief: "Thank you."

It was the old lady's turn to express surprise. He explained to her that the lawyer's profession served as an alibi.

"Who are you then?"

"A poet," he replied.

"Oh," said she.

"I keep it a secret; if men knew they would look upon me as some kind of animal."

Mélie Caron lowered her eyes at this modesty.

"Your name again?" the lawyer asked her.

"Mélie Caron."

"I don't know why," he said, "but that name brings to my mind the image of a field and the sound of a river."

At these words, no longer doubting that this was her Littl'un, the poor dear animal, old Mélie pulled from her bag the pitiful object, which she had kept, and let it hang beside her. Meanwhile the archangel, the orphan, the young man in black, went on in his beautiful deep voice, saying that it was not the sound of a river, but that of the wind in the grass, the wind whose waters bleach it white in the sun.

"Earth's back is dark and stains the hand, but when the wind passes she forgets her sorrow and, moved, turns over, showing her white belly, where the grass is soft as down, where each blade is a nipple gorged with milk."

"Poor dear," thought the old lady, "he badly needs to graze!"

"Do you sometimes hear a voice?" she asked him. "A voice calling you: Littl'un! Littl'un!"

"Yes, I hear it."

"It's mine," said Mélie Caron.

"I didn't know," said the lawyer. "Besides I cannot answer. I am imprisoned in a cage of bone. The bird in his cage of bone is death building his nest.* There was a time when I hoped to free myself by writing, but the poems I wrote then did not render my cry."

"Poor dear," thought the old lady, "he badly needs to moo."

"Are you married, Littl'un?"

The young man gave a horrified start; his archangel's wings trembled; he was deeply offended at being thought capable of anything so low.

"Quite so, quite so," said the old lady, "I didn't mean to offend you. I only wanted to find out if you were free."

"I am free," he said, "subject only to the will of the ineffable."

She handed him the hairy member.

"Then take back your tail, Littl'un, and follow me."

---

* *L'oiseau dans sa cage d'os*
C'est la mort qui fait son nid
These lines are taken from *Cage d'oiseau* ("Bird Cage") by the Quebec poet, Saint-Denys Garneau (1912–43).

She lead him to the Hôtel de la Traverse where Jean-Baptiste Caron was waiting for them.

"Old man, it's Littl'un!"

Of this she seemed so sure that the old man lowered his eyes, embarrassed. Together they returned to Sainte-Clothilde. "Well, well!" called the priest, "it's back to the land, I see!" And back to the land it was! Though they had surpassed the prophesied return. Indeed, once he had grazed, it was not long before Maître Bull had recovered his élan. Meanwhile his gown was falling to shreds. Soon there was nothing left of the fine education he had received at the Quebec Seminary. One day, at last, he was able to utter his poet's cry, a bellow such as to drive all the cows in the county mad. Faithful to his root, he had found his destiny. From that day on, before the wondering eyes of old Mélie, he led an existence befitting his nature, and left behind him in Bellechasse, where they called him The Scholar, the memory of a famous bull.

LES MÉCHINS

He practised without opium. This grieved him, for opium was his panacea: he could not bring himself to do without it. Besides, the son of a well-to-do family, educated by the Jesuits and in the hospitals of Paris, he was unable to get used to life in the settlements.* He was wretched indeed, cut off from everything he loved, so wretched that he could find pity in his heart for no one. It was a horse that saved him. He had worked nearly all the settlements and had travelled the length and breadth of the land, from one far province to another, from Abitibi to the Gaspé. He had not gone by the main highways or the King's roads, but had kept instead to the edge of the woods. Eventually, he had come to Les Méchins. Méchins was not a settlement, but a fairly old village – the proof is that it has a beautiful name. It was a village, however, where the priest had not yet managed to

---

* A settlement (in Québécois French, *une colonie*) was a more recent and generally much less prosperous community than a village. See also the footnote to the story "The Old Heathen."

43

acquire a curate, and where doctors, at least in those days, did not stay.

The first month he worked wonders. The following month, encouraged, he set out on what were ostensibly visits to colleagues, once more in quest of opium. These excursions were not always successful, but successful or no, he always managed to return in a pitiful state. By the third month he no longer had the money for a taxi, and his reputation was ruined.

What can you expect? Without opium you cannot give religion to the people. They abandoned me; they went elsewhere for treatment, to Matane, Cap-Chat, or simply reverted to paganism, to their midwives and quacks. No more consultations for trivial ills; these are the pick of the practice, the kind that fatten the purse. I spent my days rocking to and fro on my porch, opposite the Church, my hands shaking, my mind blank. Passersby would laugh loudly. I would pretend not to hear, but all that laughter was directed at me, I knew. Oh, they had me where they wanted me! I was at their mercy. They would wait until night, then come and get me out to perform the chores of undertaker, or for births the midwife would have nothing to do with. The misery I saw! But none could make me forget my own. I attended my patients correctly, doing everything according to the books, yet without giving of myself, without pity, without love. I didn't realize the treatment I gave was bad. They could see it and refused to pay me. I so desperately needed a little money. I hadn't yet been to call on my colleagues in Rimouski. Just a little money for the taxi. But they no longer gave me any. Or so little. And I went on duty in an ever dustier office.

One winter afternoon someone came to fetch me. It was beginning to snow. I climbed into a sleigh drawn by an old white horse, with bald patches where its bones stood out, a back like a ridge-pole, and a docked tail. And I let myself be carried along, the pace alternating from a walk to a trot, trot, then to a walk again, for the trot tired the horse and the walk irritated the driver, who would rise up in his seat at intervals and strike the animal. There was a great deal of energy exerted on both sides, and we made little headway for all that. Night gradually overtook and enclosed the sleigh, yet it could not shut out the wind and the snow. This darkness, pierced by flashes of startling white, with the wretched horse radiating light, was no hallucination. At last, thank Heaven, we entered a sheltered road. The wind stayed in the treetops; only the snow came down, steady and soft. The driver let the horse go as it pleased and the horse began to quicken its pace.

A log cabin overwhelmed by the season. In a corner two or three brats and a woman in labour. No lamp, just a lantern. Everything was approximate, uncertain, doubtful – except the cold; the infant came all steaming out of its mother's belly. A miserable chore.

And then, the return journey!

The storm was waiting for us as we came out of the woods. It was blowing off the sea and those sinister rocks from which the village takes its name: Les Méchins* – the wicked ones. I shivered, my eyes shut, chilled to the depths of my soul. I hadn't been paid. I so needed a little money to get me to Rimouski! Not a proper fee – I hadn't asked for that – but some payment! And I had insisted, even though I knew there wasn't an old dollar or a counterfeit dime in the cabin. "Well, if you don't have any money, you've no business bothering a doctor." That's what I had said in my anger, my

---

* Les Méchins. Ferron assumes the name to be a corruption of *méchant* – wicked, evil.

rage, my hunger for opium. I had shown no restraint. I knew no pity.

Meanwhile, the man was no longer striking his horse to make it trot, only to make it go through the snowdrifts. These drifts rose up from the sea like huge waves. One came at us side-on; it lifted up the sleigh and overturned it. While we freed ourselves, while I looked for my cap and my bags and the driver got to his feet, furious, his stick in his hand, the horse, still standing, one shaft between its legs, turned its terrified head towards us.

It was then that I had a revelation of distress greater than my own, and for the first time I felt pity that was not for myself. I loved this horse like a brother. He was my redeemer. Before that, selfish and unkind, I had deserved a thousand times to be struck down amid the rocks of Les Méchins. Since then I no longer think of myself and I thank God for it. He did not heal me, he saved me. When I do manage to find a little opium it is as though I were injecting it into that poor animal, with his docked tail, his bleeding mouth, his half-blind eyes and anxious ears. I have not forgotten him. His suffering haunts me. The storm rages about me still; the wind blows off the infernal rocks. The waves rise up towards me. The horse is encompassed by all the wickedness of the world. I must comfort him. Besides I owe it to him: did he not save me? From now on *he* is the drug addict.

TIRESOME COMPANY

I was new to the practice; with an air of self-importance I sought to hide the misgivings I had concerning my person. One day I was called out to Saint-Yvon, one of the villages in the parish of Cloridorme, in the county of North Gaspé. It was winter; the sea was a vast field of ice, with, here and there, dark and steaming cracks.

In the older counties, where the stay-at-home habitant reigns, jealously guarding his land, the only living things ever to be shared with a neighbour are the birds of the air. At Saint-Yvon it is not the same; here is felt the influence of the sea, which belongs to each and every man. This makes for a less petty way of life and encourages mutual aid and sociability. For example, cats and dogs are everyone's responsibility, and so, alas, are pigs.

These pigs remain out of doors all winter. This is supposed to pep them up. Impudent and familiar, they wander around the houses in search of scraps. On sunny days they separate into bands of boars and sows, the better to come together, which they then do with great gusto and not the slightest restraint, like real animals. Should a passerby appear, they will follow along behind him without waiting to be asked. If there is a heavy snowfall, it is they who trace paths in the fresh snow. Such are the pigs of Saint-Yvon, producers of bacon for all that, like their cousins in the older counties, and squealing their displeasure every bit as loudly when the hour for delivery comes.

I was summoned then to this village. I arrived. The mailman's snowmobile continued towards Gaspé. I went into the store to make enquiries about my patient. "Come over here," said the storekeeper, and from the window he pointed out the house, to the east of the bay, beside the shore, where the patient was waiting for me. Thus informed, I returned to the counter where I had placed my bag before going to the window. It was a fine bag, black and shiny, its ears pricked up. A mere glance would have told you it was new! "By Jove," said the storekeeper, "fine *portuna** you have there, doctor!" I was disconcerted: why had he called my bag that? Was he trying to make fun of me? With a rather inane grin I thanked him, wished him good day, and at last reached the door, glad indeed to be out of the store. Then, somewhat heartened by the fresh air, I set off, with my *portuna* under my arm, along the path of the trail-blazing pigs.

I soon noticed that my person was arousing some interest; curtains would be drawn discreetly aside in order to watch me pass, or I would be stared at shamelessly through the glass. This curiosity was in a sense justified: was I not new to the place? In order to create a favourable impression I walked slowly, with all the dignity I could muster. And for a time all

---

* *portuna*. A mystery! An archaic term of uncertain origin. Ferron uses it often, though it is extremely rare today and understood by very few Québécois.

went well. Then I heard a grunt. I glanced behind me and saw the animal. At first I asked myself, amused: "What on earth can have possessed this pig to follow me?"

My amusement was, alas, short-lived. I remembered that dark, somewhat truffled corner of my mind, which at the time I felt I was the only person to possess. Not for the world would I have admitted it was there. And now, just when I was endeavouring, with the bearing of a funeral horse, to be worthy of my noble profession, this horrid animal, with its infallible snout, was uncovering that secret corner for an entire village to behold. What to do in such circumstances? "The best thing," I said to myself, "is to pay no attention." So I kept on going, but I was not happy. The pig stayed right behind me. I could hear it grunting at regular intervals. Soon it seemed to me that these intervals were becoming shorter, and that the grunting noises were not at all alike. What could this mean? To satisfy my curiosity, I glanced once more over my shoulder: the *portuna* almost fell from my grasp: there were four of them! One was bad enough, but four! It was more than my pride could take. And I very nearly lost my head, turned on those cursed pigs and booted them in the snout. My sense of dignity prevailed. Besides, I was not yet ready to admit defeat. "If I stop," I said to myself, "perhaps they'll pass me. Then all I'll have to do is not follow them."

So I stepped to the side of the path; I lit a cigarette. The pigs had nothing to smoke, but they too stopped, and there was no indication that they might be persuaded to take the lead. So I moved on in the hope that they would remain fixed to the spot; they started off again immediately. My only hope now was to quicken my pace, forcing them to abandon the pursuit. My efforts were in vain. They would not leave me; they trotted along behind me, grunting joyfully. There was nothing else I could do. I was disgraced for ever more. The houses crowded in on me as I passed; the whole village was afforded the spectacle of a doctor of medicine being followed by four pigs.

I had the courage to continue. Besides, I was now approaching my patient's house. I knocked. The door was opened. I was prepared for the worst, prepared, for example, to hear them say: "By all means, doctor, feel free to bring your friends in."

I was received with the utmost courtesy. The pigs remained outside.

THE ARCHANGEL OF THE SUBURB

The archangel Zag was not in Heaven at the time of the famous battle between Lucifer and Saint Michael; he was on Earth. When word of it reached him, he concluded that he had been most inspired to make this trip and decided to extend his stay. So it was that until quite recently he still dwelt among us, in a shack along Chambly Road, near the marsh which then served as boundary and garbage dump for the parishes of Saint-Hubert and Saint-Antoine-de-Longueuil. To the profane he was an old anarchist, a retired vagabond, one of those likeable outlaws who are the very charm of the suburbs. As for the clerics, they didn't even suspect he was there. Zag avoided them, was distrustful of them as of the devil. With the exception of one, Brother Benoit of the Coteau-Rouge Franciscans, who often came to see him and whom he received with pleasure. Brother Benoit would bring holy pictures and religious trinkets, which Zag, out of regard for him and also as a precaution against the police, who can always make things difficult for a tramp, used to decorate his hut. But that was as far as he would go. He had said to Brother Benoit: "Why do you try to convert me?

I don't try to make an angel out of you." He would not tolerate the mention of good or evil, of Heaven or Hell; to him these distinctions were distasteful. So Brother Benoit had ceased to preach at him, continuing nevertheless to visit him, out of pure loving-kindness, good Franciscan that he was.

Now Zag, who in spite of everything was no earthling, set out one morning bright and early along Chambly Road in the direction of Longueuil. At the first crossroads he turned left and found himself on the Coteau-Rouge road, heading for Saint-Josaphat. In actual fact, he wasn't too sure where he was going. He zigzagged along as if drunk; at times his feet would leave the ground; he continued in this fashion for some distance. Apart from his flying, he looked for all the world like a wino. Meanwhile it was getting late, the suburb was waking up, three or four clandestine cocks crowed in defiance of the municipal regulations, and people began to gather at the street corners to wait for the yellow bus of their misfortune, people still worn out from the previous day's work. And now that same rattle-trap bus was heading straight for Zag, who leapt up into the air and clear over it. The driver, flabbergasted, drove right past the next stop, cursed by those he'd forgotten. Their protests brought the archangel back to his senses. He felt ashamed of himself, and returned to his shack in low spirits. But the next morning he was again excited, light-headed as a bird on the eve of migration. This time he went off across the fields and following along the edge of the marsh, soon found himself near the Franciscan monastery. The day was fine and bright. He stretched out on the grass. In the distance he could see the pink and grey haze of the city, the arches of the bridge and the summit of Mount Royal. However, there was a bush blocking his view. Zag said to it: "Cast off thy leaves." The bush obeyed so promptly that a hen, perched among the foliage, was stripped of her feathers at the same time. This hen stared at Zag in dumb amazement, and he, equally surprised, stared back at the naked fowl. They finally came to their senses, the hen protesting, the archangel laughing, and the louder the one laughed the angrier the other became. Once Zag had taken a moment to wet his whistle, he said: "Don't fret, old dear, I'll soon fix that. Only I can't promise to put your feathers back exactly the way you had them; I might make a mistake and put one of the tail-feathers on the wing or one from the neck on the tail." But the hen demanded to be feathered as before.

"In that case," said Zag, "go fetch me some dry wood-chips." The hen brought them to him.

"Now an iron rod." She brought that too.

"And last of all," said Zag, "go into the monastery kitchen; there you'll find some matches."

The hen went into the monastery kitchen, found the matches and brought them. Then Zag grabbed hold of her, skewered her, lit a fire and roasted her. Brother Benoit, who happened to be in the monastery kitchen meditating on a pot of chickpeas and herring, for it was a Friday, had had his appetite whetted and had followed after the naked fowl.

"Ah! Brother Benoit," cried Zag, "you couldn't have come at a better moment! I've a theological problem to put to you."

Brother Benoit stretched out on the grass.

"What advice would you give to an archangel in exile on Earth, who was beginning to lose his sense of gravity and jump in the air like a harum-scarum?" asked Zag.

Brother Benoit answered, "There is only one thing for him to do: go back to Heaven."

"That's all very well," said Zag, "but it so happens that this archangel was absent at the time of the Lucifer–Saint

Michael match; how can he be sure he'd have been on the side of the latter?"

Brother Benoit asked, "While this archangel was on Earth, did he seek out the company of the proud and the mighty, of aldermen and other potentates?"

"No," replied Zag. And as he spoke he handed Brother Benoit a chicken leg. The fasting Franciscan took a bite and found it to his liking. In his satisfaction he declared: "Let him go to Heaven!"

"Then farewell, my friend," said the archangel Zag. And the beggar's garment, the wino's rags fell among the leaves of the bush and the feathers of the late hen. Brother Benoit ran to the monastery, and to his Father Superior he related the wondrous story.

"What is that?" asked the Father Superior.

"A chicken bone."

"And what day of the week is it, Brother?"

"Friday," poor Benoit had to admit.

And thus it was that a great miracle ended in a confession. An angel, even an archangel, cannot spend time on Earth without falling into some mischief.

THE BRIDGE

This was some time ago. The Seaway Canal had not yet been dug. In the evenings I was in the habit of forgetting my practice and seeking out another world on the other side of the river. The bridge marked the halfway point, and was itself divided, both architecturally and according to the direction in which I was going. When I approached it from the south, crossing over to the north, no structure was visible overhead, and I hardly noticed I had left the road. I would walk under an open sky as far as the Île Sainte-Hélène. There it seemed I was already in Montreal. I was no longer aware of the bridge, so eagerly was I anticipating the night's encounters. But as I returned, tired, disappointed, my eyes could not escape the compelling power of its superstructure and the magnificent tracery of its steel girders. Night enclosed it like a cathedral. I would enter it with remorse, regretting the time I had wasted and my neglected duties. The high black arch came to an end and opened out onto the lights of the lowest stars, and those along the plain which stretches from Longueuil to Chambly, from Saint Lambert to Saint-Amable, these lights variously grouped in constellations, small villages, and large suburbs. In the midst of this glimmering rose the dark shapes of the mountains – Saint Bruno, Beloeil, and Rougemont. This sight would reconcile me to my side of the river. Each time I would vow never to leave it again.

Sometimes I would pass a horse and cart. The driver was a woman. In the cart she carried scrap-metal to Montreal, then headed back to Coteau Rouge, where she was a fellow citizen of mine. I knew her. She was one of those English women, still marked by the old world, who for some strange reason flee their race and feel happy only among French Canadians. The latter in return assimilate them. This is where we get a good many of our red-heads. One does one's best to gallicize, usually from the bottom up, while Englishness asserts itself from the top down. Nothing could have been more wretched nor at the same time more proud than this woman. The shack she lived in was divided in two by a semi-partition: on one side the horse, on the other side her family. This family: her husband, pin boy in a bowling alley, a good-for-nothing, and two rather snotty children.

There and back, her expedition took her about four hours. She left around ten o'clock in the evening. That was roughly the hour I left the south shore. And my return often coincided with hers. Now, at the time, because of a photographer friend who wanted to go into film-making, I was thinking in terms of cinema. I'd thought of using this strange group. The action of the film, its climax and its denouement, would take place within four hours. By showing from time to time the horse, the cart, the English woman, I felt I could indicate in an interesting way the precious moments allotted to the characters for their happiness or unhappiness. However, the idea was not new, and I was all the less original for having seen *The Phantom Carriage*.* Besides, the photographer did not go into films; he became a journalist instead, and I stopped thinking about my scenario. Yet I was left with the pretext for the film – this little group, which measured the passing of time and was a reminder of destiny. Today I cannot think of the bridge without remembering them. I've always had a weakness for fine words and beautiful images – even secondhand. That's probably why I write.

During the day the English woman would go along the streets of the suburb before the arrival of the garbage trucks. Old springs, the remains of washing machines and stoves, any old metal interested her. She went to a great deal of trouble and earned very little money. Perhaps it was to make use of her horse, quite a fine animal. But what do I know? What did I ever know about her? Everything was an enigma, even her age. Was she twenty-five, thirty, thirty-five? Thin, bony, red-haired, and not in the least feminine, she aroused neither desire nor pity. She seemed to expect nothing from anyone and to remain, in everything she did, an outsider. Perhaps she was mad. She had fine features and her skin was extremely white. She never struck me as vulgar; on the contrary, by a strange air of authority, she commanded respect. But this authority was due perhaps to her origins and to our own feeling of inferiority. I had noticed she was growing rather stout. One night I was called to her shack. She had given birth alone. I cut the cord and completed the delivery. She didn't utter a word or make a sound. She seemed to be thinking of something else. This third child did not prevent her from going back to her work. But a few months later she

---

* *Körkarlen* (1920) by Victor Sjöström, a classic of the Swedish cinema, based on the novel by Selma Lagerlöf.

disappeared. I still meet her good-for-nothing husband reeling along. No one has seen her since, neither her nor her horse, the last one to cross the river regularly. The cart has become, like that carriage, a phantom one. If I see it again some night on the deserted bridge I'll know I have had an accident.

THE PARROT

I f she had been vulgar, coarse, fleshy, it might not have been so surprising, but she was, on the contrary, a very prim and proper lady, tight-cheeked to say the least. What, then, could have possessed her to show her behind?

Her nephew appeared in my office, embarrassed, unsure how to go about telling me the awful truth.

"The fact is, doctor, my Aunt Donatienne has been behaving very strangely."

And he had come to ask for my help in getting her into a mental hospital. I wasn't surprised: it's the fashion now to shut people up. Faced with an undesirable who's not a criminal, we simply say he's sick, and he can be imprisoned without trial. In this respect medicine is a most useful institution, a branch of the law. Doctors themselves are generally well-fitted for their role; they make excellent jailers. All they have to learn now is the executioner's trade.

"But is she actually mad, this aunt of yours?" I asked the nephew.

"Oh yes, doctor."

"In what way?"

That he couldn't tell me. He asked me to come with him. I would see for myself in what way. So we went off together. The aunt lived out in the rural part of Coteau-Rouge.

"Stop here," said my companion suddenly.

We stopped near a signpost that said, "Rue Sainte-Olive." The sign would have gladdened the heart of any nominalist philosopher: there was no street in sight, only two or three houses in the middle of a field. The nephew pointed to one of them.

"There it is," he said.

"But that's Monsieur Comtois' house!"

"You're right," he replied, "it is."

And with a sheepish look in my direction he asked how it was I knew. I'd visited this Monsieur Comtois the year before. I remembered him well. A little old boy with whiskers in his ears, a mouthful of crude jokes, and cheeky as a monkey, who lived with his daughter and a parrot. The daughter was one of those gals who knows her stuff, wised-up but none too bright, the kind they call a floozie. It was rather surprising that she should have stayed on with her daddy. As for the parrot, he hadn't made too good an impression on me either.

"A fine parrot you have there," I'd said to Monsieur Comtois. As if in response to my words, the bird had begun to flutter its wings.

"He's a vain little fellow," the old man replied.

"Does he talk?"

"No, but he's got something he'd like to show you."

"What's that?" I asked.

I could have saved myself the trouble. My curiosity had been well received. They lost no time in satisfying it.

"Coco," said the daughter, "would you like to show the doctor what a smart boy you are?"

Coco having indicated that he would (it was obvious from his fluttering), she continued: "Go on, Coco, show him your bum. Show the nice doctor your bum."

And, painstakingly, the bird had shown it.

Once the ceremony was over, the homage paid, I'd busied myself with old Comtois, who was having an attack of colic. The case had baffled me. I'd nevertheless comforted him as best I could. That's the way I practise. I'm ruthlessly optimistic. The old boy had never called me again. So I'd assumed he was cured.

"How's Monsieur Comtois these days?" I inquired.

"Dead," my companion answered flatly.

That's the trouble with optimism: you can't keep it up for long. Even though I'd not ruled out the possibility of his dying, I'd still not foreseen that the old boy would lose his cheekiness so soon. "He must have fallen into the hands of a pessimistic doctor," I thought.

We were almost at the house. The nephew explained that Comtois had been his Aunt Donatienne's brother.

"But," he added, obviously embarrassed, "he was not the father of his daughter."

After his death the orphan had been advised to find herself another daddy, and Aunt Donatienne had taken over the inheritance. At first she seemed happy, then the parrot had died. . . . We had reached the house.

"Come in, doctor," said the nephew.

I went in first. A little old lady, modestly attired, was sitting on the edge of a chair in the attitude of a novice awaiting her bishop. The awkwardness of the position seemed to suit her. She was reading with an air of quiet contentment. We had been standing inside for some time before she deigned to acknowledge our presence. Affecting surprise, she rose hurriedly to her feet. I begged her to sit down again, which she did most readily. The house was spotless. There was an air of refinement about it, rare in this rural part of Coteau-Rouge, and I took it to be an innovation, since I didn't recall having noticed it in the days when old Comtois had occupied the premises with his floozie.

The old lady had closed her missal. We embarked on a conversation which was polite, refined, flowery, but dreadfully trite, reminiscent of those paper flowers that adorn side altars. As soon as I ventured anything less insipid, she would take fright, and her answers would become evasive. Embarrassed myself, I would take refuge again in the pious artificiality that put her at her ease. When the time came for me to leave, I had discovered nothing. In fact I was quite captivated by this aunt and could find only the most complimentary things to say to her nephew as he led me away.

"Well, she's refined all right, is Aunt Donatienne," the nephew admitted. "But there's a reason for that. She worked for thirty years with her elder sister in the millinery business – making feathered hats for society ladies. There's no trade like it for giving you airs. Then her sister died and she went into a convent. Terribly posh, shiniest floors you ever saw: you needed the grace of God to walk around the place."

"Why didn't she stay there?"

"At the convent? That's simple: at night she never slept. She wandered around the dormitories like a ghost. Or if there was a nun or a boarder she particularly fancied, she'd go sit on the edge of her bed and watch over her while she slept. She imagined she was some kind of guardian angel."

"She'd let herself get too refined."

"Perhaps so. But the trouble was she had everyone scared

to death. In the end they threw her out. I took her in. Then, when her brother died, she came to live here."

"I'm beginning to understand," I said.

The nephew gave me a searching look. He had let himself get carried away on the subject of his aunt's fine manners – manners of which he was proud – but that didn't mean he'd forgotten his plan, which was to get her into a mental hospital. Worried, he asked me, "You do think she's mad, don't you, doctor?"

"Peculiar, perhaps. Affected, certainly. But she's not mad. If that were madness we'd have to clear out the convents and the academies and lock up all the poetesses in Canada and all the nuns on earth."

He seemed surprised at my lack of discernment.

"But," he objected, "are the nuns and poetesses of Canada in the habit of showing their behinds to passersby?"

"To my knowledge Aunt Donatienne has not shown me hers," I retorted, piqued.

Now it was my turn to scrutinize him. He seemed sure of himself. Then I remembered the parrot.

"Good God, it can't be true!"

It was true. Aunt Donatienne had not only inherited the house, but the parrot too. At first she had tried to teach him to pray: "Coco, say, 'The Lord's name be praised!'"

She had been wasting her time. Coco had continued to show his behind. The old lady had had to accept it. After a while she began to enjoy it. The bird's fluttering excited her. From then on she was forever telling him:

"Coco, show me your bum."

Until in the end poor Coco had died of it. After that she had taken to showing her own. And in no time at all word had got round. She couldn't go out now without a band of children following at her heels. The more the children squealed, the more excited she got, and the more she showed them what they wanted to see. At night the local perverts prowled around outside the little house, terrorizing the lady who had once taken herself for a guardian angel.

We had stopped to talk outside the front door. It was a sunny afternoon. The window panes reflected the sunlight. A cloud passed overhead. Before setting off I gave a last glance at the window. I saw something white. It was Aunt Donatienne. It was that very prim and proper lady showing us her poor, frilly behind.

THE CHILD

A husband was on his deathbed; his beard was long; he
looked like a seal. However, he was in no hurry to
die. His wife had been sitting up for a week; she was
beginning to lose patience. It would have been different had
there been a steady decline, but no: he had ups and downs; he
was playing games with death, he was not taking dying seriously. Most of the time he stayed under water, unconscious,
hiding his hand. Whenever he came up again, suddenly
opening an eye at the surface, he would catch his wife off-
guard; she would have no time to pull herself together; he
would see her in all her weariness, just when she was beginning to hope he would stay under. Then she would put her
hand over her face; "Oh dear!" she would say.

That was not enough; she would start asking questions
again. How did he feel? Had he slept well? His only answer
was to grunt – he was not at all obliging – to grunt, then dive
under again. She resolved, rather than have a seal for a
husband, to be a widow.

The doctor had left some medicine that did not have to
be taken. She sniffed it and decided that it would be wiser to

continue giving it to him, only she slightly overdid the dose. Once, when she had been particularly generous, her hand shook. "Take it, dear," she said. The husband turned his head away. She didn't insist. But when the doctor called again: "Oh, doctor, I can't stand it any more: my husband doesn't trust me." The good doctor administered the potion to the sick man: "Come, come, this will help you."

"Thank you, doctor," said the wife.

She was a good woman, and had been a good wife as long as the husband had seemed a good man. Together they had built a house, put money aside, and in comfort had nourished fond hopes of having children. They had had none. Whose fault was it? She blamed herself; it is always the innocent who admit guilt. This had given her the strength to endure, for ten years and more, the pecking of a useless cock.

The potion had its effect, the priest had to be called in to administer the last rites to the dying man. When the ceremony was over, the priest lit a candle and went away. The wife remained alone with her husband; she fell asleep and dreamed she held a child in her arms. While she was sleeping, the poor man came up again – he was a hard one to kill – a bubble burst on the surface of the water, he saw his wife, the child, and the candle: his wife happy, the child looking at him in terror, and the candle half burned away. He didn't know what to think. Who was he? A seal? A wet cock? He was certainly no longer the husband. Then he found the strength to raise himself up, put out the candle, and die.

THE LANDSCAPE PAINTER

A lazy man in league with a half-wit, the latter thinking for the former, the former working for the latter, lived, wonderstruck, a life of long idleness. It was in that goodly province of Gaspé, which is so theatrical, where the earth has been pushed up into a pile of mountains, a pile you can lean your back against and hardly believe your eyes. This is what you see: the sky moving down, the sea rising up, and these two planes meeting to form a variable angle, and within this angle, space itself finding room enough to yawn. All very fine! However none of it lasts; it simply takes a liner to show its mast above the horizon and this geometry is destroyed. It's hard to build the sea on such fluidity: in the end the vastness you give it is no better than water in a sieve. Nevertheless, our man, Jeremiah by name, had before him a plentiful supply of air, enough to breathe in with both lungs, his mouth, his nose, however he pleased, and even enough to yawn as well. But when he yawned, matching the angle of his jaws to that of sky and sea, his opening was always the smaller, and that other space would swallow him up. He would become the boat anchored out at sea, that other boat still in the bay, or the one at the mouth, on its way out or in, advancing to the sound of cannon shots on the head of its single piston; he would become the sun, the source of all energy, yet less boastful than the Acadia engine shaking the universe with its puffy prowess, the sun whose copper propeller turns so fast it sleeps on its tip, a spinning top whose axis is the heart of the waterspout of birds frenzied by the return of the fishermen and the gutting of the fish. He would become anything he happened to see, with that preference the eye has for movement. The mêlée of birds fascinated him. How quickly he would spot a tardy gull in the distance and how impatiently watch it draw near, longing to plunge it into their midst. From then on this gull would be his; with it he would dive into the fray, in and out of the turmoil, never tiring, at times amazed to find himself emerge as a smaller gull, diving back at once in search of his identity, endlessly losing then finding himself again, swallowing some morsel in passing, gorging, excreting, caught in the movement which the radiant propeller, the top drowsing on its tip, sends up at the surface of the water – the gush of spray, the waterspout of mad wings, the cyclone of harsh cries, the fever of life, the whirlwind exposing the heart of the sea and bringing forth a raw, wild Aphrodite smelling of cod. Then Jeremiah would ask himself whose plaything he was – his own, the sun's or God's? His question disappeared in the form of a taciturn gull with its neck drawn in, winging its way mournfully into the distance, releasing one last dropping – perhaps that was the answer.

But the noise of the motor, the carrion dance of the birds, the all-powerful sun, decaying death, the arousal of life, Aphrodite, all that, and the *décor* – the land pushed back to the mountains, the village sloping down to the sea as in a theatre – was but one aspect of the landscape which Jeremiah, from the time he was a child, in all seasons, winter and summer, had painted upon the day, a sketch done in a few hours, continued the following day, the landscape he was unable to finish, irritating as life that will not die. Jeremiah was thirty-eight. His greatest success had been to gain acceptance by those around him. The concordat obligated them to give him food, clothing and shelter. For a long time they had resisted. As Jeremiah seemed to be a lazy man in league with a half-wit, the latter thinking for the former, the former working for the latter, they would speak to him very quickly, using puns and clever language, with the intention of confusing him, of "straightening him out" as they put it, in order that inadvertently the lazy man might think and the half-wit work. Jeremiah had remained intractable. Anywhere else but in the Gaspé they would have sent him away to study painting in a madhouse, for in those provinces where houses have been lit by electricity for more than a generation, they consider themselves to be in heaven already; they choose their children; the others go to prison, damned. In the Gaspé this is not yet so; people are still people. So it was that when all attempts to lead him astray had failed, Jeremiah obtained his concordat. Since negotiations had been long, it was agreed that in order to make up for the harm this could have done his reputation, they should give him nothing and owe him everything, looking after his needs in exchange for his services. This amounted to recognition of his art. They went even further; when the census was taken and Her Majesty's agent asked, "What does this fellow do?" they replied: "Sir, he does landscapes." Whereupon the official put him down as a landscape painter. This had been copied into books and circulated all over America, even as far as our most distant capitals.

There was no going back on it; the name stuck. Henceforth Jeremiah was known as the landscape painter.

All day long he yawned, caught up in that space which yawned even wider, in the colours and lines, the movement and the harmonics of the picture. When the weather was fine he would paint out of doors, when it was not, behind a window, on a pane of glass, taking care to see that it adhered to space. In the evening he was free; they would come and chat with him. Since he painted by projection – live, you might say – following with perfect accuracy the reality he embraced, onlookers already knew all about his latest land-scape, one having strolled there, another fished, and all having seen it. This participation added to the dimensions of his work, an edifice all the more amazing for being a cathedral built in a day, to be engulfed at night by the sea, an ephemeral edifice of water and air, whose beauty lay in its very fluidity. Jeremiah knew how to come down to the level of those con-federates, who when looking at his work had retained only the piquant crystallisations on its surface, the details, the triviali-ties, the accidents. Perhaps they were indifferent to the artist's inspiration, for they never spoke of it. "Not a bad shower that," they would say. "Turned out well, that wind of yours! Didn't think much of your morning drizzle." Appreciation, compliment, or reproach, Jeremiah listened to it quite humbly, for everything about his work was important to him, even a fleeting reflection in indifferent eyes. This small talk occupied the evening, then one by one the art-lovers withdrew, and last of all Jeremiah would go to bed, alone. Whereas he had once been thin, eating half-heartedly, anxious during the day, but sleeping well at night, he had now put on weight, no longer hesitated to eat his fill, and had become a fine-looking man; but at night he was uneasy. The wind off the land, which in the evening begins to creep along the mountains, gradually swelling, like torrents of strident birds spreading wide their wings to avoid the roofs of the houses – this wind seemed baleful to him. These were no longer the white wings of day crowning his creation. The malice of the night troubled him. His terrors dated from the time of the concordat; acceptance by his own had made him an exile from himself, and, unable to express himself through them as is natural in the species, he remained in torment and only found peace beneath the sun. He slept little, badly, or sometimes not at all. Often he would get up, leave the house – and what would he find? Debris, sombre masses, emptiness, the deep moaning of the wind. And he would wander till dawn along the shore, through the ruins of his work. One of those nights he drowned.

The next day and all the following week there was fog. Then the landscape reappeared. From then on it returned day after day, season after season. This was the landscape Jeremiah had painted day after day, season after season, for years, leaving behind him enough to last forever. No one recognized it. The artist had forgotten to sign.

THE PROVINCES*

There once was born a cartographer in the heart of old Quebec, which is to say in the country that lies downriver from Trois-Rivières, and since he bore a mark the shape of the fleur-de-lis just above his buttocks, everyone knew that he would be no ordinary cartographer. When he was old enough to earn his living, his parents brought him before the priest. "We don't know what to do with him, Father. He's not like the other children. All the others had to do was follow the roads that lead to Montreal, Abitibi or the Farwest. This one is a cartographer."

"A cartographer! Splendid!" exclaimed the priest. "We'll send him to our Bishop, who is also the Primate of the Church in this country."

---

* The story relies for its effect on the ambiguities surrounding the word *province*, which can have political and even religious overtones, depending on whether the perspective is federal or separatist or that of the regular or secular clergy. Of course, there are other ambiguities here too, as in the case of the words *country* and *region*, for the cartographer seems fated to talk at cross-purposes with the official spokesmen of Quebec.

72

His Eminence the Primate said to the cartographer: "Very well, then: divide the country up into dioceses." Which the cartographer proceeded to do. Each diocese had its colour. For example, Valleyfield was a magnificent blue. The others ranged all the way from yellow to black. Many were green, but not a single one was red. The cartographer presented his work to the Primate. Above the country he had put the sky, with the sun, the moon and several planets. It was a very beautiful map.

"That's a strange sun you've painted there, Mr. Cartographer!"

"I've given it a hat, Your Eminence."

"Ah, so it's a hat!"

"Yes, your Eminence. And notice how perfectly placed it is: just over Montreal!"*

"I see, my friend, I see."

"And I've also painted the diocese black, Your Eminence, to give some idea of the Sulpician influence. Your own diocese is white, with the moon directly over Quebec. The planets are for the Archbishops' palaces."

The Primate was a shrewd and very distinguished man, extremely high-minded, yet meticulous and exact as a watchmaker. "Mr. Cartographer, you've one planet too many. Valleyfield is only the seat of a Bishop!"

"Yes indeed, Your Eminence. But I thought it would please you. The Bishop there came so close to getting the Hat!† He really deserved a little planet in compensation."

---

* This is the hat of Cardinal Léger, who in 1953 became Montreal's first Cardinal.

† A reference to Bishop Langlois, who in a famous incident in 1933, was transferred to Valleyfield from Quebec, where he had been expected to succeed Monseigneur Bégin as Archbishop and Cardinal.

"Quite so, my friend, quite so."

The cartographer rubbed his hands.

"Could you grant me your imprimatur, then, Your Eminence?"

"Imprimatur, my friend?"

"Yes, Your Eminence, so that this map may be hung in every house where men fear God and respect his representatives."

"What a strange idea, my friend! We are not Caesars. We are not pashas. We may live in palaces, but these are only appearances. Our kingdom is not of this world."

"Then, Your Eminence, my Catholic, diocesan, episcopal map is not the true map of our country!"

"No, my friend."

"You surprise me. . . . But I must take your word for it, Your Eminence. What is to become of me now?"

"You will go on making maps, my friend, since that is your vocation."

Even though his kingdom was not of this world the Primate had considerable influence in the government, and he had no trouble placing the cartographer there. The Premier said to the cartographer: "Divide the country up into counties." Which the cartographer then proceeded to do. Each county had its own colour. For example, Deux-Montagnes was a magnificent shade of violet, obtained by mixing Brigadier Sauvé's colour and the flaming red of General Colborne.* The

---

* Brigadier (Paul) Sauvé was a conservative Quebec politician who represented the riding of Deux-Montagnes and served as Premier of the province from 1959 to 1960. General Colborne was at the head of the British troops who defeated the *patriotes* at the battle of Saint-Eustache, during the rebellion of 1837.

others ranged all the way from navy-blue to pink. Many were yellow, but not a single one was white. The cartographer presented his work to the Premier. Above the country he had put the sky, the sun, the moon and several stars. It was a very beautiful map.

"That's a strange sun you've painted there, Mr. Cartographer!"

"It's wearing an English wig, Mr. Premier, Sir."

"Very good, my friend. And what about the moon?"

"A coif, Mr. Premier, a nun's coif."

"Very good, my friend. And what about the stars?"

"These stars in our sky, Mr. Premier, Sir, are probably from the South."

"Very well, my friend. We'll publish your map. Your little celestial allusions don't bother me. I don't claim the stratosphere; the counties are enough for me."

The cartographer lowered his head; he did not share the Premier's view. Indeed, who is to say that a country should be divided into precisely ninety parts, and not thirty-eight or twenty-two? Is it for politics to intrude into geography? Should not geography determine politics? A country is not a piece of cloth to be cut up at will. What if onto these ninety parts some government superimposes another sixty-five? What if all the parts then begin to shift, to shrink, to stretch, to become shorter or flatter with every census? Why, soon, Mr. Pellan and Mr. Borduas themselves will be turning their hand to making maps! The cartographer said to the Premier: "Mr. Premier, Sir, I don't share your view. For me the county is a perfectly arbitrary division."

"Ah, Mr. Cartographer, I see what you're getting at! In your view the county represents an electoral corruption of the art of map-making."

"Mr. Premier, Sir, I don't deny it. What is to become of me now?"

"You must go on making maps, my friend, since that is your vocation."

The Premier, even if his kingdom was of this world, had considerable influence in the Congregations. He had little difficulty placing the cartographer with the Reverend Brothers, who are experts in geography. The Brother said to the cartographer: "Divide the country up into regions." Which the cartographer then proceeded to do. He divided the country into two parts, one cold, the other temperate. Above, he painted the different celestial regions, each with its own sign. He also indicated the various layers of the atmosphere, which are likewise known as regions. Finally, in order to exhaust all possible meanings of the term, he put on his map a shivering French Canadian with all his anatomical regions shown. The cartographer presented his work to the Reverend Sponsor, who was flabbergasted.

"Here," said the artist, "is the map that you asked me to make. All the regions in the dictionary are there except for one: the one to which men rise in certain sciences, also known by the same name, as in the expression 'the higher regions of philosophy.' I couldn't find a way of showing that one, Brother. But you'll find all the others on my map."

"Mr. Cartographer, you've misunderstood me!"

"What do you mean, Brother?"

"What I wanted were the different regions of the Province – the Gaspé, Abitibi, the Saguenay, etc."

"But those are not regions, Brother. You're using a French term in a way that is foreign to French. Those are not regions, they are provinces."

"Provinces within the Province."

"The confusion, Brother, stems not from the former, but from the latter."

The Brother was extremely annoyed. He said to the cartographer: "I shall talk to my superiors about this." His superiors were extremely annoyed. They said to the Brother: "We shall consult our Bishop." The Bishop consulted his housekeeper, who advised him to seek counsel in Rome. Rome referred the matter to the Legate, who passed it on to the Primate. The Primate sent for the cartographer. "Well, my friend, you do cause quite a stir."

"I try to do my best, Your Eminence."

"You are a cartographer, are you not?"

"Yes, Your Eminence."

"Then why don't you go ahead and make your maps as you see fit? Have I ever come and asked you how to say mass? Has my honorable friend, the Premier, ever consulted you on the subject of his elections?"

The cartographer kissed the Primate's ring, for from him he had learned that a man only works well in his own profession, and that it alone is his authority. And he set about building the country, putting it together, province by province, on beautiful illuminated maps. He works alone. There are times when he thinks he must be mad, and times when he sees himself as a prophet. He is only an artist, like so many others.

LA MI-CARÊME

I was only a nipper, a kid from the Shore. At eight I hardly knew la Mi-Carême*, since she had so far always come to our house at night. Then, one morning, my mother realized that things were going to be different for once. Speaking ever so softly, so as not to let me see her pain, she said:

"Go fetch Madame Marie."

I ran and told the old lady, who quickly began changing into a clean apron. I stood waiting for her, thinking she would simply follow me back. But no; once her apron was changed, she grabbed a huge stick and waved it over my head, crying: "You rascal! Off with you!" I bolted, needless to say. My mother, who was watching for me, gave me a questioning look.

---

* In the Gaspé legend has it that babies are brought, not by an Indian, as in other parts of Quebec, but by this imaginary witch-like creature, whose existence is made vividly real to the non-initiated. For Ferron she is as indispensable on one level as the midwife herself is on another. Indeed, he sees the two as complementary, as collaborators exemplifying the interdependence of legend and life. See also the story "The Witch and the Barleycorn."

I nodded my head in reply. A few moments passed. Another look. The same reply. At last the old lady arrived, all out of breath. She fell onto a chair and, winking one eye, sized up the situation with the other. Then, before we knew it, she had turned on us children, even though we had never done her any harm. "Out with you!" she shouted. But we were too stunned to move. So, ever so softly, my poor mother was obliged to say:

"Now run along and go next door."

When we came home, the old lady was waiting for us in the middle of the room with her stick. Behind her, my mother lay in bed, quite still, and she turned her head towards us and smiled. Seeing this, the youngest ones, just chicks themselves and barely hatched, rushed over to her. The old lady caught hold of them and sat them firmly down.

"Don't touch your mother," she said. "La Mi-Carême has been beating her."

And to me she explained: "It happened while you were all next door. I'd just gone out to fetch some wood, when all of a sudden I heard terrible cries. I rushed back in, and what should I see but la Mi-Carême, right here in the house. I wasted no time. I lit straight into her with my big stick. Well, sakes alive! She wasn't expecting that, la Mi-Carême! Away she flew, out through the doors, out through the windows, out through any hole she could find. And in her hurry, guess what she left behind . . . this baby!"

And the old lady winked one eye, watching me with the other.

"Rascal! Do you believe me?"

Yes, yes. I believed her. But already I could hear my father's footsteps coming up to the house. The door opened. My father stood on the threshold, wearing his big boots, his hands all covered with scales, and he said:

79

"I thought la Mi-Carême was in the house."

"She's gone back to the woods," the old woman said. "But just take a look at what she left us."

My father bent over the tiny bundle. When he stood up he looked happy and younger than I'd ever seen him. The herring scales glistened on his arms. He rubbed his hands and stomped his feet in his big boots. And I thought to myself, I, the nipper, that la Mi-Carême ought rightly to have beaten him.

SUMMER LETHE

O n the edge of a village, whose name I forget, a
village called after some outlandish saint who
would flee the church when the priest's back was
turned and hide out in the woods, a wild, unruly saint, eccentric in his ways, a Merovingian or an Ostrogoth, there lived a
widow who would give no thought to marriage. Her husband
had left her decently enough. She had property, a house, a
garden, a sizeable income. However, he had failed to provide
her with the essential: that burning memory of a man's touch
that makes a widow not averse to consolation and allows her
to remain faithful to the entire sex of her dear departed. This
husband, then, had been forgotten, as well he deserved to be.
No sooner had his wife taken her eyes off him than he had
slipped quietly out of her head, through one ear or the other,
and made off to the woods to join the patron saint of the
parish. He had vanished so completely that to the priest the
widow was obliged to admit: "Sometimes I wonder if I was
ever really married." The priest quoted to her from Ecclesiastes,
who says that man is in the life of woman as the bird that
passeth in the air or the fish that swimmeth through the

water. The comparison was refreshing, but offered little hold to the suitors who swarmed around the lady fair, swimming and flying. Now these suitors were none of them children. They were all fine specimens of manhood, upstanding, you might say. Yet, though they came on hard and strong, they failed to take a hold. In time the more impatient among them left to plant their hopes elsewhere. Those that remained, like Aaron, flourished. The widow's garden was the finest in the country. The priest sometimes came to read his breviary there.

This widow herself was lovely, very lovely to behold, clean, fresh, fair of cheek and merry-eyed, well-rounded, plump, yet firm of flesh, clad in the filmiest of garments, surrounded by angels and cupids, one of God's own enticements. The years passed. She did not age. Everyone had grown used to her charm and to her irreproachable sensuality. She became the goddess of the village. When she was nearing fifty she died quite suddenly. Laid out among the flowers, she seemed to be asleep. There was a great crowd at her funeral. It was the beginning of fall. The trees were bent low with the weight of their fruit, the sunflowers stood tall around the edge of the gardens. Everyone looked happy. You would have thought it was a wedding.

But the celebration did not last. Out of the woods came the wild unruly saint, the Ostrogoth, the Merovingian. He took possession of the church again. I remember his name now: Saint Agapit. Winter had begun.

THE GREY DOG

Peter Bezeau, Seigneur of Grand-Étang, had become a widower soon after his marriage, and had replaced his wife with the bottle of rum he drank each night. As the years went by he drained his bottle faster and got to bed earlier, and in this way, little by little, went into his decline. But each morning he was always up again at the very same time, tough and fearless as before. Four big black dogs went with him everywhere, and it was over their heads that he spoke to his men. As the beasts had the reputation of being vicious, his words intimidated. The fishermen and farm-workers he employed all feared him. A few respected him. No one thought of loving him.

When evening came Peter Bezeau would suddenly age. His face grew lined, his eyes glassy and wild. The approach of night filled him with alarm. It was then that he drank his bottle. When he'd finished it he would call to his daughter Nelly to fetch in the dogs. Then he would hurl himself flat on the bed and sink into a deep sleep. Nelly would let in the dogs and go to bed herself.

One morning the Seigneur woke to find among his animals a mysterious grey dog, whose red eyes and furtive manner disconcerted him. He opened the door, and the intruder slipped out, supple as a shadow. One month later it was there again. This time the Seigneur picked up a gun and pushed the door open. The animal fled. But just as he was taking aim it stopped and looked back at him, and from its eyes there darted such flames that the Seigneur was forced to lower his weapon. The dog ran on and disappeared. "Next month, flames or no, I'll shoot," said Seigneur Peter Bezeau. And shoot he did. But when the shot rang out the grey dog was no longer there to receive it.

"It must be a werewolf," he thought.

That night, after he'd finished his rum, he called to Nelly to fetch in the dogs, adding: "The dogs, mind! Not the werewolf!" Nelly thought her father was drunk. Now in the old days she would never have thought such a thing. But lately she hadn't been herself. The next day, when she brought him his bottle, he made a point of telling her so. She shrugged her shoulders. He did the same and turned his attention to his bottle.

One more month passed. The fateful day arrived. Peter Bezeau rose with a feeling of apprehension. He went down to the kitchen. His four big black dogs were there, but of the grey dog there was not a sign. He could breathe again. The nightmare was over. It was then that Nelly appeared on the scene. She was not usually about so early. Surprised, Peter Bezeau studied her closely. Her delicate features seemed smaller than before, her shoulders were thrust back, and her stomach. . . .

"Nelly!"

Nelly didn't move.

"Do you know what's the matter with you, then?"

She did not. Peter Bezeau waited to hear no more. He rushed outside, followed by his four big black dogs. To Madame Marie's house he headed. He left his dogs outside her door and went in.

"Peter Bezeau," says the old woman, "you look worried. Are you ill?"

Without his dogs the Seigneur is a pathetic figure, just an old man of sixty years or more.

"I'm not ill," says he. "I'm worried about my daughter. Come back to the house and tell me what's the matter."

Madame Marie had a look at Nelly.

"Your daughter, Peter Bezeau, is in the family way. And pretty far along she is too."

"Now listen to me, Madame Marie!" says the Seigneur, and this time he's talking to her over the heads of his four big black dogs. "Just you listen to me. If any harm comes to Nelly I'll have you dried and salted like an old cod-fish."

"Will you, indeed, Peter Bezeau? Well, I'm not good for much more than that as it is. But come back and see me tomorrow and I'll give you an answer then."

The next day the Seigneur was at her house at the crack of dawn. He left his dogs outside. He was just a pathetic figure again, an old man of sixty years or more.

"Who got Nelly in this state, Peter Bezeau?"

"I don't know."

The old woman looked hard at him.

"Are you sure?"

Peter Bezeau became uneasy. He admitted what he knew.

"A grey dog with red eyes? A werewolf, then?"

"I was thinking the same myself."

"Peter Bezeau, are you serious? You expect me to deliver your daughter when we don't even know what she's got in her belly! I don't intend to get myself dried and salted like an old cod-fish."

The Seigneur didn't have his dogs. He was just a pathetic figure, an old man of sixty years or more, in despair over his daughter's misfortune. He begged the old woman to have pity on him.

"I'll have pity on you, Peter Bezeau. But you must do as I say. Fetch me Madame Rose, Thomette Tardif, Pope Jane from Gros-Morne and Madame Germaine. With their help I'll deliver Nelly, I swear, even if she's pregnant with a unicorn."

No sooner had she spoken than the Seigneur was running toward the shore, his four big black dogs bounding ahead of him and barking in the wind. Seagulls burst from their mouths and flew out to the wharf, where they merged with the foam of the waves. Presently four boats weighed anchor and put out to sea.

The first boat would sail back from Cloridorme with Madame Rose, who was thin and cunning and knew the art of deceiving young women as to the nature of their pains, making them believe they were only stomach cramps that would soon pass, while the labour pains would not start for another nine days. She denied labour in its early stages, the better to affirm it later on, when it was nearly over. She was a very useful old lady. The second boat would come in from Gros-Morne with Jane Andicotte, known as Pope Jane, because she owned a huge English Bible. From this Bible she drew strange magical incantations that had the power to seize the soul and raise it a full two feet above the bed, leaving the belly free to get on and do its work, without any fuss or bother. The third boat would have on board Madame Germaine from Échourie who handled a babe like a piece of fine satin. And, last of all, Thomette Tardif would arrive in the fourth boat from Mont-Louis, bringing hooks he'd made himself, to be used in the event the child (or monster) got stuck in Nelly's loins.

When the boats were all in, the three midwives, Pope Jane, and the man with the hooks shut themselves up with the Seigneur's daughter. The Seigneur himself was banished from the house and stayed outside. From time to time a young man came out to bring him news. And in this way he learned that Madame Rose had finished her little deceits and that Pope Jane had replaced her and was reading from her big book. The hours seemed long. At last, as day drew to a close, the young man came out, beaming.

"The women have sent Thomette away," he announced.

The Seigneur looked at him over the heads of his four big black dogs.

"Who are you, young man?" he asked. "And how do you know so much?"

"I am your manager. Don't you recognize me?"

"I don't like my managers. They're too ambitious. They all want to steal my estate."

The young man didn't answer. Night was falling.

"Monsieur Bezeau," he said, "come to the store. We'll be more comfortable waiting there."

The Seigneur followed him. They sat down inside the store. The four big black dogs began at once to sniff at the cellar door.

"What do they smell?"

"I've no idea."

"Open the door and we'll soon see."

The manager opened the door and the Seigneur saw a grey dog with red eyes that he knew well.

"Whose animal is this?" he asked.

"Mine," replied the manager.

At that moment someone came to inform them that a son had been born to Nelly in the most felicitous manner possible. The two men went back to the house, which was all lit up. When the lamps had been blown out, the Seigneur asked, "Who will bring me my rum?" It was the able young manager who brought it. Peter Bezeau emptied the bottle, hurled himself flat on his bed and fell asleep as usual. In the days that followed, however, he seemed changed. Now everyone saw that he was a pathetic figure, just an old man of sixty years or more. He died soon after.

His four big black dogs searched for a time around his grave, then, finding nothing, they too disappeared from Grand-Étang. The grey dog took their place.

THE DEAD COW IN THE CANYON

I

François Laterrière, the fifth son of Esdras Laterrière of Trompe-Souris *rang**, Saint-Justin de Maskinongé, came of good stock. When he was sixteen years old he already looked twenty. His father said to him:

"You're not a child any more."

"No," he admitted.

The conversation went no further. Several months passed, and the old man continued:

"Well then, my boy, seeing as how you're not a child any more, have you thought what you're going to be in life?"

---

* *rang*. In Ontario, a "concession." The French word, referring to the adjacent farms along a country road running parallel to a river, is typically Québécois and has been kept throughout. A rural parish generally encompasses a village and several of these *rangs* (literally "rows"), which, because of the narrowness of the lots and the proximity of the farmhouses, are like small communities in themselves. The term dates from the earliest days of the seigneurial system in New France and, like "habitant," has no true equivalent in English.

"Yes, Pa: a habitant like you."

A strange idea, this, coming from the youngest son! The old man made up his mind to give it some thought. A year later he asked his son:

"Hey, François, who was it put such an idea into your head?"

"What idea?"

"Lord love us! The idea of becoming a habitant."

"The priest, Pa."

The priest. Now that was a serious matter. Esdras Laterrière, his brow knit, realized the going could be tough. "Whatever I do," he thought, "I must be sure and not rush things."

"François," he said, "I have great respect for the priest. You know that. But the more I think about it, the harder it is for me to understand. Why ever would he advise you to become a habitant?"

"Because that's what you are, because that's what your father was, and because we must preserve the heritage of our ancestors."

"The heritage of our ancestors?"

"Yes, Pa."

The old man waited to hear no more. He hitched up the old grey mare, jumped onto the cart, and with a "Giddap!" was off to the presbytery.

"*Monsieur le curé,* I've come to pay my tithe."

"There was no hurry, my friend."

When the calculations were completed and the arithmetic done, the habitant did not budge from his chair.

"And there's something else," he said.

The priest had suspected as much.

"There's my son François," the habitant continued, "he's stirring up trouble at home."

The priest expressed surprise. The habitant explained.

"But there's been a misunderstanding!" the priest objected. "François has no intention of ousting his eldest brother! The land will go to him, whole and undivided. François knows that as well as you and I do. He simply wants to follow in your footsteps and become an honest farmer himself, Monsieur Laterrière."

"He doesn't want my land?"

"No, he doesn't, I can assure you."

"Then I have to agree with you, Father. He's not a bad boy at all."

The habitant, however, was not entirely reassured. He had nothing against his son becoming a farmer, but where was he going to get his land?

"That's a mere detail, Monsieur Laterrière!"

"A detail! There's no land left in the parish, and there's none in the county either."

The priest rose to his feet.

"There was no more land in France. Our ancestors found it in Canada. There's no more in the county, no more in the province, you say? Your son won't let that stand in his way. He'll find land somewhere else!"

"Where?" the habitant asked.

"In the Farwest,"* the priest replied.

Esdras Laterrière had never heard of any such country. The Farwest, Patagonia . . . they were one and the same to him. But no matter. His worries were over. His boy would not be setting himself up at his expense. Back home again, he said:

"François, I've found you some land."

---

* Here, as elsewhere, Ferron writes *Farouest*.

François thanked him. The next day he set out for the Farwest. Two years later he arrived in Regina.

"*Monsieur,*" he asked the first man to come along, "is the Farwest still here?"

"No," said the man, "it's moved to Calgary."

The lad from Trompe-Souris was beginning to find the Farwest a little too much for him. In Toronto they had told him it was in Winnipeg; in Winnipeg they had said it was in Regina; and now he had reached Regina only to discover it had already moved to Calgary. The land of Esdras Laterrière had never shifted an inch. True, it was very well fenced. . . .

"It's a strange country, this Farwest, *Monsieur!*"

The first man to come along agreed with him politely, then bade him goodday. This man was followed shortly after by a second man, but François did not speak to him, nor to any of the others who came his way. Without further pause, he continued on to Calgary.

Calgary is a city with wide avenues, where there are no longer any horses to be seen. There are, however, a great many horsemen, whose sleek boots, thick belts, steel spurs and high hats all attest to the fact that they have left their mounts at the city gates. The avenues themselves tell you nothing you do not already know, show you nothing that cannot be seen elsewhere. But close your eyes for a moment and you hear the hard jangle of spurs on the pavement. In an instant the ordinary world is abolished, for the place is surrounded by a thousand horses, impatiently pawing the dust. You breathe the air they blow from their ardent nostrils; it is the air of the Farwest. François inhaled it with satisfaction, but before long his throat was dry. He went into a tavern.

"I'm happy," he said to the landlord.

The landlord slid two glasses his way.

"Why two?" asked François, whose tastes were modest.

"In my tavern that's how it is, my boy," replied the landlord. "You have one drink because you're happy, and I offer you another because I'm happy to see you happy."

This friendliness, the beer, and the joy he felt at finding himself at last in the Farwest put the young man in a confiding mood.

His chin over the glasses, his hand in his mane, a faraway look in his eyes, he began to tell his story. The landlord interrupted him, banging on the counter with his fist. The glasses jumped, but the young man did not flinch.

"You're from Trompe-Souris?"

"Yes, *Monsieur.*"

"And you want to be a habitant in the Farwest?"

"Yes, *Monsieur.* A habitant like my father, like my grandfather, like all the Laterrières, because we must preserve the heritage of our ancestors."

The landlord leaned over to Timire, his assistant.

"Take off your apron," he told him. "Run and tell the Chief:* the Chosen One has arrived."

Timire took off his apron and hurried out. François, however, protested that he was not the Chosen One. The landlord hastened to reassure him.

"You're from Trompe-Souris, I'm from Crête-de-Coq. You're from Saint-Justin, I'm from Sainte-Ursule. We're from the same county. Could I possibly wish you any harm?"

"No, not if it's like you say."

---

* Ferron takes particular delight in gallicizing English in this story. His spelling for "Chief" is *Tchiffe.*

"If it's like I say? It's even better than I say. Why, I wouldn't be surprised if you weren't my cousin. My name is Siméon Désilets!"

"Well, how about that! My mother is a Désilets!"

"Her first name?"

"Wait now. . . ."

"Georgina?"

"No."

"Valéda?"

"No. . . . Wait now. . . . I've got it: Victoria!"

"She's my sister; I'm your uncle."

The landlord wasted no time. He seized a glass and filled it. Uncle and nephew raised their glasses. The drinks overflowed; they were deeply moved. The beer spilled onto the counter; the landlord mopped it up, himself scarcely able to hold back the tears. When you're a French Canadian you can't possibly know all your relatives, but you're over-joyed to make their acquaintance all the same. Family spirit is strong!

When they had drunk, the landlord asked for news of the old country, then he continued:

"You're not the Chosen One, Nephew. I know that as well as you do. You're no fool and I've still got my head screwed on. But we can make the Chief believe you are."

"The Chief?"

"Yes, the Chief. One of the feathered breed, a kind of Iroquois. When I first arrived here I traded with him. Then I bought my tavern. A good-hearted fellow, but not much of a head for business. I owe a lot to him. He's right at home here. I let him drink as much as he likes. He's always paid me. If he weren't my friend, I sometimes think he'd be my best customer."

The landlord drained his glass. François did the same. With the glasses empty the acoustics were much improved.

"Why should we make him believe you're the Chosen One? I'll tell you why, Nephew. He has a daughter. Her name is Eglantine. He wants to marry her to a white man. The fellow's nuts. He says the spirits have spoken to him. The spirits, they're the good Lord's flying *curés*. When they command, you have to obey, otherwise you go mad. So there's the Chief, looking for a white man. Not that there aren't plenty of them about. You can find white men of every race and religion in the Farwest. The trouble is my friend is fussy; to him all whites are savages. He wants to obey his priests, but he doesn't want to give his Eglantine to a savage. He's in a right quandary. So what does he do? He comes to see me. 'You good white,' he says to me, and to the good white he offers his daughter. Now, if ever any man has cheated, robbed, taken advantage of the old Chief – I can tell you this, you're my nephew – that man is me. Hearing him talk like that just about breaks my heart. 'Chief,' I says 'I'm good, all right, as good goes. But that doesn't mean I'm the man to marry your daughter. I'd consider myself lucky, make no mistake, but alas, I'm old, the tavern ties me down, and then there's Beauty Rose,* my Irish girl. You know her: she'd spit the fire of hell in your face if she heard of your offer.' Before I could finish my speech the Chief was in tears. It was the first time I'd ever seen him in such a state. I was touched. I said to him, 'There, there, don't cry. I'll pray to God and ask him to send you my cousin, a fine lad from Maskinongé, not savage at all, and white as milk. We'll marry him to your Eglantine.' That was the promise I made to the poor Chief out of the

---

* Ferron writes *Biouti Rose* throughout.

goodness of my heart. Tell me, François: wouldn't you have done the same?"

"Yes, of course," replied the young man.

"Ah, Nephew, you are indeed the son of my sister Victoria, the kindest girl in the world!"

And the landlord proceeded to fill the glasses.

"To your mother, to my own kind heart, to the goodness of the Désilets!"

They drank.

"After hearing my promise," the landlord continued, "the Chief went away rejoicing. I can see him now. And that was more than two years ago. He went away, but he came back. At the end of every season he'd come down from his canyon to ask for news of the promised cousin. I'd do what I could to keep him happy. The last time, at my wits end, I promised him he wouldn't have to wait much longer. The old boy went home. The season ended. Yesterday he arrived with his Eglantine to greet the Chosen One. There wasn't a cousin anywhere I could lay my hands on. I didn't know which way to turn, I cursed my promise. But I didn't have the heart to disappoint them. They were so happy, so trusting. So I said to them, 'Come back tomorrow.' Oh, what a night I spent! And then morning brought me you, dear Nephew! Even if you're not the Chosen One, you must admit you couldn't have come at a better moment!"

The landlord paused for a moment and banged his fist on the counter. The glasses jumped. François did not flinch.

"Thanks to you," cried the landlord, "your uncle's word will not be broken!"

The young man was uneasy. He'd have liked nothing better than to help an uncle keep his word, but it wasn't for that that he'd walked for two years, crossed four provinces, worn out fifteen pairs of cow-hide boots. Besides, the Commandment that told him to honour his father and mother made no mention of any other relatives, least of all an uncle with a tavern in the Farwest, who he hadn't even known existed until one day, feeling particularly dry, he'd entered this tavern to wet his whistle.

"What's the problem, Nephew?"

"The problem, Uncle, is that I'd like very much to oblige you. . . ."

"I know that."

"It's also that I didn't wear out fifteen pairs of cow-hide boots and come all this way just to meet an Indian maiden from the Farwest."

"Now you're talking! Have another drink, you deserve it."

And the landlord slid one over to him.

"All the same, Nephew, what would you say if this Indian maiden, a fine-looking girl, as it happens, also brought you a canyon the size of a whole parish for a dowry?"

"A canyon?"

"A piece of fine land surrounded by mountains as high as the sky."

"Hey," said François, "then I'd ask to see her."

He saw her, found her to his liking, and the next day they went to the church. A priest with carrot red hair, not one inch a Metis, married them with a wave of his sprinkler. The ceremony continued at the landlord's tavern. After eight days of revelry, the Chief stopped drinking, pushed away his glass and said:

"It's no good."

He still wasn't drunk. His thirst was intact. So why go on drinking? This wasn't the first time he'd tried. His previous attempts had all ended in failure. He'd never managed to get himself drunk. To bring him to his senses, it had always been necessary to knock him out. With age he'd grown wiser. This time, before he lost patience, he'd cut short the drinking, thus avoiding the final fury.

"It's no good," he repeated.

The landlord, who knew his Chief, having had occasion to bring him to his senses in the past, was careful not to insist. He made haste to end the celebration and had the horses brought up. When the animals were at the door, François asked:

"And what about the cows?"

For François Laterrière, shaken though he was by the little jolts of marriage, still held fast to his resolve.

"Yes, Uncle, the cows. I cannot become a habitant like my father, like my grandfather, like all the Laterrières before them, and preserve the heritage of my ancestors, if I don't have at least one cow to put in my canyon."

"What did he say?" asked the Chief.

The landlord explained his nephew's demand.

"Pooh!" said the Chief.

"What did he say?" asked François.

"He didn't make himself very clear," replied the landlord, "but I think he has a rather low opinion of cows."

The lad from Trompe-Souris, touched to the quick, flashed an indignant glance at his father-in-law, who continued:

"Cows! Pooh! Buffalo in canyon."

"What did he say?"

"Instead of a cow he's offering you a herd of buffalo."

The young man refused. Who had ever seen a buffalo on a habitant's land? It was a cow he needed. The Chief raised his arms to heaven: a cow would never be able to climb up to the canyon.

"He's right," urged the landlord.

But François took no notice. Disdainful and proud, he remained deaf to anything that might deter him from his mission. Blood will tell. Like all French Canadians he was a descendant of Madeleine de Verchères. He was a hero. All that mattered to him was his cow. They suggested a doe: a fig for their doe! A goat: fie! and for shame! Eglantine was growing anxious, the Chief impatient. Suddenly the landlord cried:

"A heifer!"

There was some sense in the idea; our hero considered it; he hesitated. Pressing his advantage, the landlord slapped him on the back. A heifer, after all, was only different from a cow for a few months. And what were a few months to a determined young man who had worn out fifteen pairs of cow-hide boots, crossed four provinces and found his way at last to his uncle, Siméon Désilets?

"Come on, François, come on!"

François gave in at last.

"I give in," he said, "but I'm not giving up. I'll accept the heifer but I won't forget the cow. I'll give satisfaction to the Farwest, but I'll remain faithful to the traditions of my ancestors."

"Bravo!" cried the landlord. "God has inspired you. You speak like a true *curé!*"

They all applauded and everyone was happy. All they had to do now was find the heifer. The gods smiled on them: she was found at once. François took her in his arms and leapt onto his horse. The party moved off. Siméon Désilets stood alone at the door of his tavern.

"Whew!" he said.

Then he went inside and poured himself two drinks, one because he was feeling happy, and the other because he was happy to see himself happy.

"You're laughing," exclaimed Timire in amazement.

"And you would be too," replied the landlord.

II

Once they were out of Calgary François cried:

"Hallo!"

He was echoing that distant hallo that the rising mountains call to the plain.

"Hallo, plain," they say, "give up your illusion: the earth is not flat."

The lad from Trompe-Souris was astonished. The mountains drew nearer. His astonishment did not lessen, but his apprehension grew.

"The canyon isn't up there, I hope," he inquired.

They showed him, between two dazzling peaks, the pass they would have to cross to reach it. He felt no pleasure at all at the sight. Like La Vérendrye, he would gladly have turned back. Nevertheless, he continued. It was a long climb. When he finally reached the canyon he vowed never to come down. One year later he started down again. You can be sure of nothing when you've a heifer in your care.

By spring the heifer had already become a cow. She took no notice and continued to graze. However, she was gaining less now and grew more slowly. Summer came. She stopped growing altogether and was amazed.

"Why should I bother to eat any more?" she asked Eglantine.

"Eat, my girl, eat," replied Eglantine. "You'll not regret it."

Enigmatic words, which the cow was to ruminate for a whole month. At the end of the month she wanted to know more. Eglantine proceeded to instruct her. From then on, her ears aquiver, her neck strained, she lived in expectation. She forgot to eat her due. There, amid the juicy hay, hunger gnawed her, and she began to wail. It was pitiful to hear.

"What's wrong with her?" François asked.

"She claims," replied Eglantine, "that your hay tastes bad."

This insinuation was not well received. The hay was from good millet and identical in every way to the ancestral hay. How could it possibly taste bad? The cow was an impudent hussy and was lying shamelessly. To satisfy himself François went and examined her closely. When he came back he announced:

"Wife, there's nothing the matter with my hay. It could feed more than a cow; it could feed a whole herd."

"In that case," inquired Eglantine, "why does she wail, poor thing?"

"There's another reason. We must go down to Calgary and bring back a bull calf."

At that same moment the Chief emerged from the bushes. He had been gone since fall and had spent the winter hunting. His pelts had been rich; he was carrying a roll of bills as fat as a girl's thigh. The roll redoubled his valour; his children were on their way to Calgary; without pausing for breath, he set off behind them.

"Well!" thundered Siméon Désilets, "this is a big surprise!"

The Chief put his roll on the counter.

"Count," he ordered.

The landlord felt it.

"It's velvet to the touch."

"You keep," said the Chief, "if you find way to get me drunk."

Thus challenged, the landlord felt every confidence in his ability to get him drunk. He brought out his very best mixture: white lightning, beer and rubbing alcohol. One week later, the Chief was hollow-eyed, but he still sat upright in his chair. "Wait a moment, my good Chief," said the landlord, "you won't be sitting like that for long!" And he placed in front of him the decisive glass, filled with straight rubbing alcohol.

"Just taste that now and tell me what you think."

But the Chief didn't seem the least bit curious. He didn't even touch the glass. Perhaps he needed a little encouragement. Siméon Désilets, acting out of the goodness of his heart, went to give him a friendly pat on the back. . . . He remained rooted to the spot, his hand upraised, extremely surprised. The Chief had spun round, lithe as a cat, and plunged a knife into his belly. No allowance had been made in the itinerary for any such stabbing. Having come down to Calgary for the sole purpose of acquiring a bull calf, François and Eglantine had intended to go straight back once the calf was acquired. They were obliged to attend the landlord's funeral, then the Chief's trial, and finally, his hanging. These family duties kept them in Calgary for more than three months.

Meanwhile, above the canyon, the sun never blinked from morning to night. In time it grew very hot; the springs stopped running, the water in the trough dried up, and in a cloud of dust drought descended on the land. The little cow soon found herself in difficulties. Whenever she took a step, thousands of grasshoppers would fly up, and with their shrill call warn the grass to flee still farther. Imprisoned in a moving desert, she could find nothing at all to eat. Her skin was loose, her bones unsteady. She had grown so thin she looked as if she were wearing her big sister's coat. Ridiculous and pitiful, she wandered about, saying to herself:

"If only I could get a drink."

It was her sole concern. A hundred times a day she returned to the trough, and always came away disappointed. Above the grasshoppers, the hawks hovered; higher still, the vultures. Neither bird was a good omen. At last, her courage failing, the unfortunate cow said to herself:

"My hour is come."

And, so saying, she let herself fall onto the burning ground. After a time, however, discovering that she was not quite dead, she opened her eyes and strained her ears. . . . And what should she hear but the sound of running water!

"My hour is not yet come," she cried.

And with this she struggled to her feet, poor creature, and rushed off once more in the direction of the trough. But the effort this time was tremendous; her strength gave out; she staggered; a thousand suns were spinning in the sky. To regain her balance, she stopped, but her skeleton kept right on going. She was blinded by the dust, deafened by the grasshoppers, the hawks, and the suns. A vulture landed on her head. The skeleton was still going; it was already well ahead of her; she didn't know what to think. She shook the hat and the vulture flew off; she had lost sight of the skeleton now, concluded that she must be dreaming, and continued on her hallucinating walk. She arrived at last at the water trough; on the dried up mud lay the skeleton of a cow. She was not dreaming; it was her own.

"I am dead," she murmured to herself.

Death has as a rule a most devastating effect on life. In this case, the opposite was true; the result was exhilarating;

the cow felt better dead than alive; freed of needs she could no longer satisfy, harassing needs, more terrible by far than hawks or vultures, she once more took pleasure in herself. The impression was a strange one: she almost felt alive again.

At the same moment, the sun blinked and rain transformed the landscape. As soon as they were wet the grasshoppers fell silent; reassured, the grass came back, soft and defenceless. The carrion birds, lords of the drought, had disappeared; green silences replaced their harsh cries. Although she was indifferent to this renewal, the little cow nevertheless felt inside her a joy that grew with each new day. Her courage had returned, her skin fit once more. True, she still had no skeleton, but it hardly noticed; her appearance was most respectable. She wandered freely through the canyon. Every now and then she would pause to take a mouthful of grass; not that she was hungry – it was pure caprice. Sometimes she would go over to the water trough and there, occasionally, she might take a drink; not that she was thirsty – it was just a lapse; she simply wanted to see the reflection of the spectre her joy had brought to life.

When they returned to the canyon, François and Eglantine were delighted to find her, to all appearances, in the best of health. They ran to her, embraced her fondly, then introduced the male calf they had brought back with them from Calgary.

"He's a nice little animal."

There was no glow of passion in her eyes.

"Nice, he is," Eglantine replied, "but that's not all. Just wait: a year from now, burning with passion, a little bull he'll be."

The cow remained cold.

"What's the matter with you, little sister?"

"I'm dead," she replied.

Eglantine burst into tears.

"What's wrong?" asked François, who understood nothing of the language of cows.

"She says. . . . Oh, God! it's dreadful."

"Well, what?"

"She says she's dead."

Surprised, François walked around the animal, then looked up, skeptical. Eglantine, offended, brushed away her tears.

"How could you have the heart," she cried, "to doubt the word of a poor dead cow?"

To which he replied that he, for his part, had heard no such word.

"Is it my fault if you're deaf?"

"If I'm deaf, Eglantine, then maybe you've too much imagination."

Then she asked him if he thought she was crazy. No, he didn't think she was crazy. But he did disapprove of her listening to the blather of animals. She argued back; he refused to climb down. She called him a savage; he called her a squaw. In short, they quarrelled. When they had finished, the cow motioned to them to follow her: she led them to the water trough. The skeleton was there, irrefutable.

"Well?" said Eglantine.

François, shattered, could find no reply.

"Now do you dare to say this cow is not dead?"

He did not dare.

"But," he added, "dead or not dead, what's the difference, as long as she'll calve?"

"What do you mean?"

"Let's leave the little bull to sort things out."

A year passed. The bull calf, now every inch the animal required, began to lift his eyes in the direction of the cow. One day, emboldened, he lifted his legs instead. The cow, already suspicious, had seen him coming; she jumped sideways and the bull fell to the ground.

"You should be ashamed of yourself," she said.

He picked himself up, his forehead bristling, all ready to try again.

"If you want to know the truth," the cow went on, "you disgust me."

Round-eyed, he stared at her.

"Fool, can't you see I'm dead?"

The poor chap swallowed his saliva. He was sincere in his intentions, but, blinded by passion, he had not noticed the sad condition of his companion. In his innocence, he had wanted to serve her. Since she was dead, he did not insist. He walked away. Not for the world would he have defiled her. And his ardour, with no outlet, turned inward against him now. His head became swollen, his eyes shot with blood; he longed to crush his bones against a rock; the canyon shook with the sound of his bellowing. Until in the end the little cow took pity on him.

"After all," she said, "I may be dead, but that doesn't stop me from taking a mouthful of grass here, a drink of water there. Why shouldn't it be the same with the other little necessities? There, poor boy, don't look so sad now. You can do what you like with me. Feel quite free: it's really all the same to me."

Now it was the bull's turn to be disgusted.

"Thank you very much," he replied, "but I don't need your cold carcass!"

And with that they were estranged, estranged forever, sadly, foolishly, all because of a few thoughtless words, estranged for no good reason! For they could have been reconciled; indeed, they should have been. Love is the coming together of life and death; it is perfectly natural for one party to be cooler than the other.

Meanwhile, François himself had not been idle. Having talked at first for the sake of it (which improved his voice) he found at last the word he had been looking for. And so it was that the virtue of the race, at first inoperative, one day bore fruit. Eglantine, mysteriously touched, smiled as she grew heavier. In spite of her condition, she continued to look after the animals. Her shoulders thrust back, portly as an ambassador, she went from the bull to the cow and from the cow to the bull, mediating as best she could, but unable to make peace between them. This failure, however, did not trouble her unduly, for she had already achieved within herself the reconciliation of opposites. François, for his part, was preparing the nest. He was putting the finishing touches to a house, the perfect replica of the Laterrière farmhouse in Trompe-Souris, in the parish of Saint-Justin de Maskinongé. He had thus reconciled future and past, heir and ancestors, and was on the point of transplanting to the Farwest the traditions of the Quebec people. It was too perfect to last.

One morning, Eglantine, on one of her diplomatic missions, spied the bull, normally quite standoffish, coming towards her with blood-shot eyes, his head low.

"What's the matter, little bull?" she asked.

He did not answer, but kept on coming. Then Eglantine, guessing his intentions, uttered loud and piercing screams. Her emotion only proved to the animal that she was indeed alive. Frustrated by a dead cow, he needed nothing more. The morphology of the two parties did not lend itself to their union. The fair Eglantine died. François, who had rushed to the scene, now furious at finding himself a widower, killed the bull, then collapsed himself on the two bodies. When he came to, he heard a wail. It was a baby girl, lying there, kicking, in the blood of her mother and the monster.

François Laterrière left the canyon that same day. It was the dead cow who moved into the house, that perfect replica of the ancestral home. She felt quite happy in it. But there were times when she would climb up to the attic and there, with her head thrust out the window, gaze nostalgically into the distance.

III

Fleeing his canyon, François Laterrière left behind him, like an absurd dream, a house built in the Quebec style and haunted by a dead cow. The chorus of ancestors tried to hold him back, but he refused to stop, thinking it was the cow. For two days and two nights he walked. After which, already much distressed by the death of Eglantine and the failure of his mission, he had completely taken leave of his senses. God guided him. At the end of the third day he reached Calgary, a city large enough to get lost in. But God did not abandon him: he found his way to the tavern of his late uncle, Siméon Désilets.

The last client had left, and Beauty Rose and Timire were in the process, she of totting up the day's cash, he of wiping the tables. Any moment now they would be closed. The door opened; a man walked in and placed on the counter a tiny bundle of soiled linen. Automatically, Beauty Rose slipped him a glass; he emptied it in one gulp. She slipped him another; he emptied it just as fast; then a third, and a fourth. . . . He was clearly very thirsty. Beauty Rose, her interest aroused, said to herself:

"Something tells me I know this man." But she could not put a name to him. Suddenly the tiny bundle moved.

"Lord, it's moving!"

"So what?"

"What is it you've got all wrapped up there and moving like that?" she asked him.

"Dunno," he replied.

She took pity on him.

"Come along with me," she said.

He followed her to the Tourist Rooms adjoining the tavern. She pulled off his boots and put him to bed. A maid appeared, enticed.

"Is this one for me, Ma'am?"

"No," replied Beauty Rose, "he's not for you, nor me, nor anyone. He hasn't a cent and he's sick; his own mother wouldn't want him now."

When the servant had left, Beauty Rose thought to herself: "Perhaps he really hasn't got a cent." She checked; she was right. But what should she find in his pocket but the rosary of Siméon Désilets, her late husband.

"It's my nephew, François," she said to herself. "I thought he looked familiar!"

She left the room. To the maid, she said:

"It's my nephew, François. Something terrible has happened to him."

"Poor you," said the maid.

"Something terrible. And he's changed, changed! I recognized him by his uncle's rosary."

"Poor you! What a dreadful thing to be so changed!"

Cutting short these ancillary condolences, Beauty Rose went back downstairs. The bundle was still on the counter.

"Timire," she called.

Timire arrived.

"Unwrap this bundle, Timire. I haven't the heart to do it myself."

He unwrapped it. She clutched her hands to her breasts.

"Lord Jesus! Just as I thought: it's a girl, a lovely little girl! Timire don't just stand there with your mouth open! Come on! Do something."

Do what? Timire had no idea.

"Why, baptise her, of course! Can't you see she's cold? You never know; she might have caught her death, the poor dear little creature."

Timire, beer in hand, said:

"I don't know what to say."

"Poor fool! You say: 'I baptise you in the name of the Father, the Son and the Holy Ghost.'"

Timire was about to touch the baby's forehead with his glass. Beauty Rose stopped him.

"Fool! Precious fool! It's not beer you use to baptise a child! Do you have no principles, then?"

She handed him a bottle of white lightning.

"It's white lightning!"

Once the ceremony was over and the way to paradise opened to the poor dear little creature, the widow of Siméon Désilets regained her composure.

"Now," she declared, "we must see to it she doesn't die."

Timire called the maids. They came down to the tavern.

"This," the widow told them, "is the child I've been promising you. She's my niece. Her name is Chaouac."

Their joy was amazing to behold. The child was handed over; her weight seemed to reassure them. When they had taken her away, Beauty Rose asked Timire how he felt.

"I'm very glad," he replied.

The next day, although he had fully recovered his senses, François Laterrière did not recognize the grimacing little frog he had found lying in the blood of a monster and a woman; they showed him a clean, well-fed baby, asleep on the breast of one of the maids. This breast, alas, reminded him of another.

"Aunt," he said, "Eglantine is dead."

"I'd guessed as much," replied Beauty Rose.

He told her the tragic story. She said:

"François, your daughter is my daughter. Stay here; we'll bring her up together."

At such generosity the young father lost his composure and fell down upon his knees. Seeing this, his aunt lost hers, and burst out laughing.

"Get up off your knees, you silly boy! You owe me nothing. It's a favour you're doing me letting me take your daughter."

He got up.

"There are three reasons why you owe me nothing. Just listen to them and you'll stop your genuflexions, you'll see!"

And Beauty Rose explained that she had not always been a person of staid disposition, having first been driven by wanderlust for many years. Born in Dublin, she had acquired her Irish education in haste and had left in search of adventure by the time she was thirteen years old. Her travels had brought her, by a thoroughly capricious route – via Australia, China and Russia – to Canada, where she had at first sojourned in the ports of the east. After which she had moved to the Yukon, and from there to the Farwest.

"Nephew," she went on, "I paid my own way. For a long time I had the means. As I grew older, however, I found it more difficult to make a living from my looks, and I was soon in desperate straits. From then on travel became difficult. I have very unpleasant memories of the Yukon: men there are quite unreasonable. When I arrived in Calgary I was exhausted. Siméon Désilets came along. He needed a wife, I deserved a rest, we were married. He was a strong man, your uncle! He kept me where he wanted me and there I stayed! And I became staid, oh so staid! We lived together five years, then his friend the Chief did him in. He's gone now; but he left me his memory, Timire, his tavern and his morals. That's the first reason why you owe me nothing, even if I am helping you out."

But the inheritance was not all pure gold. There was also, in the widow's estimation, an element of wastage, understandable if one considered that Siméon Désilets had not come to Calgary via Australia, China and Russia. He had held on to certain of the prejudices of Sainte-Ursule de Maskinongé, which Beauty Rose had been obliged to dispense with after his death. On the subject of the sexes, for example. Not for anything in the world would the landlord have encouraged contact between them. He had every occasion to do so, however; beer awakens a client's generosity; after two or three bottles he very often feels the need to bestow his favours on some poor disadvantaged girl; in this case, why not help him to find her? Besides, collaboration of this nature is always profitable.

"Your poor uncle always refused."

François Laterrière had not travelled via Australia, China and Russia either.

"By God," he exclaimed, "my uncle was right."

"After his death I gave in."

"You betrayed him!"

"Precisely," said the widow, "and that, you see, is my second reason. I've been unfaithful to the principles of your uncle. I'm sorry, even though I didn't approve of them. You're his nephew. I'll help you and so make amends."

François, indignant:

"Make amends some other way. Don't count on me any more. I'll have nothing to do with your acts of fornication."

Beauty Rose, taken aback:

"Fornication?"

"Yes, fornication."

"I don't understand, Nephew. You're forgetting that I have morals."

"Morals? You must be joking!"

"Morals that I got from your uncle. If I hadn't had them, I'll admit, I'd have gone in for a brothel; but I had them, and so I made do with Tourist Rooms."*

François had spoken too hastily.

"Tourist Rooms, that's different," he conceded.

"Just a modest little enterprise: ten rooms, four maids. So help me, I don't see where you get your fornication, Nephew! I employ the maids to look after the rooms; in between chores they have time to spare; I don't ask them how they spend it; that's their business. I collect the money for the rooms. What could possibly be wrong with that, Nephew!"

"Why, nothing at all, Aunt Beauty Rose."

"Besides, I'm never in the place; I stay in the tavern. There, after the second or third bottle, a client will sometimes ask me for a girl; I offer him a room, I promise him nothing; I tell him if he's lucky the maids will like his pretty face. If he still takes the room it's at his own expense, and not theirs,

---

* Tourist Rooms. A euphemism to begin with, it becomes the singular *un touristeroume,* and thus even more amusingly evocative, in Ferron's "French."

because he never has a pretty face. I personally select the clients; the pretty faces always go elsewhere to be admired."

"And the third reason?" asked François, who was beginning to weary of his aunt's dialectics.

Beauty Rose hesitated.

"To be perfectly honest," she replied, "when the client goes upstairs I'm not as confident as I let on to you. True, I've personally selected him; he never has a pretty face. But then, I'm not that well acquainted with my maids either; they just might have poor taste. And so, to calm my fears, I've insisted that they all have milk."

François, aghast:

"Milk!"

"Yes, milk."

"Hmm," said he.

"Of course," Beauty Rose went on, "a maid can't have milk without having previously experienced a certain misfortune, and I tell myself that the milk will prevent it happening again. That's my third reason: we'll have more than enough to feed your daughter, you lend her to us, we'll care for her, and you can keep your genuflexions for another: your daughter will pay us back."

The young father, horrified:

"How?"

"By sucking," came the reply.

Having milk is not everything; what matters is being able to keep it. To achieve this end, it's best that it be drunk, since breasts are so made that they will fill up only as they are emptied. For a while, before the arrival of François Laterrière and his daughter Chaouac, this generous paradox caused Timire great concern, for it was he who had been put in charge of the milk-maids' welfare. Day in, day out, morning, noon and night, he had to provide them with hungry children. He chose these children with the greatest of care; they were nevertheless always taken off the streets, where children have a tendency to be more talkative than elsewhere. And so it happened that certain parents came to hear what repast was being served in the Tourist Rooms, and they were most upset, for parents, it is well known, are always more or less corrupt; these felt obliged to forbid their children the healthiest, the noblest, if not the most humane of all foods. As for Timire, they talked quite simply of hanging him. Timire would hear nothing of it, but he was anxious all the same. He had no difficulty approving the adoption of Chaouac.

François Laterrière also approved it, but with less promptitude. First he had to listen to a debate in his conscience between his daughter, the said Chaouac, on the one hand, and his priest, Monsieur de Saint-Justin, on the other. The priest spoke first; he affirmed truths to which François listened, but which he barely heard, since the acoustics of a "tourist room" in the Farwest are hardly as conducive to such things as those of a farmhouse in Trompe-Souris. Then it was Chaouac's turn; her speech was short and to the point; she was thirsty. With her first cry François heard her and felt the torment of her thirst.

"Oh, *Monsieur le curé,* forgive me," he cried, handing the child to Beauty Rose, "I have no other choice!"

"Not so fast, there, Nephew!" replied Beauty Rose. "I may have my morals, but I'm not a *curé* yet!"

One of the "tourist rooms" was made available to the young father and it was suggested that he might like to help Timire in the tavern during the day. He accepted the room but refused the job, happy to be able to sleep next to Chaouac, but not the least bit inclined to get himself breathed all over by drinkers of beer. Not that he despised these drinkers; they were his brothers, exiles like himself, and for the most part of the same origin. Indeed, the Tavern is the only place in America where a French Canadian can speak his language freely. But François Laterrière was not one to indulge in conversation. He was a serious lad, who had no time for idle talk and knew that, as far as essentials were concerned, everything had already been said long ago by persons in authority, and in particular by Monsieur de Saint-Justin. And so he preferred the open air.

He went to work on a ranch. No speeches there, just grass and wind, and sometimes a cloud or two, or else an empty sky and the backdrop of monotony against which simple, uncomplicated souls, inclined to melancholy, seem to thrive. François found peace there, if not happiness. They hadn't given him a lasso; he had no idea that he'd become a cowboy. The ranch seemed to him like one vast Trompe-Souris, a free and unfenced version of the lowlands of Maskinongé County. He wished for nothing more. At night he came back to sleep at the Tourist Rooms; in the morning he returned to his cows. He took care, however, never to go near the tavern, which he believed to be a haunt of the devil. On the ranch he felt no cause for anxiety. Yet it was there that a sinister encounter awaited him. One day he found himself face to face, not with Satan, but with a white bull, an animal utterly lacking in subtlety, who was nevertheless to have a most disastrous influence on his soul.

Both parties began by examining one another coldly. The landscape was green, almost blue. Then a strange heat was felt, as a cloud moved aside, unmasking the sun, which was yellow, almost red. And in that same moment both turned coward. Each took a step forward in the hope that the other would take a step back, then keep on going, leaving fury triumphant and carrying off in his retreat the cowardice of both. But the other party also stepped forward. So there was no alternative but to fight it out. François was the madder of the two. His fury triumphed. With his neck wrung, the white bull turned coward and died. "Bulls and I," said François to himself, "just don't seem to get along!"

He had to admit that he, for his part, detested them, for the very good reason that one of their kind had forced him to leave the Canyon, where he had found his mission, where Eglantine lived, and where his ancestors and his children would together have brought about his certain happiness. But he refused to allow for the existence of any such sentiments on the side of the bulls. Yet the bulls had every right to feel this way, since they considered their brother in the Canyon to have been guiltless, laying the blame for Eglantine's death on the dead cow and responsibility for the bovine fury on François, who, they claimed, could have prevented it by removing the offending organ. In short, as is always the case, both sides had excellent reasons for carrying on the war. And the war continued. Ten more times, pitting his strength against an ever renewed enemy, François Laterrière emerged victorious, thus demonstrating the superiority of the lad from Maskinongé over the bull of the Farwest. This was not quite what the boss had had in mind.

"You'll go far, my boy," he said. "Ten bulls in one week is a mighty fine start! Carry on the good work anywhere you like, but keep off my ranch!"

So François took himself elsewhere and, at the expense of another boss, proceeded to repeat his demonstration. Before long a nasty reputation had overtaken him. Thrown out a second time, he was unable to get himself hired on a third ranch. After which, on the advice of Beauty Rose, he went to see old Jesse Crochu at the Calgary Stampede. Crochu took him on immediately, but on one condition: he was to change his name. Frank Laterreur he became.

Not long afterwards, who should arrive in Calgary but Monsieur de Saint-Justin, on an apostolic mission. He was accompanied by an academician – a ferret-faced pinhead – none other than the famous historian, Ramulot.* They had come from Edmonton where, on behalf of the Committee for the Survival of the French Agony in America, they had been inspecting the few remaining houses where the French-Canadian lingo could still be heard. In Calgary there was no one to visit. And so, to the Calgary Stampede they went. There, the said Frank Laterreur greatly impressed them, both by his courage and by the extreme simplicity of his technique. Indeed, without picadors, without banderilleros, alone in the ring, and unarmed, without the aid of a red cape, or a lance, or a spear, with only his bare hands, he slew the black bull. This beat† anything Europe and its toreadors could do.

"Oh my! Oh my!" exclaimed Monsieur de Saint-Justin.

"Hooray! Hooray!" cried Ramulot, his mouth watering.

After which, still hungry for more, they decided to go congratulate the champion on behalf of their Homeland and to present him, *honoris causa,* with the emblem of the fleur-de-lis. In the wings they bumped into Jesse Crochu, who

---

* Ramulot. In this name can be heard the words *rat* and *mulot* ("rat" and "field mouse"). Ferron is mocking the right-wing Quebec historian Robert Rumilly.

† beat. Ferron's sly invention *il bite* hints at François' own bull-like qualities, making visible the French noun *bite* – a popular term for the male genitals.

asked them, "Who're you?" They gave their names and listed their titles. The Academy? Old Jesse had never heard of any such thing, but, putting two and two together, guessed what it must be. "I reckon that's what those fellas down East call their Rodeo," thought he.

"Anyhow," he said, "don't go getting ideas about taking Frank away from me. Bulls, now – that's okay. If you need some, I can let you have all you want. But not Frank. He's mine, and he stays right here with me."

Ramulot thanked him: the Academy was not in need of bulls. As for the said Frank, they had no desire to hire him. They simply wished to congratulate him and pin a fleur-de-lis on his chest. Jesse Crochu, reassured, saw no reason to stand in their way. Let them congratulate, then, and decorate, let them fleurdelisate to their heart's content!

François saw them approaching. Like most priests when they travel, Monsieur de Saint-Justin was not wearing a cassock. François caught sight of his collar. "Bah! it's a clergyman!" thought he.

As for Ramulot, he was wearing a tie, a blue one, distinctly on the gaudy side.

"You, my pinhead," said François under his breath, "you can pay for the heresy of your friend."

And drawing in his neck like a bull, he advanced towards him.

"Mr. Laterreur!" cried the Academician, "I have the greatest admiration for you. Please stop and allow me to decorate you with the fleur-de-lis!"

Now, in the Farwest, this symbol is used for branding cattle.

François: "Just you wait! I'll show you who's the calf around here!"

But Ramulot had no wish to wait. He turned on his heels and fled, and all went well until a terrible boot with a deadly aim caught him from behind, raising his lower quarters high off the ground and causing his upper quarters to plunge accordingly, so that he sailed through the air, a ferret-faced Icarus, in the direction of the nearest manure pile. There he landed, pinhead first, and sank so deep that François abandoned the fight in disgust. And turning to Monsieur de Saint-Justin:

"Mr. Clergyman," he said, "take back your shit-faced friend."

So ended the encounter of François Laterrière and his parish priest in Calgary. They met again in Saint-Justin twenty-five years later, but this time, the priest having assumed his cassock and François his real name, they recognized each other.

"So!" cried François, "the clergyman was you!"

"So!" cried the priest, "the toreador was you!"

And they burst out laughing at the memory of Ramulot. He alone had kept his identity. And a fat lot of good it had done him.

"God can't have wanted us to recognize each other," the priest concluded.

"Still, there were a lot of things I'd have liked to tell you, *Monsieur le curé*."

"You can tell them to me, now, François Laterrière. It's never too late."

And François did. There was Siméon Désilets and his tavern, there was his marriage to the Chief's daughter, the canyon and the dead cow, Eglantine's death and the birth of Chaouac, Beauty Rose and her Tourist Rooms, and the Calgary Stampede.

"Upon my soul," thought Monsieur de Saint-Justin, "I foresaw nothing like this when I sent this boy to the Farwest!"

François also told him about the milkmaids, but out of regard for his listener, he arranged the episode in such a way that it appeared edifying.

"There you have it, *Monsieur le curé*. That's the story you'd have heard in Calgary if by chance we'd recognized each other."

"Very well," said Monsieur de Saint-Justin, "but what happened next?"

What happened next presented François with certain difficulties of narration. It had come to pass that the said Frank Laterreur, having constantly to pit himself against the bulls, had ended up resembling them in one very significant way, the consequences of which are easy to imagine when one considers that he was spending his nights in the Tourist Rooms and that more often than not the four chambermaids whom Beauty Rose reserved for her clients also slept there. He took advantage of the fact that they were his daughter's wet-nurses and insinuated himself into their company, with the result that the clients soon ceased to receive the attentions they were accustomed to. The affairs of the Tourist Rooms declined, seriously damaging those of the adjoining tavern. All of which would have given Beauty Rose cause to complain, but Beauty Rose herself had no time to think about it, being, in spite of her age and her morals, just as well served as her maids. The honeymoon lasted four years. After which business picked up again and improved from month to month. Two years later, Tourist Rooms and tavern were flourishing as before. It was the said Frank who had gone under. The bulls had stopped hating him, he himself no longer detested them, and from there it followed that everything else was changed. Jesse Crochu had fired him. Beauty Rose now did the same.

"Your daughter is six years old," she told him. "There's nothing to stop you putting her in a convent now. I'll not be able to help you any more. As it is, I've given you far more than I need have done. I've paid off my debt to the late Siméon. Farewell, Nephew!"

François Laterrière, ex Frank Laterreur, fallen champ, now not even worth his weight in beef, left Calgary, taking with him his Chaouac, his bright little flame, his only passion. In Regina and Winnipeg he worked as a butcher, in Toronto, as a gangster.* When he reached Montreal, Chaouac was turning fifteen. She was well educated and beautiful. Together they opened up Tourist Rooms, and fortune smiled on them. . . .

"Very well," said Monsieur de Saint-Justin. "What happened after that?"

"After that . . . well, er. . . ." What happened after that, it seemed, presented certain difficulties of narration. Here was the gist of it.

With a sweep of his hand, François indicated, over by the presbytery, the huge black limousine, in which he had driven up like a prime minister.

"My, my!" said the priest. "What a big car! I'm very glad indeed. Then the advice I gave you wasn't so bad after all!"

"It was good advice, *Monsieur le curé,* and I thank you for it. However, I must tell you that I didn't carry out the mission you entrusted me with."

"What mission? I don't remember any mission."

"To be a habitant in the Farwest, a habitant like my father and my grandfather and all the Laterrières of Maskinongé county."

---

* The gallicized spelling is *gagnestère.*

"Forget it, François, forget it! You've kept your faith. You've kept your language. And you're rich. What more could anyone ask?"

François Laterrière was sad, for he knew himself to be unworthy of the priest's approval.

"Besides," the priest went on, "even if you didn't succeed in putting down roots there yourself, the conquest of the Farwest by our people is going well."

He pulled out some photos of his trip, showing the various houses in which, twenty-five years earlier, French was still being spoken.

"What do you think of this one?" he asked.

François recognized his own house in the Canyon.

"Doesn't it look just like one of our own?"

"Yes, indeed, Father."

"When we visited it, the owner was away. A cow had climbed up into the attic, and she was standing there, with her head out the window, mooing and mooing. I said to her: 'Now stop your mooing. Your master'll soon be home.' And I blessed the house."

François Laterrière took leave of Monsieur de Saint-Justin. The village around the church had not changed. In his big car he drove through Trompe-Souris. Trompe-Souris had not changed either. The parishes of Quebec took on their definitive shape in the last century. Since then they haven't budged, hardening like cases around their habitants and retaining always the same invariable number, the number they held one hundred years ago. François found his child-hood still intact. And yet, in spite of this, he was a stranger in the village and in the *rang*; his place was no longer here. But then, had it ever been here? Temporarily, perhaps, until such time as he could grow up and be expelled to an absurd

Farwest. For he belonged to that surplus humanity that the Quebec parishes have continually to reject, in order to preserve their traditional face, the one they put on for the benefit of foreigners, and exploit and sell, the grimacing face of the puritan prostitute.

When François Laterrière left Saint-Justin the first time, wearing his cow-hide boots, he wept, and could find no solace till, in a far-off canyon, he had managed to recreate the likeness of his Homeland. When, thirty years later, in his big black limousine, he left the village for the second time, no tear blurred his vision. He knew then that he had never been loved. He also knew that a country that values itself more highly than its children and doesn't hesitate to get rid of them, sending them off to the cities, to the mines, to every corner of America, without thought for their fate, concerned only with the preservation of its own old togs, is a country that does not deserve to be loved. And he was perhaps sadder than the first time.

When he got back to Montreal, he sold his Tourist Rooms. No one has ever enjoyed running a brothel, and François Laterrière was no exception. He had been driven to it out of necessity. After the death of Eglantine and the failure of his mission, with nothing left to guide him, he had understandably sunk very low, low enough to collect the wages of sin and to bounce back onto the highways in a big, black limousine, like a prime minister. This limousine he also sold. Soon he was free to go as he pleased. He returned to that absurd and unlikely canyon, which was the place in all America where he felt least like an exile. Meanwhile, at his side, with staring eyes, her head stuck out the attic window, the dead cow mooed in the direction of an unattainable Trompe-Souris.

ENGLISH TALES

ULYSSES

After Ulysses' return to Ithaca, an island in the Ontario countryside – Ithaca Corner to be exact, ten houses at a crossroads, grouped round the one-time blacksmith now turned gas-pump operator – his wife, Penelope, continued to embroider. Why stop? Her embroidery had stood her in good stead. But as she no longer undid it at night, it soon became very clear what was on her mind, for she would write it, embroidering the words with appropriate motifs, little birds and bleeding hearts. No sooner was a piece finished than she would put it on display: "Home sweet home" – "No wife in the home, no sun in the sky" – "God bless this happy union." And she had a long litany of them. What was she doing? Simply this: publicity for Penelope.

Her embroidery adorned cushions, pillow-slips, aprons, nightgowns; framed, it covered the walls of the house, from the basement to the attic. And she went on and on, the dreadful woman, stitching, stitching, thin as a spider too.

With a marriage so explicitly, not to say deliriously happy, ostentatiously so at any rate, all garnish and no meat, Ulysses, like the Englishman he was, could find no fault. He acquiesced, content and wretched. At times a faint smile would cross his face, a distracted gleam appearing in his glaucous eyes. Ah! he was all but done for. The long-drawn thread was tightening round him. Yet a little and he would be caught, chewed, digested. By chance he too began to embroider. This saved him – at least for a time. And he embroidered at night, on the back of Penelope's canvas.

Here is how he went about it: he would pour himself a glass of rum, toss it back with a "God save the Queen," then go to bed, snore, and as soon as his wife had fallen asleep, suspecting nothing, he would hand the organ pipes over to her so he himself could set to work in silence, like a real werewolf. Swiftly he would slip back to his golden years, to the barbarous provinces of the East, to Moncton, Pictou, Quebec, to Montreal especially, that city where, though a Sergeant-major, he had been a little less virtuous than he would have liked. His conscience troubled him. A little less – even that was too much. Only just a little less, but the opportunities for sin had been tremendous.

Snore, Penelope, snore!

Yes, tremendous. *Ouonnedeurfoules,** to use his exotic expression. He took them one by one, these chances he had missed, and embroidered as he dreamed, embroidered as one can after the event, when life has passed one by, with libidinous verve, and that love of the sensational characteristic of cowards and fools.

And in this way, little by little, he created the Odyssey of his life.

---

* *Ouonnedeurfoules.* Ferron's own "exotic" spelling of "wonderful." The English adjective has even acquired a final "s" to denote agreement with the plural noun, as required in French.

During the day he did not undo his work; on the contrary, he advertised it, confronting Penelope's version with Ulysses' version – a publicity battle, you might say, in true English style. That race is taciturn, but it delights in billboards.

But whereas Penelope stayed indoors, Ulysses operated outside the home. He would go and relate his adventures to the blacksmith cum gas-pump operator. Ithaca Corner is a forgotten island. Few people ever pass through, and no one stops. To Ulysses' story the gas-pump operator added his own nostalgia for horses. Sometimes, so it seemed, girls and animals would come together, and then, in the respectable Ontario countryside, centaurs would appear. Not long after, lean Penelope, peeping out through the venetian blinds, saw the cows being brought back to the shed.

THE SIRENS

And then, one day, the blacksmith cum gas-pump operator, who was beginning to have a bellyful of the Odyssey, said to Ulysses: "You've been back in Ithaca all of fifteen years. Why not take a little trip down East? Montreal isn't that far. You talk and talk, and perhaps the setting of your adventures has changed." It was a great idea! But how to get away? There was no war on and Penelope was too old to be left alone; who would make a fuss of her? The Legion very conveniently provided the excuse: they were organizing parades of one-eyed, limping and bemedalled veterans in the barbarous cities of the East, which were showing signs of unrest, with the idea of restoring calm and demonstrating the might of Her Majesty the Queen. The Sergeant-major took part in the expedition. After all, one *ouiquène** was not the Trojan War. Penelope let him go.

So once again old Ulysses appeared in the Sirens' quarter, lashed to his foremast. With his royal sail rising in his head,

---

* *ouiquène*. Ferron's version of "weekend" – another mischievous attempt at gallicized spelling of English.

puffed out by the winds that had gathered during those fifteen years at Ithaca Corner, he sailed down the middle of the ill-famed streets, listening for the sweet, erotic strains of a French chant that had once drifted from the now silent windows. Saint-Dominique, Berger, de Bullion, Hôtel-de-Ville, Sanguinet – he patrolled them all, but the Sirens were no longer there.

"*Ouèredéare?*"* he enquired.

"*Hou?*" they asked.

"The Sirens."

The Sirens? They had never heard of them. You sure meet some nutty Englishmen! Can't help liking them though. Sirens, just imagine!

"Come have a drink, old chap."

"Me, a drink!" said Ulysses, shocked. What did they take him for? No, thank you! He only got drunk at home. Or at the sergeants' mess, in the good old days, when the war was on and he could feel right at home in the heart of French Quebec. Ah! he drilled his conscripts then, did Sergeant-major Ulysses!

They had taken advantage of peace to make a great breach in that quarter of the city. Dorchester Boulevard they called it. Cars dashed along it from one red light to the next, as in Toronto. To Ulysses this was not a good omen. However, he crossed the boulevard; there was still the lower part to patrol, as far as Craig. He set off without much enthusiasm, his royal sail now drooping, his foremast unsteady. His quest was unsuccessful, as it had been farther up. All he met was a veteran from Alliston who was also looking for the Sirens. And the fellow hadn't even bothered to unpin his medals. The

---

* *Ouèredéare? Hou?* For "'Where are they?' (Where they are?) 'Who?'"

shame of it. Probably an Irishman. Ulysses tried to avoid him. The veteran nabbed him.

"*Ouèredéare?*"

"*Hou?*"

"The whores."

Yes, he was Irish all right. Ulysses was extremely shocked: the whores! Did he look as though he'd be hunting whores? And he did not hide his indignation from the Irishman. Really! The man was disgusting!

"And what about you, brother; what are you hunting?"

"For a start I'm not your brother and furthermore I happen to be looking for the Sirens. Yes, the Sirens! And for a worthy motive. Lashed to my foremast in order to resist their call."

The Irishman burst out laughing and slapped his thighs. Ulysses walked on. He felt old and weary. Ah! the Odyssey! How far away it all seemed. His foremast tilted, then fell. Ulysses picked up his royal sail from the street and put it in his pocket; it was now only a soiled handkerchief.

THE BUDDHIST

Vernon is a peaceful little town, green and extremely British, situated in a valley whose slopes have remained untouched and wild. A spur at the base of the mountain forms a plateau; this plateau overlooks the town; it is arid and shrill with grasshoppers. There grazes the austerity of war: the herd of young males separated from the female, to be banded against the enemy, to gain instruction and stature, and to receive, in place of Nature's tool, a great steel rifle, or else a machine gun, which arms they clutch all day long, acquiring in the end the jerky gait of maniacs. It was on this lunatic plateau that I became a Buddhist.

I hadn't studied theology, but rather was in the process of forgetting my catechism, so that in the ten commandments I would jump from five to seven, resolutely, and was even promising myself a tea-time visit with the little ladies of number six,* six which is spelled the same in British Columbia

---

* In a French rhyming version of the Ten Commandments, found in the old catechism, number six warns against lust of the flesh. Ferron's French parodies the style of this well-known text.

as elsewhere. But I had learned, shortly before leaving Quebec, that there was in Beauce County a Buddhist lawyer, and this had greatly amazed me. Arriving at Camp Vernon and finding myself as a result very far from my priest, I decided that even though I was a doctor, there was nothing to stop me from doing the same, and I put myself down as a Buddhist! This done, I hastened to inform my companions. "You must be mad!" they said to me. The lawyer had amazed me; now it was my turn to amaze them, and in my delight I asked myself why the deuce I hadn't thought of taking up Buddhism before.

Things went no further. A few days later I had already forgotten the matter when I learned, with astonishment and, I confess, some dismay, that the Adjutant of the camp was waiting for me in his lair. I was in no position to refuse, so I went. This Adjutant was an energumen of a kind never seen in our streets; he was wearing a green beret, a ginger mustache, a pleated skirt, two hairy legs, all of this emerging from large boots — heels together, of course — and standing stiff as a ramrod from end to end. I said to myself: "This is surely an Englishman." And it was. But what I had not anticipated was that at the sound of my name he would begin to come undone, stoop, bend, sit down, take a pipe from his drawer and say to me, cutting short my formalities: "Very well, sit down!" Which I did, humbly, first on one buttock, then on the other, then, while he filled his pipe and lit it, on both. And when his pipe was lit, what did he do? He smoked, in no hurry to reveal the subject of our interview.

At last he said, "So you are Lieutenant Laurendeau from the goodly province of Quebec?"

"Yes, Sir."

"And you're a Buddhist!"

With these words I saw the light. Everything became clear and rather amusing. "I'll bet this Englishman is a Buddhist himself," thought I.

"For the moment, yes, Sir."

"Then you are not really one?"

"I mean," said I, taking my time, "that I might one day be converted to another religion."

I didn't want to become too involved with Buddhism, about which I knew very little, nor to vex a man of his importance, an energumen into the bargain, who might himself be in it up to his neck. With an Englishman it's always advisable to be prudent: you never know what madness may be brewing behind that screen, what Punchinello his phlegm conceals. Not only might mine be a Buddhist, but even worse, and without its being obvious, continuing all the while to carry out his functions as Adjudant of Camp Vernon, the Buddha himself. My situation was clearly a delicate one.

"Be converted? So might I. But for the time being I'm a Presbyterian."

This confession restored my confidence: so he was a mere Protestant, a Punchinello, a conformist, an Adjudant! I adopted an air of superiority.

"Sir," I said, "what appeals to me in Buddhism is that the Buddha, having gone up to Heaven, should have come back down again. As a matter of fact, I'm a bit of an atheist like him."

"The Army does not recognize atheism."

"That, Sir, is precisely why I am a Buddhist."

"We find this very distressing, for we have no bonze. Perhaps you would care to join our army in India?"

"I believe my family would object."

"Your family is not Buddhist?"

"No, Sir."

"Then why not agree for the time being, without committing your conscience, to be preached to by one of the many ministers, priests and rabbis we keep here? We have a very wide choice. Do be obliging, Sir!"

I noticed that he had called me "Sir"; this flattered me, I must confess, coming from a superior.* But on the other hand I could not help thinking that this deference was due entirely to the fact that I had declared myself to be a Buddhist.

"Consider for a moment my responsibility," he added. "I must provide every one of His Majesty's soldiers with the religious services his soul requires. I do the best I can. But in your case it is impossible. The only bonze I could find is in San Francisco. And he's apparently a very bad bonze – always drunk. I've made enquiries: I wouldn't recommend him."

The idea of having a personal bonze struck me as very funny, particularly a bonze who was none too catholic.† Did he sense my amusement? Was he shocked by it? Was he, after all, as I had at first suspected, a Buddhist himself? Or did he take me for a practical joker? He drew himself up to his energumen's height, stiffened piece by piece, from the big boots to the green beret, and on the way up the little pleated skirt,

---

* In the Canadian Army in 1945 the term Adjutant referred to a staff position normally filled by an officer above the rank of Lieutenant, a senior captain, for example. Since Ferron himself spent time at Camp Vernon in 1945, it is probably safe to assume that the story is set around that time.

† catholic. In French, *pas très catholique* is a set phrase meaning "louche" or "disreputable," which makes for a richer resonance than is possible in English.

which I forgot to mention was black, and shouted: "You may return to your ranks!"

The following Sunday I was not too surprised to find myself with my companions at the Catholic mass. "And what about Buddhism?" they asked me. I replied that it had not worked for me. They were not surprised and I was not sorry, for it is true indeed, as La Bruyère says, that there is no better religion than the one into which we are born.

ANIMAL HUSBANDRY

I took my lessons in private school at the far end of Fontarabie *rang*. The mistress was a little widow with a bad reputation and familiar ways, nicknamed *l'Allumette* – her touch enflamed. She showed me the moon and the stars and the underside of life. My visits made me melancholy; I would leave for home, a doleful elephant with a drooping trunk following after me. The good people of Fontarabie, seeing me go by like this, found my behaviour extravagant. There was nothing I could do about it; I was overcome with embarrassment. But then, to cure me, didn't the elephant fall sick – sick in the trunk, naturally. I took him to Montreal to visit a doctor. The doctor told me the malady was *h*onourable – an *h*onour* for him to treat – and his treatment worked so well that I found myself rid of the elephant, mounted on a unicorn, galloping back to the beautiful county of Maskinongé. Three big black dogs accompanied me, their eyes red, their mouths ablaze. This was more than I had bargained for. So,

---

* A play on the words *honorée* ("honoured") and *gonorrhée* ("ghon-orrhea"), as in the story "Cadieu."

when I arrived in Sainte-Ursule, instead of continuing on to Fontarabie, I made a beeline for the presbytery. The dogs plunged head over tail into the flowerbed. I went in alone, with my unicorn.

"A fine animal," said the priest.

"A fine animal, to be sure, and straight to hell he's taking me."

And I showed him the black dogs in the flowerbed, on their haunches, raging, their mouths ablaze – regular hellhounds.

"It's time you were married," said the priest.

One week later, it was a done deed. My wife gurgled like a Charlesbourg mouse.* She called me her rat, her big white *r-rat* – nothing could have been more restful after the elephant and the unicorn! I was content, I was happy. My wife did with me whatever she pleased. One morning, on her pillow, she found a rat, a big white rat: it was me. That put her completely at her ease: at last she could open the closet, where, surprised by my offer of marriage, she had locked her lover a few days before. The lover came out, my wife dusted him off. They were happy to see each other again. I strolled about on the pillow.

"Who is that?" asked the lover.

"It's a big white rat," replied my wife.

"I've nothing against big white rats, but couldn't he stroll about somewhere else?"

"No," said my wife.

---

* gurgled. In French, *grasseyer,* a verb which means, literally, "to roll one's 'r's in one's throat," as in the accent of Paris. The word for "rat" can be heard in the verb's first syllable. Charlesbourg is a working-class district of Quebec City.

The lover was surprised.

"It's my husband," she added.

The lover was no longer surprised. I continued to irritate him all the same. If he forgot me for an instant, I would nibble his ears. After one week of this, no more love between him and my wife. He was on constant alert; his whole expression had changed. Why was he watching me this way? Innocently, I came over to see. All claws, he pounced! But I was ready for him: I let out a bark straight away. Was he surprised! He didn't recover. It was a cat who ran away and not a lover. I chased him half-heartedly, just for the fun of it, to get a little exercise, then came back and placed my muzzle on the lap of my unfaithful wife.

"Silly fool," she said, "why don't you just show me you're a man?"

I was only too happy to oblige. And so it was, after a few digressions, that I became a good husband.

THE WOMAN NEXT DOOR

A silly little thing! If it had been up to me I'd never have spoken to her. Her high-pitched voice, her nervous laugh irritated me. I'd had enough of listening to her all summer. I couldn't bring myself to look at her now. And I didn't notice her hanging around my husband. Besides, even if I had noticed, I wouldn't have been particularly worried. My husband isn't one to have his head turned by a woman, and since I'd never let mine be turned by a man, it didn't occur to me that there were women around like her, susceptible enough for two.

I'd come home from work early. Mondays are quiet at the office. The manager knew my husband was off. He always takes his holidays in September. His colleagues all want to grab the summer. He lets them fight over it. He prefers the fall. The children are in school then. He has the whole day to himself. He stays in bed late, cooks all his favourite dishes, and gets quietly on with the housework for me. It's the same every year. "Just leave," the manager had whispered to me, "I won't even notice."

When I arrived, Leo was up on the stepladder. He gave me a funny look. I said, "The manager let me leave early." He just went on painting. That's when the woman next door appeared. She pushed the door open and called in. "Leo, have you finished painting yet?" With my hat still on, I confronted her. "Since when do you call my husband Leo?" She said, "Oh! You're not working today!" and ran off. A silly little thing! I was angry. Otherwise I might have felt sorry for her.

Leo had stayed on his stepladder, his paintbrush in his hand. For a moment I waited, hoping he'd put it down and get off. But he kept a firm grip on the handle and was soon painting again. He's not much of a man for words. I took off my hat. I'd have liked to make a scene, but it's not my style and I didn't dare. So we didn't talk about it. I got the supper ready. The children came home from school. They did their homework and prepared their lessons. At six o'clock we sat down to the table. Then, the children, who until that point hadn't noticed anything unusual, looked up at us. Leo was being nice to my favourites and I to his. They couldn't understand why we were exchanging roles like this. They found it amusing, nothing more. When the meal was over, they rushed to the door. It was the same in all the other houses. Soon the street was full of shouts.

I cleared the table and started washing the dishes. Leo had gone to sit by the window, without his newspaper. He was just smoking a cigarette. Then I heard the nervous laugh, the high-pitched voice of the woman next door. She was complaining to her husband, telling him she couldn't stand being shut in any longer. Soon afterwards I saw her come down the steps into the yard, all dolled up, prancing like a little warhorse. When she reached the window where Leo was sitting, she turned back to face to her own husband. He'd come out onto the doorstep after her, holding the baby. "If you feel like joining me, I'll be at the movie, on the corner." Leo must have known who the remark was intended for. He didn't let out so much as a sigh. He picked up his newspaper with the air of a man who hadn't the slightest desire to go out.

A few weeks later, it was raining and the last leaves were falling. A truck backed into the yard. Our neighbours, who had arrived in the spring, were moving out again. I said, "Poor woman!" Leo replied, "She's a silly little thing. Her husband's the one to feel sorry for." And I understood then that things had come to an end between them the night of the movie, when he'd seen the cuckold standing there with a baby in his arms. Do that to a man! He'd felt outraged and hadn't forgiven her. When it comes down to it, we only really love our own sex. As for me, it was at that moment that I went from pity to remorse.

I wondered if perhaps it was me she'd been reaching out to all along, when I was avoiding her, and if she'd only turned to my husband afterwards, out of spite. What could he have given her that she hadn't already received? If she irritated me, poor girl, it was because I was indebted to her. Insecure and unhappy, she allowed me to feel myself different, proud of my own strength and assurance. Why didn't I let myself like her? I'm the guilty one in all this. The uneasy feeling that comes over me whenever I hear a nervous laugh, a high-pitched voice, and turn around to see if she is there, convinces me of it.

THE FLOOD

A habitant and good farmer, who had managed to obtain from his wife thirteen children, all well grown though of unequal size, lived with his family in a farmhouse which was a strange kind of house, for every year in winter it would float on the snow for forty days or more; yet in spring it would become a house like any other, returning to the very spot it had occupied before, in Fontarabie *rang*, Sainte-Ursule de Maskinongé. This house had two doors; the front door opened onto the King's road, the back door onto the habitant's land. Now one spring the eldest son went out the back door and began to help his father, whose heir he subsequently became. That door was never used again. Every spring from then on the children went out by the front door; boys and girls in the flower of youth, they set out one by one on the King's road to sow their seeds elsewhere. The habitant shook hands with each and every one, saying: "Bon voyage, my pigeon, bon voyage, my dove. Come and see me at Christmas; I'll be expecting you." But these children bore more resemblance to the crow: they never came back. With the exception of one. When he appeared in Fontarabie, having failed to found a family elsewhere, the old man was sitting on his front steps, his beard bristling, his stick between his knees, raising himself up from time to time to get a better look at any creature that happened by. When he saw his son he asked himself whose offspring this runt could be, for he looked familiar. He started with the most distant families, then, having no success, worked closer and with some apprehension began to go through local names and names of relatives. "You don't understand," said the runt, "I'm your son." The old man did not deny it; it was quite possible.

"Have you come to see your mother?" he asked.

"Yes," replied the son.

"Well, you're out of luck; your mother's dead and buried."

The runt took the news very well; he had been away for a long time.

"I haven't married again," added the old habitant. But so saying he raised himself up with the help of his stick, peering into the distance to see if by chance a woman had appeared on the horizon.

"What about you, son; have you got any children?"

"No," the poor devil replied.

The old man grew thoughtful.

"And your wife, what's she like?" he asked, without getting up, but tightening his grip on the stick, his beard flashing sparks. He was thinking that his runt of a son might invite him to his house where he would be alone all day with a young daughter-in-law. The answer shattered his hopes.

"Have you at least been to the city?"

"Yes," replied the son.

Then the old man, who knew perfectly well, having seen it in the papers, that in the city there were hundreds and hundreds of girls herded together in an enclosure, raised himself up on his stick, filled with the greatest indignation:

"Stay here," he shouted, "I'll go in your place!"

And off he went. Winter was not far away. Soon the snow came down and the strange house broke loose from Fontarabie and began to float; it floated slowly over the lost generation, an absurd ark, raft of the helpless; it floated over the old man, who, from the depths of the flood, brandished his terrible stick.

THE PARAKEET

The departure of her eldest had never upset her, for she had always managed to replace them as she went along. But there came a year when she was no longer able, having, as it turned out, produced her lastborn the year before. This was the end of her family. The lastborn grew and, growing, nudged the rest, who, one after another, went their way.

"Soon they'll all have left."

"I hope so," said the old man.

The wife looked at this husband of hers and thought what a fool he was, what an old fool. What disconcerted her was that he had always been this way and that she loved him. He was of the opinion that as long as you'd done your duty by your children, and they weren't in poor health, they should be made to fend for themselves once they were of age – or sooner, in the case of the smartest ones; after that they didn't belong to the parents any more, but to the whole world, and to the good Lord; you had to let them go, and even, if necessary, show them the way.

"Even the lastborn?"

The lastborn was no different from the rest, for the old man was poor and hadn't the means to keep a single one. So in due course he, too, left, and the mother fell ill.

"Very well," said the old man, "but I'm warning you, old girl: if you die, I'll take a new wife."

He thought himself clever. She thought what a fool he was, what an old fool. What disconcerted her was that he had always been this way and that she loved him. She couldn't bring herself to leave him to another, and recovered. This changed nothing in the house, which was as sad as before. Even the old man was not happy.

Then, one day, they received from a daughter, who had never married, two parakeets in a white cage, birds the like of which had not been seen in the county, blue birds with masquerade beaks, which spent their time teasing, petting, nestling together to sleep, never tiring of love – two birds of paradise. As soon as they entered the house the sadness left it. The old couple were delighted. Soon the cage got in the way. They opened it, and the parakeets flew about the house. The only drawback – the holes pecked in walls and ceilings. The old man had a hard time repairing the damage, but he was only too happy to do it.

"Damned birds! I'll cut off their heads!"

The old woman looked at him and thought what a fool he was, what an old fool. What disconcerted her was that he had always been this way and that she loved him.

One winter afternoon, when the old man went out to fetch wood, one of the parakeets followed behind him and found itself burning in the icy air. Frantic, it flew straight for the sun. The old woman had rushed outside. Together on the doorstep, husband and wife watched as the bird fell, and they each took it to be a sign that their own end was near. They went back inside. In the parakeet that lived on, the old man saw his bereaved wife, the old woman her widowed husband. Each was broken-hearted. Their last days were spent doting on the bird; by lavishing attention on it, they encouraged it to live. Each partner hoped in this way to lessen the other's pain.

Each morning, the old man would say to himself: this day will be my last. At his side, the old woman would think: this will be mine. After a time, however, they changed their chronology, instead of the last day, preferring to say the last week, then the last month. When a year had gone by, and they still hadn't died, they didn't know what to think. Above their heads, the blue parakeet, with which they had become one, hovered motionless, sardonic as an idol.

THE WEDDING BOUQUET

In the evening after the rosary, while the mother was putting the children to bed, the old man would sit down to smoke a last pipe, the best one of the day, and he would say to Hortense, his eldest daughter, "Daughter, go bring in a little wood for breakfast tomorrow."

Hortense would go out and return with a few logs; she couldn't carry much, it was all her arms would hold. And the old man would say, "My, what short arms you have, daughter!"

It was the same every evening. Then Hortense would go off to bed, blushing.

One Sunday afternoon a tall fellow came up to the house. Who did he want to see? The tall fellow didn't say. Hortense offered to go and tell her father. The fellow was in no hurry. "Don't bother him. I'll wait for him here." Not wishing to be rude, Hortense waited too. When the old man came back he saw the beau and was not pleased. That evening after the rosary, Hortense asked him, "Shall I go and fetch some wood?"

The old man replied, "No, daughter."

Then Hortense went to bed, blushing a sight more deeply than usual.

The wedding was held two months later. By the end of the evening the house could hold no more – everyone was tight. The bridegroom's carriage was brought up to the door. As Hortense was climbing in, the horse reared, she dropped her bouquet. With a crack of the whip the bridegroom brought the animal to its feet.

"Remember who's boss," they called to him.

His only reply was to brandish his whip; then he slackened the reins. Hortense wasn't laughing; they were carried away at a fast gallop.

As he came back from his chores the next day, the old man's brow puckered into a frown: someone was coming across the fields in a wedding gown. He went into the house and said to his wife, "I think the priest administered the sacrament wrong. Look who's coming home: it's Hortense heading back across the fields."

The wife said to the old man, "Smoke your pipe and stay quiet."

Hortense opened the door. With her short arms she was pressing to her a sorrow much heavier than the logs. When she saw her father, impassive, hiding his feelings behind a cloud of smoke, her arms fell to her sides. But this made no difference; the sorrow was firmly attached.

"Hello, daughter," said the mother, "I expect you've come to fetch your bouquet? Here it is. I picked it up out of the dust: the wheels of the carriage had run over it."

Hortense took the bouquet. The mother said to the old man, "Go harness the horse and drive your daughter back home."

So the old man drove her home. All the way he smoked his pipe and said not a word. And beside him, in the rain, Hortense clutched her crumpled bouquet.

MARTINE

HIS WIFE

She was ugly, undeniably, uncompromisingly ugly. Yet, by making the most of the night, she managed to bear a child each year. Her husband was my father. He never went to bed sober. I could understand why.

She would have preferred to call me Angèle, but my father refused and to silence all argument put his fist in her face. After which, proud of his authority, he went off to get drunk. His wife only had one dress, and that was full of holes. She stayed home. Every time I heard her call "Martine!" I would lower my eyes, ashamed, for my name ought to have been Angèle. I was wrong, she was right, and right was unforgiving. Beware of the broom in her hand!

"Your wife beat me," I would tell my father.

He in turn would beat her. And so we would reason. Did it make any sense? At the time, perhaps, but soon we would have to start all over again. In the end, by dint of reasoning, I acquired a mind of my own. I resolved never to marry. There appeared to be a connection between marriage and having children.

THE COIF

I attended a convent. I wore a black dress. I was in mourning for my childhood. Nuns with pointed coifs, who at first looked all alike to me (it was a while before I lowered my gaze to the level of their faces, and I never did get as far as their smiles), told me things of grave importance. I listened absent-mindedly, attentive only to their coifs, which stood tall, white and impeccable, awakening in me the notion of perfection and the earnest desire to wear one myself. So great was my desire that I would gladly have endured any sacrifice and, plagued though I was year round by fleas, would even have foregone the privilege of scratching.

The convent was a long way from our house. And there and back I had to listen to the sniggering of the boys. They showed such contempt for my sex that, having at first considered it natural, I came in the end to feel ashamed of it. And I went from the house to the convent, from the convent to the house, furtively, an orphan, bereft of my childhood, bereft of myself.

THE TOM-BOY

My brother Ernest with the bandy legs sought to assert himself at my expense, but his timing was wrong. I lost patience and with unaccustomed vigour put him in his place. He was amazed, and I was even more amazed than he.

From that day on, the road to the convent never seemed so long. I sniggered at the boys and paid them back their blows. Their contempt ceased and there was nothing now to stop them admiring me. Before I knew what had happened, I found myself the only girl in a clan of the opposite sex. It was the girls' turn to despise me. They exchanged vague whispers behind my back.

Although it was not apparent, the nuns had ears, and the whispers reached those ears. From them I learned something I'd never known, namely that I was possessed by the devil. I also learned that they were praying for my deliverance. I couldn't help feeling a certain pride. Because of this pride their prayers were in vain. I remained a tom-boy.

"Very well," they said, "a tom-boy you shall be!"

They cut off my hair in front of the whole convent. They intended to humiliate me. They delivered me from my fleas.

THE STARS

I was going on for twelve. Jeannot was the same age. Blond, frail, shy, he was almost feminine. Dark and resolute, I had the masculine role. These temperaments led us to taste of a precocious love. As night fell we would slip into darkened alleyways.

Joined together in an unending line, the houses divide the neighbourhood into two distinct zones. One is the street, with its lights, its even paving and its tumult. The other, shapeless and shadowy, is the backyard zone, with its piles of broken pots, its garbage and its rubble. It was in the second zone that we found our refuge.

Jeannot would lay his head on my shoulder. I would lean mine against the wall, and before my eyes there would stretch the incorruptible sky I never tired of gazing on. The city was reduced to a distant murmur and the startled rats stopped short of our living flesh. What a strange thing is night in between the houses of two parallel streets! At the touch of Jeannot's body and the warmth of his hand in mine, I was filled with a joy so pure it can only have come from the stars.

THE MUSEUM

Then his head no longer fit the hollow of my shoulder; he began to be afraid of the rats. My protection wasn't enough. Without a refuge, ours became a fugitive love. We wandered the streets in search of something nameless, something that at every turn my friend would think he'd found – a ring perhaps, a watch, or a trinket, that would catch his eye in a store window and fill him with delight.

Swept away with admiration for this exquisite taste, I found myself in league with him, finding beautiful whatever he thought was so. And sometimes we would leave our neighbourhood, walking on and on until we reached St. Catherine Street, the department stores, the famous jewellers, where we would stand and gaze for hours on end.

Since that time I've often formed relationships with artists, who have taken me around museums for the good of my mind. I've never given them any cause for complaint. On the contrary, they've praised my patience and the respect I've shown for Art.

THE PINK BOX

In the school there was a pink cardboard box at the feet of the statue of the Sacred Heart. The toes of the statue were all the same colour, except for one that was chipped and white. Through a little slot we dropped pennies into the box. The nuns encouraged us; it was for the Holy Childhood.

In Canada, we were lucky: we ate pigs. In China, it was different: pigs ate children, at least those children whose parents hadn't managed to sell them to the missionary. If the missionary didn't have twenty-five cents to give them, they would throw them to the pigs. And the poor missionary, whose beard was long, would weep because he hadn't been able to save them.

Full of compassion, I'd bought a great many of these Chinese babies. The Sacred Heart, unmindful of the chipped toe, gazed down tenderly at me. Once they'd been baptised in my name, these babies had promptly died. As well as my angel and my demon, I now had their souls to hover round me. But they were of no assistance in keeping me from temptation.

One evening, very casually, I lingered after school. The corridors were soon deserted. I tucked the pink box under my arm, glanced up at the Sacred Heart, and was reassured to find the tenderness had not ceased. I kissed the chipped toe and walked calmly away.

THE PERFUME

Jeannot had a weakness for luxury and adornment. He was vain without knowing it. Born, like me, into the poorest of milieus, he had natural refinement. His hands had a whiteness about them, his features were delicate. He was a kind of prince, lost in a city where there were no palaces, in a neighbourhood of unrelenting ugliness. The best in these conditions can become the worst.

I had never been so sad. The only way I had to express my feelings for him was by becoming his accomplice. In my attempt to stay close to him, I was helping him grow away from me.

One night, he was wearing perfume. "How good you smell, Jeannot!" There was a hint of reproach in my voice, and I couldn't hide the expression of scorn that lingered on my lips. He smiled gratefully at me and, delighted to receive the compliment, pulled out a tiny bottle, which he uncorked and sniffed ecstatically. I, too, had to go into raptures over the powerful scent, which I loathed, which I still loathe, and which is perhaps the source of the repulsion I feel for all artificial paradises.

DESIRE

Of all men, artists are the kind I've loved most often. They always find me yielding, eager to serve them. Each one interprets this inclination in his own manner, and that manner is generally born of conceit. For artists believe me to be in love with their genius, when in fact what I love is the artifice itself, the painting, the book, the play, in which the object always remains true to itself, its strangeness, as it were, intact, and beauty, for all its extraordinary prestige, is never something to be desired.

As usual, in front of a store window, Jeannot had found a thousand innocent reasons, a thousand subtle pretexts for preferring one piece of jewellery to any other. At such moments he could attain true eloquence in his effort to win me over to his choice; his eyes would shine with pure rapture; he was never prettier than then. Suddenly, as he spoke, he gestured toward the object of his delight, a ring, and in so doing caught sight of his own hand. He stopped speaking, studied it and looked back into the window, where, against a background of blue velvet, the gold ring gleamed. Surprised by his silence, I looked at him; his eyes had grown dull and an ugly shadow passed across his face, revealing his desire.

THE BRASS RING

I opened the pink cardboard box and found inside the equivalent of three Chinese babies. For this sum I obtained a brass ring. It was light and flimsy but in shape quite similar to the one Jeannot had coveted. I hoped by offering it to him to cleanse his face and restore to his eyes the innocent flame, the rapture, that had endeared him to me.

He wasn't at our rendezvous. I didn't see him until three days later. There were dark circles under his eyes, and his look was sullen.

"Where have you been, my Jeannot?" I asked. He shrugged his shoulders. I'd become a nuisance to him. He did, however, deign to show me his finger. On it shone the object of his desire, the gold ring. His nails were daubed with red.

I couldn't bear to look any more. I took to my heels and fled, pursued by a terrible grief, which overtook me at last in the foul-smelling, rat-infested yard that was the scene of my lost love. There, as darkness fell, I abandoned myself to my tears and my cries.

I kept the brass ring. I still wear it at times. It's light and it's precious. Sometimes I think I see on its gemless surface the reflection of three captive souls.

THE RAT

The loss of Jeannot and my new-found grief taught me the inexorable laws of nature. Even in the midst of my tears I fell asleep. I was awakened by something warm and soft on my stomach; it was a young rat, attracted by the heat of my body. My heart beat once, then stopped. I would have screamed, but I remembered Jeannot, his red nails, his gold ring. How in such a moment of sorrow could I have forgotten him and fallen asleep? I understood then that life is fickle, and I felt such a loathing for my kind that I had nothing but sympathy left for the rat. I kept perfectly still.

The stars had moved, but their radiance was undimmed. Impassive witnesses to my conflicting passions, they shone with indifferent brightness on my joys and on my tears, showing them to me in all their vanity. I felt misunderstood and forever lost. With no one to love, ignored by the heavens, rejected by myself, I found my only consolation in consoling a rat. And I fell asleep a second time.

The next morning, on my stomach, there was no trace of the rat. The sun was laughing. I was hungry. Perhaps it had been a dream?

BRAVERY

The pink cardboard box was important. A great deal was said about its disappearance and a great deal more about the author of the crime, who was accused of all the sins of Israel and even blamed for the white toe of the Sacred Heart, broken off, it seemed, "in a fit of sacrilegious malice."

My disillusionment inclined me to confession. I had no fear of the consequences. Let them beat me, break my bones. Indeed, I could imagine no torture cruel enough, for I wished to die. So I was brave. And since bravery is a noble virtue, I felt proud of myself, proud to the point of not knowing to whom I should denounce myself. The nuns seemed to me to be unworthy, with the exception of one, who was still unknown to me. Haughty, much feared, she was the Mother Superior of the convent. I knocked on her door. She let me in, and I found myself in a room crowded with furniture and books. On a small bench stood an aquarium.

This room, which was to be the scene of my torture, was strangely calm. A kind of peace filled my heart, and my bravery vanished, leaving me simple and natural, yet astonished that my morbid desire should have led me to look up into a human face.

THE PRALINE

The nun's face, beneath the pointed superstructure, was broad and austere and quite without softness. The nose was pinched, the mouth dry, the skin thin and taut. Only the eyes had youth and life. They glowed with a gentle irony at my confession. She said, "Martine, kneel down." I obeyed, but she was not satisfied with my position. She had me move round to face the aquarium. Then, her irony never fading, she proceeded to read and to take no more notice of me.

Time passed. Kneeling stiffly, I braced myself to withstand fatigue, the goldfish and my tears. This resistance became my sole preoccupation, and I was taken aback when the nun, putting down her book, asked me suddenly what I thought my punishment should be. I could only stare stupidly, unable to think what to say. Then she walked over to me and put a praline in my mouth.

This praline melted slowly, and with it my pride. Soon only the almond was left, and my distress. I felt my eyes swim and tears run down my cheeks. I myself was swimming into shame. I was nothing more than a goldfish now, beneath the steady gaze of a great lady.

MARTINE CONTINUED

*O*nce *the city was not so tightly sealed; the countryside could penetrate it.*

MARTINE

At one time my father was an exuberant man, whose generous wife gave him a child a year and never uttered a complaint. She had kept her good looks and her rosy cheeks and was comely as the house, which stood clean and bright under the willow trees. We owned a few acres of land around the house, enough to feed a cow, her calf and a few pigs. I grew up with these animals, which is why my health is good. But all the while the city was encircling our domain, and soon it began eating into it insidiously. My father let one piece of land go, then another, then a third, till in the end the cow ran short of hay. Her milk dried up. And what can you do with a cow who has no milk but eat her? Which is what we did. The following spring we had no calf. My father sold off the last remaining plot of countryside on rue Mont-Royal, since now, without the cow and her calf, it had lost its usefulness. Finally, it was the turn of the pigs. When the last one had been eaten, the neighbours closed in on us. Houses were pushed up tight against our own. We were caught inextricably in a larger whole. And my mother began having difficulty breathing.

The countryside that had found its way through the breaches into the very heart of the city, with the cows, the pigs, the chickens, the vegetables and the trees, now gradually withdrew, taking with it its animals, the clean air and the joy. Welded together, the houses served not only as dwellings, but as walls. The breaches were closed. No more escape, no more space. The city was tightly sealed.

THE WINO

There was a time when I was not a wino. I was someone far more honorable then. A vagabond. Not the kind who frightens women, the kind you'd give a penny to just to ward off bad luck, but the vagabond known throughout the province, who is welcomed with joy and even asked to stay, for in his pack he brings wisdom and dreams. As long as the warm weather lasted I was on the road. When evening came I would stop at some house, and there, long into the night, I would sit and conjure up before the eyes of my hosts a world that had no reality, but through which they could glean an understanding of the other world that darkness had swallowed up. The next morning, as I set out again, I would sense that my visit hadn't been in vain, and that I was leaving behind me more meaning than before, a brighter day, farms more clearly drawn, faces more human. No, I was not a beggar. I asked for nothing, and what I received could not be compared with what I gave. I was a tramp, but I was also a kind of mighty lord wandering the world to give it a little more substance, a little more style.

THE WIDOWER

When I was young, a stranger passing through our village looked behind my ears and predicted to my father that I would never be happily wed. My father remembered this when it was time to marry me. He chose for me the sweetest and humblest of girls. Never in all the world was there a more tender wife. But she died, and I loved her. The stranger had spoken true.

THE WINO

When winter came, I would return to the city and meet up with others like myself, the vagabonds of yesterday, the winos of today. We would exchange wisdom and dreams while waiting for the flood to end. For winter is a flood. Each house becomes an ark, where the memory of spring is kept alive. That is why spring returns. We would watch for it, and as soon as the air began to tremble with a nameless desire, as soon as its luminous sign appeared in the sky, we would hurriedly say our goodbyes. Each of us would take up his pack of wisdom and dreams and go quietly out of the city. The winding roads were well suited to wandering. Walking was still possible then. A horse doesn't travel much faster than a man, and the difference isn't worth the bother of an extra animal. So we went at a lively pace. Sometimes in a single season we would travel the whole province. Then the horses vanished and machines appeared in their place. The roads became straight and hard. From then on walking was impossible. How do you expect a man to compete with these speed machines that tear through space on ribbons of smoking asphalt? Walking gets you nowhere. You might just as well stay put. And so we've stopped our wandering. Without our tales the country has fallen into confusion once more. We

never leave the city now, and we've traded our packs for the
bottle. We've traded wisdom and dreams for the bottle.
Wisdom and dreams have no place in the city and the bottle
gives us a foretaste of the great escape.

MARTINE

When we'd eaten the cow, the calf and the pigs, my father
began to drink, and misfortune entered the house. His wife
became a hideous thing, a withered bag of sagging flesh, who
still had strength enough to wield a broom. And you know
the rest of my story. What I've been through! Yet I can't forget
my childhood, and happiness for me is still a cow chewing her
cud by the side of rue Mont-Royal, or a cup of warm milk
with a hint of froth on top, just enough to leave a white line
under your nose.

*The countryside entered the city at the same time as the wino,
with his pack on his back, was leaving it. Between the country
and the city there were exchanges of wisdom and health. The
exchanges have ceased now. The city keeps what belongs to it, the
country does the same, with the result that both have lost everything, wisdom as well as health. You can't have one without the
other. Some exchanges are necessary. Here is a fable that will help
you understand.*

THE WINO

Once upon a time there lived a man who was a widower, and
this man had large ears and an only daughter. The daughter
was courted by a boy who was the son of another widower,
and the second widower had ears that were just as large and
just as red and just as shameful as the first. Which is not at
all surprising, since people with uncommonly large ears have

a predisposition to widowhood. Friendship provided them with consolation in adversity, and this tender bond not only made possible their children's friendship, but also enabled the two men to work more productively. Co-operation is necessary within continents, and it was all the more so on the desert island where these two widowers had landed one morning, each with a child on his back, sole survivors of a shipwreck. They had landed separately. The widower with the daughter had built his house on the north of the island, while the widower with the son had built his in the south. Then one day, while out exploring, they had met and had become fast friends, soon agreeing to combine forces to farm land in the middle of the island. Theirs was a friendship based on equality. Neither had further to walk than the other. Meanwhile the children kept house, one in the north, the other in the south, and it was only by chance that they came to know each other. On the shore the boy picked up a little compass, washed up from the wreck of his father's ship, and it led him straight to the girl. Love itself could not have guided him better. For which we should be glad, for otherwise he might have drowned. There are attractions that can lead as surely to life as they can to death. Love is one of these. This time, thanks to the compass and the positions of the two houses, love was right on course. While the fathers laboured in the middle of the island, in the house in the north the children practised to become lovers. The boy grew a beard, the girl heaved a sigh. The days passed and their passion increased. The girl sighed so long and so deeply that in the end her bosom swelled, pushed out by a sigh that could find no release. This rounded bosom, this sprouting beard, called forth other arms, and the young lovers, ready at last to do battle, were on the point of confrontation, when, most inopportunely, the widowers with the big ears caught wind of something and, instead of continuing to work in harmony in the middle of the island, took off the masks of friendship and discovered hatred in each other's eyes. The battle had nothing to do with them, so why didn't the old fools just mind their own business? Widowers have strange ways, and because their children were falling in love, ours set about trying to kill each other. Then they thought better of it and decided to go home, one to the house in the south, the other to the house in the north. And there, in the north, the second widower found the son of his new enemy, booted him unceremoniously in the backside and sent him flying out the door. Boy and girl were separated. It was the end of their romance. The blossom, for all its promise, brought forth no fruit. The widowers confined the lovers, and each one proceeded to clear a garden around his own house. The middle of the island, untended now, became wild and overgrown with bushes. So too did the lovers' hearts. After two years of living this way, the widower in the south had for a son a vague, nervous, sickly creature, who was no longer a boy. The widower in the north had for a daughter a vague, nervous, sickly creature, who was no longer a girl. And in their anguish the two widowers strained their ears. One night they caught the sound of footsteps. The next morning, in the bushes in the middle of the island, they found the two children, who had come together to die. The fable tells us nothing more. What became of the widowers? Were they changed into donkeys? Probably so, but the fable doesn't say. It has nothing to add once it has made it plain that among human beings certain exchanges are necessary.

Exchanges are necessary between lovers, between mind and body, between city and countryside, but a thousand walls surround the city, and the imprisoned lovers can only meet in death. The wedding procession loses its way in the underbrush, and the funeral procession follows in its stead. No one can cry out. The substitution has been made without a single protest. In the anguished silence diligent undertakers profit from the mistake. Exchanges are necessary between the two shores, but the bridges have been destroyed. Willows reach out from either bank but their branches no longer intertwine above the shared waters. The arch that spanned the walls has collapsed and hands stretch up to the sky without touching. Exchanges are necessary between men, yet men come together and remain alone. They long to be understood, yet cannot speak. They arrange to meet, then shut the door in each other's face. Imprisoned inside himself, each man is his own jailer. Some, in a burial vault, observe their own agony with the eyes of undertakers. In solitude man is his own prey. Solitude is a sign of our times. There are no more exchanges, there is no more society. A grotesque misunderstanding reigns. And in the rarefied air, nothingness casts its darkness over the world.

THE WINO

I no longer dread its coming. For a long time now I've heard the whistling of its wing. Haven't you noticed it?

MARTINE

It's a wing of shadow and blood, sweeping the herd before it. Men come to me, absurd and pitiful. At least rats, when they panic, hurl themselves in their droves into the sea. But men keep up appearances. They stay in line, despite their anguish, hat in hand. And they come to me seeking some kind of deliverance, as if I could open the door of the world to them, as if love, for them, were a last escape. They press against me, they jerk me up and down. In vain. These little jolts may trigger great emotions, but they cannot shatter fate.

SALVARSAN

If nothingness casts its darkness over the world, then men, for their part, are breathing madness into the air. We live in strange times.

The world evolves, but the forms in which we conceive it have hardly changed. To conceive it this way is naturally to end up conceiving nothing, and it follows that a mind without nourishment breeds a quiet unease.

SALVARSAN

I found I was getting short of breath. "I'm growing old," I thought. And my attitude changed. I felt greater pity for my patients, and my joy, when they recovered, was keener. When they paid me I felt like the girl who has given herself willingly and finds it hard to hold out her hand. The money I took diminished me. My patients were not rich. Poverty and the abjectness of a lowly condition are the cause of many illnesses and even of some premature deaths. Whenever I witnessed one of these deaths I felt I was taking part in a human sacrifice. Behind the social system I began to discern, more clearly every day, a bloodthirsty god, greedy for little children and for young men and girls. I called him Baal. I could just as easily have found another name.

My perspective had changed, and medicine began to seem a futile pursuit.

THE WIDOWER

My wife accidently swallowed a germ, which stuck in her chest and wouldn't budge, even though she took all kinds of drugs. As the doctor said, medicine is still an imperfect science. But the day will come when they'll have a drug for every kind of germ. Men will go on dying, but they'll die naturally. A natural death is the flower of old age.

SALVARSAN

Once upon a time there was a man whose son had been condemned to death – for what reason, I don't recall. Mad with grief, this man imagined that he could save his son by killing the executioner. It was simple enough. He killed him. And it was a second executioner who put to death both the father and the son.

THE WINO

Another time there was a young prince who lived in the most beautiful castle in the world. His father was king of the land. When he was twenty years old he lapsed into a strange kind of lethargy. He lost interest in everything. Even the most exquisite foods filled him with disgust. The king summoned his doctors; their knowledge was useless. In desperation he summoned his wise men; they were as useless as the doctors, with the exception of one, who said to the king: "Sire, there is in the city an old woman, who is dying of hunger. Save her life and you will save your son." The old woman was given food, and the young prince regained the will to live. But the next day he had lapsed once again into the same strange lethargy. The king summoned his wise man. "There is," said the wise man, "a baby crying in hunger. His mother has no more milk and his father is too poor to buy him cow's milk." The baby was given milk and the young prince recovered the will to live. But the next day he had lapsed again into the same strange lethargy. "There is," said the wise man, "a young girl who has been wronged and. . . ." The King interrupted him, protesting that there would be no end to it if they went on this way. "No, indeed," said the wise man, "for there is no end to human misery." And the king, who more than anything loved his palace and his feasts, let his son, the young prince, die.

No one uses new cloth to mend an old garment, for new cloth pulls away part of the garment, and the tear becomes worse. Neither is new wine stored in old casks. . . . To preserve the old casks we have sacrificed the new wine. The blood of our children flows in the mud.

(1948)

ARMAGEDDON

The ambulance men had refused to pick him up. "He's dead."

"No, he's not."

"If he's not dead, you'll soon find out, Captain. You can give us another call. We'll come back."

And the ambulance men had driven off with the injured. As it was they couldn't have taken any more. Didier was lying on the pavement, between two cronies. There could be no doubt about these two; they were already growing cold, frozen in their melodramatic poses, like ham actors. Didier's act was far more subtle and discreet. He was still warm. Lying on his back, with his eyes closed, he could almost have been in bed, pretending to be asleep, holding his breath. His charcoal grey suit and his starched white collar were still spotless. If he was dead, you'd have been hard pressed to say what he'd died of. If you pulled back his lids, the eye still seemed moist and not completely insensitive to light. The Captain was like that: he'd never trust a habitant. And Didier was one all right. The Captain stood looking at him. "Listen, buddy. If you expect me to put my reputation on the line and send you off to the morgue in that phoney sleep of yours, you've got another think coming!"

The accident had occurred on the wide turn leading from Chemin Neuf into Montée de Sainte Julie, just above the right angle where the two roads used to meet. You couldn't have found a more perfect setting. On either side a line of cars could be seen stretching for a mile or more. The new arrivals left their headlights on for a moment or two, then switched them off, one by one. At night the roads always seem deserted, but you only have to block them for an hour or so to realize how busy they really are. I started up the line, keeping doggedly to the left, like an Englishman. It wasn't long before I came to a policeman waving a flashlight, who shouted insults at me *en canadien,* like a Frenchman. I said nothing. In the end he recognized me, this usher. It was as if I'd shown him my special invitation. He motioned to me to go on up to the stage.

It made a darn good scene.

First of all, centre stage, the main protagonists – two old cars that had collided head on, then come to a stop, their motors welded together, while the most impatient of their passengers just kept right on going, through the open doors, and even through the windows. The other passengers had stayed inside, some to be knocked unconscious or receive nasty cuts, others to simply die outright. The Didier in question was one of those who had not taken flight. It had rained the day before. They had brought him out and laid him on the clean pavement along with his two companions – one of them his son, the other Lafleur, a man he'd never met before, but who needed no introduction to the Captain or me. Then, facing this heap of metal and these corpses, training their headlights on them and bathing the whole scene in the red of their flashing lights, four police cars and two fire trucks, arranged in a semi-circle. And the effect was all the more dramatic with the injured no longer there to distract attention. Driving up, I'd seen the ambulance, across the fields, in the distance, leaping from bush to bush as it fled along another road. The crowd completed the circle, hushed and still. Three woolen blankets had been spread out, red patches on the black road. I was taken over to view the statues. They unveiled them for me, one by one, letting me admire the artist's handiwork. The last one was Lafleur. It shook me to see him lying on his side, with sand in his startled eyes, this man of violence, this invincible daredevil, the tough guy of the suburb. "At least we know what this one died of," said the Captain, moving the head to one side. Lafleur was lying on his injury; the jugular and the carotid were severed. On the pavement, between the head and shoulder, a little pool of blood, a tumblerful, no more.

"Come on now! He didn't die of that. He'd have made one bloody mess if he had! No, he died of something else, and instantly. His heart just stopped beating. It was much cleaner that way. Only the blood from his head spilled out, a little tumblerful. The head doesn't run on blood."

"What does it run on, then?" the Captain queried.

"How should I know? Electricity, maybe."

"Electricity!" the Captain said. "In that case Lafleur had a current all his own."

"That's for sure," I replied.

We came back to Didier. In spite of his phoney look, he was well and truly dead. But what of? It was a mystery to me.

"And I thought he was just trying to catch me out!"

"You don't know habitants. They're a crafty lot, I grant you. But nothing means more to them than their dignity."

The Captain: "Well, this one's kept his dignity all right."

"Under the circumstances he couldn't have done better. Just look at him, Captain. He's made a fine job of it."

"A fine job of dying – you reckon that's possible, do you?"

"Captain, if it weren't for the fact that I'm not a believer, I'd say you weren't very religious."

We had unbuttoned Didier. Under his white shirt his vest looked distinctly grey. We felt a little embarrassed. When we'd finished examining him we quickly did up his buttons. I said to the Captain, "Somehow I don't like having to hand him over to the morgue. It would be so much better if we could just send him directly back to his village."

"It'd certainly be a lot simpler," the Captain agreed. "They could lay him out, then, just as he is."

A response perfectly in keeping with the scenario. But it had the effect of annoying him. When it came to cinema, he had ideas of his own. Perfection was silent, all masterpieces were pageants. He had said too much. It was my fault, of course. Having said it, he shook his head. A fly was buzzing in his ear – a parasite at this pure spectacle. And besides, it was a fact that his nerves were always frayed and ready to snap when he hadn't any alcohol on hand.

I felt I should say something. "Just as he is? He's still soft and warm. By the time he's cooled off he mightn't look so nice. You never can tell."

The Captain shrugged his shoulders. We were wasting our breath. We were just a couple of third-rate actors. And his whole attitude was one of disdain – very honest disdain, intended for himself as well as for me. I shrugged my shoulders too, but not so high. Mine drooped – it was more a question of pulling them up.

"Okay, that'll do," said the Captain. He didn't stand on ceremony with me, nor did I with him. In public I was no match for him, but in private I had the upper hand. While we spoke the police had slackened their hold. His men had moved closer to us in an attempt to catch what we were saying, and the spectators crowded in. Bold eyes were already invading the stage. The Captain swung around to face them – tall, thickset, an imposing figure, with a mask and grey eyes, a well-fitting uniform, badges, stripes, and gold buttons that glared in all directions. He didn't have to say a word; the spectators backed away into the night like a pack of frightened wolves.

It was time for me to go. My role was finished. I was left with this character I was hardly cut out to play. If it hadn't been for my diplomas I might easily have taken myself for a charlatan. I couldn't believe I was a doctor. But no one had ever doubted me. In the end I had come to feel at home in the part, and played my stock character with a kind of nonchalant ease.

I picked up my bag, in no great hurry to leave this fine theatre, where there were still two or three good scenes to come. In the crowd I spotted one of my clients, a decent sort, holding his eldest daughter by the hand. They looked like a couple of lovers. I still had another call to make. Right after the police, Mr. Coldmorgan, his voice faint, had phoned to say he was waiting for me.

"All right, but be patient. It'll be a good half hour before I get there."

"I can't wait!"

"Just hold on!"

I explained. He understood. A police call – no doubt about the priority there. You stand aside. Especially if you're a veteran of North Africa, still fired with the light of the desert, thrilling to the call of Ogou-ferraille,* sickened by the oil of tanks. Police – you think of the army. At your command, General Rommel! A German, and a bit of a crank, a mechanic with Pratt and Whitney, and a Jehovah's Witness in his spare time. His wife was one too – but she never let up for a minute. And their three children seemed normal. . . . Bravely he had held on . . . a touch of diarrhea! But that was how dysentery had started at Tripoli. Two comrades had died of it. Not much glory. A lousy way to go. . . . Canada, he knew, could be just as deadly. Fear had shot through his gut, sent a shudder rising to his heart, wrapping it in black velvet. It's too dry for the heart, velvet, quite intolerable in fact, worse than pericarditis.

He felt very sick, did Mr. Fritz Coldmorgan. And alone, with no one to comfort him. Mrs. Coldmorgan considered him a defeatist, possibly an atheist. She hadn't known thirst, the stench of corpses and tank oil, hadn't heard the cry of the vultures. She could easily think herself immortal, even with her hairy thighs.

"A defeatist? And who was it that surrendered? Who was it that cried for mercy in the night? You! I felt more like whistling. Oh no, Mrs. Rommel! Don't think you can keep me at my post. Standing up for Jehovah – I'm through with that now. The salt water in the desert poisoned me. God can work his miracles tomorrow. Today I want the doctor, the little French-Canadian doctor. Maybe he's an Iroquois? Anyway, he knows the secrets of his country. I'm only a poor foreigner. He'll deliver me from the spell of Tripoli."

Mrs. Coldmorgan beseeched Jehovah to overlook her husband's weakness.

---

* Ogou-ferraille. Ogou is an African god, Ogou-ferraille the Haitian god of war.

"But why doesn't he come?" cried the Witness.

"He'll come, Fritz, just keep calm. You're tired. Trust in Jehovah."

And, worried, she asked herself how he would ever get through the terrible battle of Armageddon if he couldn't put up with a few stomach cramps.

When I'd arrived on the scene of the accident and come face to face with the Captain, the lights had gone out for a second, the film had stopped running. Whether Didier was dead or alive was no longer the question. The question now was in a look: "My son?"

"Your son? No news."

He hadn't opened his mouth. I'd answered him in the same way. When we were really talking we were more formal, on account of the subalterns. The Captain looked at me. I looked at him. Not a word had been spoken, and everything was said. Then the show went on – for him an hour or two of grace, three if he was lucky. After that his son would fill his thoughts again, his son for whom he had left a prestigious job at Bordeaux prison and come to rot in a suburb whose police force and administration were notorious. He had lowered himself, but had still been unable to follow him. The son was gone now, lost from view, and he felt more guilty toward him than an assassin.

Gaily I said to the Witness of Jehovah, "I've just come from the battle of Armageddon!" The walls were covered with quotations. This one, for example: "He that believeth on him is not condemned. He that believeth not is condemned already." John 3-18. The sentence struck me as rather funny, in view of the privileged one's diarrhea. "You're not con- demned – so shit away!" I thought to myself – or words to that effect – mirth bubbling in my throat. But there was no danger of my laughing outright – I, a doctor above all else, my features composed, my expression faintly grieved, sympathy guaranteed. "Come on, Mr. Fritz Coldmorgan, let it come! You'll have me feeling sorry for you."

While I was at it I decided I'd wind things up with a whore. A pretty shabby one she was. As I worked on her, I suddenly wondered just who the innocent was under this innocent.

"You bringing up your child?"

"Yes, he costs me a fortune."

"How old?"

"Five years."

But under the child? I didn't know. The target was unsteady. I couldn't fire. If I'd been a Christian I'd have made it all the way with Jesus' help. . . . God, no! What a thought!

On my way back I stopped at the police station. The Captain was getting himself drunk, methodically. It hardly showed because of the uniform and the gold buttons. He told me he'd like to go to the moon and direct traffic under a black sky for the robots and cosmonauts.

"Go on, Captain, old friend, go get some sleep."

"Are you crazy, doctor? I wouldn't want to miss the end of the world."

The Sergeant came in to get an order. The Captain gave it correctly. You had to know him well to see that this handsome, imposing man was drunk and unhappy.

"It'll be an accident, just another accident, the same as all the rest, with sirens and flashing lights. Except that when it's all over, I won't need to come back to the station, and you won't need to go chasing whores."

THE WOOL NIGHTSHIRT
AND THE HORSEHAIR TUNIC

The Queen was so pure and white that the King had felt no desire for her. They had been married a year or more, and still she had not lost her lily. One night the King had a dream: the Queen was lying as she always did, chastely covered, her face grave. But at the foot of the bed there was a long line of little rams. Their presence puzzled the King; what could they be waiting for? He looked more closely and noticed a wriggling under the sheet, "Perhaps the Queen has fleas," he said to himself. But nothing showed on the Queen's beautiful face; it was as grave as before. The King was wondering what to make of this, when suddenly, in the hollow of the Queen's neck, he spied the top of a little ram's head. Moments later this ram jumped from the bed and ran off, only to be replaced by another, who made his way up under the sheet from the foot of the bed. All the little rams had a turn, and God knows there were enough of them! The King went to sleep trying to count them – he who was already asleep – and he didn't wake up until the next morning. He went to find the Queen, who asked him if he had slept well.

"Yes, my love. I slept like a top."

She shook her head and sighed. She was still as white and pure as ever, and the lily was at her breast. The King felt no desire for her. However, because of the rams, he was less indifferent than before. The Queen was knitting.

"What are you knitting, my love?"

"Sire, I am knitting you a nightshirt."

"Of wool?"

"Yes, Sire, of ram's wool."

When the nightshirt was finished the King wanted to try it on. It looked so well on him that he asked the Queen for permission to sleep with her. But the wool could not warm him up. He went off to sleep like a baby and snored like an ogre. The next morning the Queen asked him how he had slept.

"Don't ask," said the King. "Your nightshirt is useless, my love!"

"Perhaps I knitted it wrong side out," said the Queen.

So she unpicked the nightshirt and began knitting it the other way round. It took her a month or more. Each day the King came to see how she was getting along, impatient to try it on again. He had great faith in ram's wool. When the nightshirt was finished, the King put it on and asked the Queen for permission to sleep with her. But the wool could not warm him up. He fell asleep like a baby and snored like an ogre. The next morning the Queen asked him how he had slept.

"Don't ask," he shouted.

He was very angry. He was furious in fact. He tore off his nightshirt and trampled on it. He was a very hairy king; his hair was thick and black, like horsehair. When the Queen saw him in this state she was afraid and began to swoon. The King took her in his arms. He was quite terrible. She lost consciousness, and when she opened her eyes two hours had passed. Her beautiful lily was gone.

The next night the King had a dream: the Queen was lying as she always did, chastely covered, her face grave. But at the foot of the bed there was a long line of little kings. Their presence puzzled the monarch: what could they be waiting for? He looked more closely and noticed a wriggling under the sheet. "Perhaps the Queen has fleas," he thought. But nothing showed on the Queen's beautiful face. It was as grave as before. The King was wondering what to make of all this, when suddenly, in the hollow of the Queen's neck, he spied the top of a little king's head. Moments later this little king jumped from the bed and ran off, only to be replaced by another, who worked his way up under the sheet from the foot of the bed. All the little kings had a turn. And God knows there were enough of them! The King went to sleep trying to count them – he who was already asleep – and he didn't wake up until morning. He went to find the Queen, who asked him if he had slept well.

"Yes, my love, I slept like a top."

She shook her head but did not sigh. She was still as white and pure as ever, with just the shadow of a lily on her breast. The King seemed very pleased. As the Queen was knitting, he asked her, "What are you knitting, my love?"

"Sire, I am knitting you a horsehair tunic."

"A horsehair tunic?"

"Yes, Sire, for you to wear to war."

When the horsehair tunic was finished, the King wanted to try it on. It looked so well on him that he asked the Queen for permission to go to war. But the tunic could not protect him; he was struck by an arrow. They brought him back, bleeding, to the palace. The Queen asked him how he felt.

"Don't ask," said the King. "Your horsehair tunic is useless, my love!"

"Perhaps I knitted it wrong side out," said the Queen.

So she unpicked the horsehair and began knitting it the other way round. It took her a month or more. Meanwhile the King's wound had healed. He put on the tunic and asked the Queen for permission to go back to war. Either way round, the horsehair could not protect him. He had no sooner arrived on the battlefield than an arrow pierced him through and through. He fell down dead. The Queen no longer felt any desire for him.

LITTLE WILLIAM*

*In pedes procidere nascentem contra naturam est, quid
argumento eos appellavere Agrippas ut aegre partos.* †
— Pliny

The young woman refused to stay on her back. No matter how many times we turned her over, she would look up at us through blurred eyes and then roll onto her side again, tucking her knees up to her stomach, hiding her face in the pillow, sulking her way through labour. I stood near the bed, gloved to the elbows, looking like a priest stalled in the middle of his *Dominus vobiscum*. I was all at sea, being both impatient (it's a fatiguing way to stand) and disconcerted, because for things to be ship-shape according to

---

* Original translation by Ray Ellenwood (*Impulse* 3, 2 [1974], pp. 11-12). Revised, with permission.
† It is against nature to be born feet first; this is the reason why the designation "Agrippas" has been applied to those so born – meaning "born with difficulty." (Errors – or deviations – in Ferron's transcription of the Latin have been corrected.)

my rites, the young woman should not have been capsized. The old lady who was helping me didn't say a word, waiting snide attendance. When finally I asked for her advice, she said, "Take off your gloves, Doctor dear, and make yourself comfortable." Then she ordered her cohorts to bring a cup of tea. Stripped of my gloves, I was at her mercy.

"Drink up, it'll do you good."

"I'm sorry," I said, "but in the hospital we don't have complications like this. The women are strapped down the way we want them."

"What a shame!" said she.

Before I could open my mouth to object, she asked me how the tea was. Was it good? "Excellent," I replied. She seemed pleased. But not just at my satisfaction.

"Look at the length of those thighs," she said, pointing to our patient. "The late Cotnoir, your predecessor, liked them that way. I think he was right. Me, I've got short ones and I've never brought a child through my labours, just lucky to save my own skin. That's why I became a midwife. Drink your tea, doctor. The late Cotnoir was in the habit of drinking two or three cups while he was keeping an eye on a patient. Look how well this one's pushing with her head in the pillow. After all, we don't need to see a pretty face to do our little job, do we Doctor?"

I had to agree. But all the same it seemed to me she would be better off if she turned on her back. It was an obsession with me and there was nothing I could do about it. To deliver me thereof, the old woman began telling me how there had once been an English doctor on the Shore.

"A boat brought him, a boat took him away, and in between he set up practice as an accoucheur. People made use of his services. One of my aunts was his assistant. And you know, he had his own special way of doing things: first of all he never put his finger in the proper place, and secondly he made the woman lie on her side, with her knees pulled up to her belly, in the exact same position as this little one here."

With my nose in my cup, I was drinking my lesson, and the old lady did not hesitate to make it clear. I didn't really mind, since I was fascinated by exotic practices of all kinds, and God knows I'd never heard of the English position.

"And did it work?"

She seemed surprised at my question.

"Of course, it worked perfectly."

"Shall we try it?"

"Now, Doctor, that's just what I was going to suggest. There's only one problem . . ."

But the labour was getting hard and I didn't have time to hear about any problem. Judging from the baby's damp crown, which was now showing, the young woman needed us, even though she was still sulking. We let her sulk, and we delivered her on her side – on her side but turned a little toward the front, with her face in the pillow, which in fact meant from behind. And everything went well. When it was all over, she rolled onto her back and looked up at us through wide, clear eyes as if nothing had happened. We placed the baby next to her. She seemed surprised: she'd had it with her back turned, and maybe she thought it had just dropped from heaven. That's the big advantage of the English position.

"What's the problem then?" I asked the midwife.

"Why, the poor babe will have to be called William."

"After all," she went on, "he's a little Englishman, so to speak."

THE OLD HEATHEN

They were father and son, widower and orphan, an only father and an only son; they detested each other and were all the more alone. This went on for six months, just long enough for the old man to have outlived his wife. Then, with the old man gone, the son became boss of a farm finer than any in the settlement,* without a single stump or rock, well fenced, with sturdy buildings and all of thirty cows, a farm the like of which can still be seen in the very

---

* settlement. The French word "colonie" has particular significance in Quebec, where in the late nineteenth and early twentieth centuries much of the population moved away from the fertile but already overcrowded farmlands of the Saint Lawrence Valley to cultivate new land in regions of the province previously unsettled or only sparsely settled. *Colonies* often sprang up in areas totally unsuited to agriculture, and while some eventually prospered, they seldom achieved the status of the "older parishes," with their connotations of stability and opulence. Here the term "settler" is used in opposition to "habitant," for the role of the traditional habitant farmer was the ideal to which all settlers aspired, but which few in fact attained. (See also the story "Les Méchins.")

oldest parishes, though there they are the work of several generations, while this was the work of a single man. He had put all his energy into it, sacrificed all his days. Truly it had been his whole life. And so, after he died, he came back there, much to his son's despair, and to his own. It was the priest who was right in the end.

And yet they had given the old man a lavish funeral, the kind of funeral he had earned for himself, creating heaven on earth out of sixty acres of wilderness. His salvation seemed assured. Every one took it for granted he would go straight to heaven. And the people of the settlement had crowded into the little wooden church, not to mourn him, but to sing his praises. The first settler to become a habitant, he was an example to all, well nigh a saint. It was more than a funeral, it was a celebration. The son, in the very forefront of the cere-mony, was beside himself with joy, delighted to be rid of the old man and to be presiding over this great assembly. Clearly they were here to pay tribute to him, for from now on he was the habitant. Only one person was uneasy, peeved, annoyed, and that was the priest. At the moment of absolution he slipped his hand under the catafalque to give the old man the key to paradise. "Take it, you bastard!" was what he said. In Latin, of course. But everyone could see he was not happy about it.

The priest knew his man. A regular heathen. If he'd gone to mass on Sundays, it was only for appearances' sake; his spirit had stayed on the front steps of the church or back at the village store, planning his next transactions or stocking up on supplies for the week; if he'd made sacrifices to the Lord, it was only to ward off bad weather or some scourge that threatened his crops. And it was to this unbeliever that he'd had to hand over the key to paradise. Religion's task is far from easy in the settlements.

But what angered the priest most was that he was not at all sure of his man. He insisted on going with him to the cemetery. There he spoke to him sternly. In Latin, of course.

"I've given you the key to paradise, you old heathen. In a more civilized parish you'd never have got it, and you know it! But since I've given it to you, I'm expecting you to use it. Your place isn't here any more. Go up to heaven, and tell God I'm sorry I've nothing better to send him. Understand? Answer me, you bastard. Tell me you'll do as I say. It's for your own good and for the good of the land. You've done all you were ever meant to do here, and you've done it well. Don't go getting ideas about coming back. Do you hear? Answer me."

The old man did not answer. He was a stubborn old cuss, a regular heathen. And, as was to be expected, when the ceremony was over he never budged from his grave. He just lay there, letting himself slowly rot away. Then, rid of his old meat and his old bones, he came back to the farm that had been his whole life. The son, who detested him, got wind of him right away. So he stopped farming the land. He ate the cows one by one. He let the house and the farm buildings fall into ruin. Alders, poplars and birches grew up where the millet had been. And in the bushes the old man began to wail and moan. His whole life had been wrecked.

That is what comes of having no religion!

BACK TO KENTUCKY

The towns of Europe were the side-aisles of the war which was raging then, monumental, gigantic, world-wide at the expense of a single continent. There the soldiers came on leave, in the same uniform, rogues and heroes alike, and incited girls to deeds of daring, the better to undo and conquer them. In war the odds are never equal. There was disproportion there at any rate. Mars was as mighty as the world, Venus delicate as Europe. And so, in nave and aisles they fought their battles, in the nave confronting death, in the side-aisles life.

In Louvain a girl met an American soldier. They stopped side by side, and love trained its camera on them. The girl was no pin-up, but pale, graceful, tender as the mushroom that grows among dead leaves, an orphan brought up by nuns. As for the Yank, he had spent his childhood playing cowboys and Indians, then had gone to the movies to discover his world, a world in two dimensions, where for want of the third one everything was unreal. The orphan had all three – this disconcerted him; he realized he had them too – a technical revelation, you might say! And he was just an ordinary conscript, neither rogue nor hero – a dutiful son, something of a Quaker, something of a nudist too, and a chemist by trade. The camera began to roll.

At the crossroads of her three dimensions, the girl was at a loss to know which direction to choose. She had never been to the movies and was not familiar with the scenario. The American took her by the arm. Love's camera tracked them. As they barely understood each other it was a silent film, shot against the hubbub of the street. And then they got married, of course, and came to Canada. To a suburb of Montreal to be precise. But whereas their encounter had been sudden, the camera fortuitous, their marriage a surprise, this choice of abode was, on the contrary, preconcerted – "scientific," the American would say.

"My wife has so little talent for languages that after fifteen years of married life she still hasn't learned to pronounce her husband's name. At first, if you asked her to, she'd blush and get embarrassed. In all fairness I couldn't take her to Kentucky. As for me, I had no desire to learn French. So we had to find a place that would put up with our linguistic deficiencies, and where each of us would feel at home. We poured over the map of the world, we bought books. We nearly opted for Lowell in New England. Human geography evolves fast in America. Our books were already out of date. Too late, Lowell! We arrived just in time in Montreal."

I was rather curious to see what would come of this eccentric love in our clime. It produced children, and these children had measles and chicken pox like any others. With one small difference, however: the discussion between the parents, each one claiming the illness, he for Kentucky, she for Belgium. "*Rougeole?* Never heard of it." "*Mizeule.*" "Oh, measles!" The word would reassure him. The children would smile. The Walloon would shrug her shoulders: "My husband's a bit dotty, you know. He won't hear anything but English: a real duck in a chicken roost." "Dotty? And what about you, my dear? A duck? Perhaps, but a duck you'll become. The house, the family, the parish, all that's of little consequence. The children will grow up. Beyond Saint-Hubert is the world. I'll be waiting for them there. I'm in no hurry. They'll teach you English, my dear!"

It was wartime then and that war is not over yet, the war of the world against the smallest of the continents. What are we but one of Europe's marches in America? Europe lost. It was quite natural that an American soldier should come and complete his victory here. Montreal is only a stop on the way from Belgium to Kentucky.

THE SEA-LION

The doctor spoke encouragingly; he might have reassured me if the next day the children hadn't begun putting flowers in my room. When I'm resting I feel quite well. I read, I pray, I build bridges between my daydreams. The flowers fade, they replace them. They'll grow tired of that after a while. Behind the house there was an orchard. When I think of my childhood I see my parents, my friends, the schoolmistress, the minister, but it's like one of those picture albums filled with photos we've taken ourselves: I'm never there. It's the same with my youth. The orchard was in bloom. A kind of pink cloud still prevented me from seeing myself. I was there, though, all the time. Johnny took me by the hand. I came out of my confusion. . . . With all these bouquets around I feel I'm about to slip back in.

A doctor was all very well for the wife and children. Johnny would have nothing to do with one himself. The doctor did try to warn him: "Take care, Mr. Waterworth, you've a thick neck." But Johnny only replied: "Doctor, you'll not get me!" The doctor didn't get him. He simply came and pronounced him dead. "He was a man," he said. This respect,

this admiration, made me think that we can't abandon ourselves to another person's care or caresses without automatically incurring their contempt. That didn't stop me from
calling this same doctor as soon as I began to feel unwell
myself. In the end it's only the doctor who is degraded by his
art. He put me to bed with kind words. If I'm careful not to
move I don't feel ill at all. I dream, I read, I pray. It keeps me
busy. I tidy up my soul, just as I used to tidy up my kitchen.
I fall asleep, my prayers said, just as I always fell asleep, after
the bustle of the day, gently, easily, almost indifferently. And
I read, just as I once listened to my husband tell me about the
world, absently.

They say women feel revulsion under the weight of a
man. It's perfectly understandable. But it never happened to
me. I made love as best I could, experiencing neither pleasure
nor disgust. I left all the passion to my husband. Sometimes
he would rise up above me like a great sea-lion, his head
thrown back. I used to wonder if he was going to bellow. The
thought of it almost made me want to laugh. He, a gentleman, a good Christian, a true Presbyterian! Then he would
fall asleep. I would lie there, thinking, and in the end it
would occur to me to get up and wash myself off. It gave me
real pleasure.

Johnny often flew into a rage. Perhaps it was because I
was so placid. Perhaps it was his temperament, too. Sometimes
his rage was red, sometimes white. It was all a matter of cir-
culation. As he grew older, his blood became more sluggish:
his rage turned blue. In the black waters of the night his sea-
lion made little choking noises. I didn't feel like laughing any
more. . . . Oh, Johnny Waterworth, I never knew the name of
your anger, nor the name of your love. And yet, when I saw
you lying there on the floor, all blue and black, stiff, and quite

dead, I wasn't surprised. I thought then that you must have been preparing this last gasp for a long time.

Perhaps the sea-lion was death looming above me. Johnny, who were you then in the night? And who was I to you? What is love? Will I ever know? I've never known convulsions of any kind. I'll probably die just as I've lived, just as I've always made love, patiently, quietly, almost indifferently. My children have been like any other children, easygoing, comforting. They've hardly caused me any worry and, since I've never doubted they would, they've all turned out extremely well. Now they bring me flowers. I'm going to die. It will be a lot simpler than going on living. I'll die easily, almost indifferently, and I'll even die content. If it weren't for the fact that I was dying, I might think I'd never loved.

THE JAILER'S SON

The jailer's son was the liveliest boy that ever was. He would chase after himself and at the same time run away. He even tried hopping and changing feet, but it was never any use; he would still get ahead of himself and come down on the wrong foot, the one that got away. He was forever giving himself the slip like this. And it was just as well. The child he'd have caught up with was an only child, half orphan. The jailer himself trod warily, with measured steps and all the gravity of a hairy, cautious man. He was proud of his son and loved him dearly.

When the son turned thirteen his father made him a present of a bear-cub. The cub had been given to him by a hunter from Ferme-Neuve. "Sir," the hunter had said, "I'll never be able to repay you for all the kindness you've shown my poor uncle."

"Your uncle?"

"Yes, old So-and-so. He's been in your care for ten years now."

"Ah, yes. Old So-and-so. A very special case, requiring very special care." That was what he had said, but who the uncle was, he hadn't the faintest idea. Clearly though, the fellow's prospects must not be very bright.

The bear-cub was chained to an elm tree which grew by the prison wall. One day, while the jailer's son was playing in the shadow of the wall and the tree, he heard a strange noise, which made him stop still in his tracks, his heart pounding. Perhaps it was the elm tree suffering? Or the cub? The sky, it was true, had been clear all summer; a fierce tawny sun devoured its creation; only the blue of night brought respite to the stricken green. But just at that moment it had begun to rain. The tree received all the water its roots could drink, and the cub, who had been dazed by the heat, perked up and began splashing in the puddles. It rained so hard the grass-hoppers turned green again. But still the noise persisted. The child stood motionless, not knowing what to think. His double, sad and lonely, and half orphan, caught up with him.

The jailer, a ponderous man, was proud of the quick-silver in his son, and it disconcerted him to see him stand so still. He asked what was wrong. The child seemed surprised. Wrong? But there was nothing wrong. He was just a little tired from running. "Then rest a while, my boy," said the jailer, only half reassured. In fact, the child had stopped moving in order to listen. Summer ended, and still he had not discovered the cause of the noise. One fall evening, while he was playing outside with the cub, he happened to press his cheek against the prison wall. Then, unmistakably, he heard a low, muffled voice calling for help. Quickly he chalked a circle on the wall by his ear and went inside to bed, still afraid to trust himself, and determined to make absolutely sure, since he knew he could rely on no one else.

The next morning he ran back to the wall and pressed his ear against the chalk circle. The voice was still there, low, muffled, monotonous. "Help!" it called. The child cupped his hands to his mouth and shouted into the thick wall: "I can hear you!" But it was no use. The voice did not let up. So he banged on the wall with a stick, a hammer, then a pickaxe. All his efforts were in vain. He realized then that he was only a child. He fell sick, sick with the helplessness of his years, and nearly died. He spent the winter in bed. April brought him back to life.

One afternoon he got up, still shaky, from his bed, and went over to his window. Under the elm tree he could see no sign of the bear-cub. When his father came to see him, he confronted him, his eyes flashing with anger: "Where's the cub!"

"There's no cub any more."

"You've killed him, haven't you!"

The jailer laughed: "I ate him!"

"You ate him!"

"Yes. Fur and all: I was hungry." Then he added, stroking his son's head, "He's changed, your cub has, just like you. He's a big boy now."

"Where is he?"

"In a hole at the foot of the elm tree. He's spent the winter there, sleeping, just like you."

As the bear seemed in no hurry to come out, it was the boy who went down to the yard. Dazed, he made his way over to the edge of the dark hole, where the bear's chain hung. He bent down and peered inside. The hole was no pit, but a kind of underground tunnel, winding steeply down toward the prison wall, with the roots of the elm tree, like wayward arches, criss-crossing to form its vault. And from it there rose up, as from some ventilation hole, waves of warm air and a barnyard odour that could not have been produced by a single animal. The jailer's son went back to the house, lost in thought. The next day he decided to pull on the chain. He had recovered his strength. The chain was long but he got to the end of it, got, that is, to the bear's collar, in which there was, however, no bear's neck. Instead, there appeared a shaggy, white head, an ashen brow, the screwed-up face of a blind old man, the gaping jaw of a demented convict, a bundle of filthy rags. Instead, it was the uncle of the hunter from Ferme-Neuve who crawled out into the blinding light, staggered to his feet, swayed, and fell moaning to the ground. Help! Help! Help! The boy let go of the chain, slipped into the opening and made his way along under the roots on all fours.

The passage opened onto a small cave, shaped like a cone, the base of which was the prison wall. It was probably here that the bear had spent the winter. But there was no bear now. On the floor of the cave lay a huge squared stone, a kind of platform. The boy hoisted himself up and found himself peering into the hole from which the barnyard odour was rising. The cave was perhaps only an anteroom, leading to some vaster and possibly infernal halls. The hole was as wide as the entrance to the tunnel. The boy managed to squeeze through it, and so through the prison wall, landing, surprised but relieved, on top of his bear, who let out a growl. He was exhausted. The bear's growl was answered by titters, shouts and moans. Huddled against the animal, the boy slowly recovered from his exertion, and little by little his eyes adjusted to his new surroundings. He was in a vast underground room, lit feebly by tiny electric bulbs with yellow filaments. Milling about this cellar were forty or so old drunks, all of the same breed, it seemed, as the one he had pulled up on the end of the chain. On the other side of the room there were bars, and behind the bars a guard sat dozing, his head in his hands.

This guard, in his torpor, was not unduly surprised by the appearance of the boy. Already he had accepted the bear as just another hallucination of the crazy old fools in his charge. He did the same now for the boy. Through intermittently open eyes, he saw the new arrival shake the bear, like a second illusion come to challenge the first, and the bear reluctantly get to its feet and in a single bound disappear – quite the most natural thing, he thought, for such a bear to do. He also recorded, through one eye then the other, as in a series of camera shots, the gradual disappearance of his patients. This caused him not the slightest dismay. "Good thing too!" Before long the room was empty. The guard could rest in peace.

The jailer's son was the last to come up. He unchained the first lunatic, whose cries, now that he could no longer hear the muffled echo of his own voice underground, grew even louder and more shrill. Help! Help! Help! His companions, startled by the soft spring light, thought they had fallen into a trap, and began to shout with him in terror. The boy pushed them all in the direction of the road. They moved off in a long procession, the uncle of the hunter from Ferme-Neuve in the lead, the bear taking up the rear.

Out on the road the highway north sped past on a ribbon of asphalt. The ribbon came to a stop. The motorists, their eyes wide, their mouths agape, dared not blow their horns. The blind procession, like a worm dug up from its decay, lost amid the walls of limp and unresisting air, as in a labyrinth, wound back and forth across the road, drawn now to drains, now to cellar windows, unable to find its way. At last, after much twisting and turning, instinct guided it in the right direction. It left the road and moved into the prison drive. By now the shouts had become howls. The police on duty piled sandbags behind the door and aimed their machine guns. Taken by surprise, they thought they were being attacked by the great army of the mad, the blind and the innocent, marching behind the sword of justice. They were determined to fight for their lives, knowing that in defeat there would be no mercy.

Luckily, from his house outside the walls, the jailer had seen everything. He appeared in the drive. He did not run, but walked, with short, hurried steps. He shouted to the police inside the fortress: "Don't shoot! They're our lunatics." He finally managed to make himself heard. The huge door swung slowly open and the procession passed through. When the bear was inside, the door closed. That same day the tunnel was sealed. The bear was never heard of again. As for the jailer's son, he had little choice but to live. But they never did make a decent citizen out of him.

BLACK CARGO SHIPS OF WAR

A widow loved her son too much. One day he left her. She began to wait for him. The years passed. Even after he had died she went on waiting. Because of this he remained in Purgatory. Saint Peter had said to him: "My poor boy, I cannot take you: your mother is waiting for you." So he too had begun to wait. And the years had passed. He wandered in Flanders, held back by his grave. On foggy nights he was able to go as far as the sea. On the other shore, in the land of his birth, an old woman never lost faith. Her son was her whole life. Of her own accord she would never have died. And the wide ocean lay between them.

When the French Canadians arrived in the Gaspé from Montmagny, l'Islet, Cap Saint-Ignace, from parishes no longer wild, where the landscape had long since been tamed, they felt anxious, diminished and wretched. In their despair they sought shelter. They built small gabled cottages, so very small, in fact, that they were diminutions of the diminutive. There are still a few here and there along the coast. They go back three or four generations, perhaps even a century. They have lasted well, all of squared logs, solid of frame, inordinately sturdy. Inside, one dark, low-ceilinged room, a veritable retreat. From whom, from what were they protecting themselves? From the cold, from the isolation, from the untamed country and its terrifying spaces. But little by little they regained their confidence; they rose to the challenge, built larger dwellings. The little pioneer house became the summer kitchen, or the pantry, or else a shed, a stable, a pigsty; or sometimes, abandoned, open to the winds, a poor demented shack, wailing the terror of those first winters. Others still served as homes, the refuge of eccentrics. It was in one of these that the widow lived. She had been there for many years, for longer than even she imagined. Whose widow was she? No one knew. She was called Gélinas – not a Gaspé name. She came, so it seemed, from far away, from a province up river from Quebec City. In any case she was an outsider.

Her cottage was situated on the edge of the small bank overlooking the shore, the only dwelling at that level, for it was an area reserved for the fishermen. It was there that they put their boats ashore when the season was over. In spring, when they took them out again, the cottage would remain alone, between the village and the sea, surrounded by the flakes and nets, amid the commotion of waves and gulls.

Her son, a good little fellow, would have wanted nothing better than to become a man. She had prevented this by her constant wheedling. He had ended up a kind of ne'er-do-well. One day he had made up his mind, he who had never been allowed to go fishing or go into the woods, because it was dangerous, because it was rough, and he had gone off to war. The widow had been waiting for him ever since. Her hut had only one window overlooking the sea. Sometimes in fine weather, as she looked out, the glass would merge with space, and she would be filled with the immensity of this fusion, which reached from the horizon to the very depths of her eyes. Then, beyond the bay and the boats out fishing, she would see the Gulf coasters, and beyond them huge black cargo ships, deep laden, their smoke hanging low, toiling towards the west. They alone interested her. Where else could they come from but the war, bringing soldiers home? But she never dared suppose her son might be one of them. She had waited for him for so long that she was content to go on. As long as there were cargo ships she could believe in his return. That was enough. Two or three went by each day. She would watch them pass. When they had disappeared she would remain with her forehead pressed to space, paying no heed to the gulls, to the return of the boats, to the activity of the fishermen on the shore, gazing instead beyond the horizon, remembering a face now far away, the lock of fair hair, the blue eyes, pansy-centred, with black, amber and brown flecks, in a ring of velvet petals. When he was angry the blue would grow pale, his eyes would harden, impenetrable as steel. Oh! he knew his own mind, the little fellow! He'd wanted to go to war and he'd gone. If he didn't come home, that was how he wanted it; he was probably well on the way to winning his epaulettes. When he'd won them he'd come home; no one would be able to stand in his way, no one! His mother had not. . . .

When their day was done the fishermen would see the old woman in her window. They would say: "Look! old mother Gélinas is on the watch." It was a sign of fair weather. But they would say no more. They would continue in silence or change the subject. The old woman grieved them. Her son had been their companion. He had gone away. They had married and already had children old enough to leave.

When the fishermen had come home, the sun would go down. Its rays would make the air tremble. Then suddenly the cleavage would occur, space would become detached from the window-pane, and the widow would find herself behind a glassy surface once more. In place of her son's face she would see her own, so old and sad she hardly recognized it. How old was she now? Fifty, seventy? She had no way of knowing, having lost her bearings. All she knew was that this war had lasted a long time, longer than she cared to think.

In the early days of her vigil she had noticed that her son's companions, whom she saw each day, were growing older. Soon she no longer recognized them, taking them for their fathers. And they ceased to interest her. But she had watched a little fair-haired boy grow up. She did not know his name. Yet he caught her attention. Each time she saw him she felt sick at heart, until she managed to remind herself that he was not her son, that he was much too young. Then, just as he was about to become a man, this boy had disappeared, and she had forgotten him. . . . The fishermen continued to come and go near her cottage. The gulls too, the crows and the dogs. To her they were all the employees of the seasons.

Each spring they pushed the boats down to the water, and in the fall pulled them back up with the help of the winch. She would hear the creaking of the cable, then nothing more: winter, the long nights broken by intervals of blinding light, the sea abandoned to the ice, heart's respite, the numbness of waiting. This would last until the first spark of sunlight kindled the melting crystals, until the trickling of water was heard under the snow. Then she would be overcome by a feeling of urgency, and this feeling would last until summer. But in the Gaspé spring is short – barely a few days in May. Still the old woman would have time to do her spring-cleaning, to make cakes and goodies, and to wrap in fancy paper the bank notes she had hoarded, a present of which she was justly proud. She was certain then that her son, her Paulo as she called him, would soon be home.

Once these preparations were finished, summer would come and her frenzy would subside. The big cargo ships would start to go past. She would press her forehead to the window, the glass would dissolve into space, and she would watch them disappear in their smoke. Then the face of her son would reappear, his lock of fair hair, his blue eyes, pansy-centred, velvet when he was pleased, hard as steel when he was angry. He was a demanding boy, and his moods had often puzzled her. She loved him too much; she was afraid of him. And so, as summer wore on, she would become less impatient for his return. She would put it off until the following month, then the following year.

Out of the cheque she received each month she would take what little she needed to live on; the rest she would keep. One day there were two cheques. She thought there had been a mistake. "No," the storekeeper told her, "it's your old-age pension. You're not young any more, missus." But she, who trusted no one, told herself that this cheque, like the first, came from the army, and consequently from her son. This meant for certain that he'd won his epaulettes. A boy who knew his own mind. A private when he'd left, he'd come home a captain. And every month from then on she was able to put by a fairly tidy sum. So she was in no great hurry to see her son return, she who lived by waiting, for the longer he stayed away, the more handsome her present would be.

One spring excitement gripped her as usual. Most unwisely, after counting her dollars, she said: "I do believe he'll have enough." The snow had almost melted. Each night the warm wind from the mountains pushed the ice away towards the north. Soon the sea was completely clear. Then, one day, what appeared to be a last piece of ice was seen floating on the water. It was minute. Suddenly it took flight. It was the gull of spring. They had begun to take the boats back down to the water. Two or three cargo ships had passed. The last one had not reached the horizon: its pink and brown smoke had spread, closing space, opening the way for night.

The widow had gone to bed. Impatient knocks shook the door. She lit the lamp and went to open it: in the doorway stood her son, in battledress, bareheaded. But he no longer had his lock of fair hair: his head was shaved and his eyes were like steel. She was frightened, she was infinitely happy and she could not say a word. She could not even cry: "Paulo, my little boy!" He said to her: "The money." This brought her to her senses. The money, yes, the money. What he saw would surely soften his gaze. Paulo, your eyes will be two pansies again, with big black centres, and smaller flecks all round, amber and brown, in a ring of blue petals. She rushed over to the package, which was wrapped up like a box of candy; she felt an agonizing pain in the nape of her neck; everything went black.

Her spirit joined that of her son, wandering in Flanders. Their long wait had been their Purgatory. Together they went to Heaven, so true it is that love will heal all ills.

LITTLE RED RIDING HOOD

An old lady who had been much chaperoned in her youth, with the result that she had married a domineering man who, mercifully, had left her a widow, was living out her days, unattended, free and happy in a little bungalow in l'Abord-à-Plouffe. She was an impeccable person, very nearly perfect. She had only one fault: she was afraid of dogs. And dogs rarely come alone.

One of her granddaughters was her favourite: she worshipped the child, though she hardly knew her. As for her other grandchildren, she knew them better, loved them well enough, but gave them little thought: solitude had made her detached from them. On her somewhat dry heart a fine crack had appeared, an unfamilial pain which solitude, far from healing, had caused to go deeper. The old lady could not think of her favourite without feeling it, without putting her hand to her chest: a nagging pain against which she was helpless. The only remedy was to say to herself: "She'll come tomorrow or the next day." But when the little girl did arrive, all innocence, having taken care to tie up her dog behind the shed, the grandmother felt no relief. The little person intimidated her. She didn't know how to talk to her, was afraid to broach new subjects, afraid of saying too much or not enough. And so she would repeat in falsetto the same refrains: "What beautiful cheeks you have, my child." "All the better to blush with, Grandmamma." "What beautiful lips!" "All the better to open my mouth with, Grandmamma." With her finger the old lady would gently stroke these cheeks, these lips, caressing and cajoling the child, who was amazed by such a show of love, a little impatient too, for it seemed it would never end.

Meanwhile, behind the shed, the dog strained at his rope, filled with hatred for all that lay beyond. The little girl's father, a travelling salesman, had brought him back from one of his trips. "And what about my mother?" his wife had objected. "Bah! She'll never see him." And she never did see him, for they had decided that he should stay behind the shed. Nevertheless, the first time the little girl came to l'Abord-à-Plouffe accompanied by the dog, the grandmother said to her: "What a strange smell, my dear." Then she grew accustomed to it. At least she never mentioned it again. But by a strange coincidence her granddaughter, who until then had seemed no different from the other children, became from that moment special, unique and irreplaceable. On her old heart appeared the tiny crack, which solitude, far from healing, only caused to go deeper.

One day the travelling salesman had brought back from Ontario a case of good margarine. The mother said to her daughter: "Put on your little red riding hood and take this present to your grandmother." The little girl, who was always bored, wherever she was, didn't have to be asked twice. She put on her cape and set out for l'Abord-à-Plouffe. "Don't play about on the way, or the margarine will melt," her mother had told her. So she hurried along, accompanied by her dog, who bared his teeth. The rogues on the street-corners dared not come near. But they called to her: "Hey! Are you Little Red Riding Hood?" She, her nose in the air, said to herself: "My mother thinks I'm still a child," and she wiggled her hips to show that she was not. The cape was too short and it accentuated the movement of her little behind. The rogues sniggered. The dog did not like this. However, there was nothing he disliked more than going to l'Abord-à-Plouffe. He soon realized that was their destination and this time rebelled at the very thought. He said to Little Red Riding Hood: "You go by way of Parc Belmont; I'll take the bridge road; we'll meet behind the shed." And he ran off, leaving the little girl unprotected.

Now, there was an old scoundrel, a regular gallow's-bird, who happened to be hunting in the neighbourhood. He got the scent of fresh meat and soon spied Little Red Riding Hood. What he saw of her from behind convinced him that the prey was worth viewing from the front. He quickened his pace, caught up with her and hastened to inform her that while she did not know him, he knew her and was delighted to have this opportunity of paying her his compliments. Not knowing what to think, she made a polite reply. "And where are you going, my little maid?" "I'm going to visit my grand-mother in l'Abord-à-Plouffe." "Yes, to be sure." "So, you know her then?" "Why, yes, as you can see." The little girl, reassured, decided that she could have nothing to hide from a friend of the family. So the scoundrel soon had the information he required. Then he stopped, unable, much to his regret, to accompany her further. Little Red Riding Hood went on alone. He hailed a big black taxi which got him in less than no time to the grandmother's house. "Who's there?" asked the grandmother. "Your granddaughter." "Have you got a cold?"

"Yes, Grandmamma." "Take the key from under the doormat and come in quickly." He went in, holding up the palms of both his hands. "Don't be afraid, good lady: I simply need a gown and a night-cap." "What for?" "Never mind!"* When he had put on the gown and the bonnet he locked the old lady in the cupboard and climbed into bed, gloating as only a scoundrel can gloat when he knows his scheme is about to succeed. He had left the front door ajar so as not to be given away by his voice. "The little girl will enter without permission, and without permission I shall make her mine." And the bed fairly shook with his glee.

Meanwhile, Little Red Riding Hood was trotting along at her usual pace. The dog was first to arrive behind the shed. There, the sight of the ring to which he was normally tied reminded him that he was alone and free. This time the rope did not hold him back. He bounded forward, ran round the shed and saw the bungalow amid the flowers and shrubs. His hair bristling, he drew near; he jumped onto the steps; the door was ajar; he pushed it with his nose and in a flash was inside. When Little Red Riding Hood arrived the dog was not at the appointed place. She called him, but there was no answer. Not knowing what to think, she walked on round the shed. And what should she see but her dear grandmother, so refined and so well-bred, with her night-cap in her hand, her gown pulled up about her knees, fleeing on long, hairy legs as the dog, in hot pursuit, snapped at her rear. Horror-struck, she opened her mouth, but to no avail. When she did manage to utter a cry the grandmother and the dog had already

---

* The French text gives: *néveurmagne* – Ferronesque for "Never mind." It is a spelling already sanctioned, however, in Germaine Guèvremont's novel, *Le Survenant*, of 1945.

disappeared over the hedges of the neighbouring gardens. The poor child clasped her little pot of margarine to her heart, greatly distressed. The bright sun, the shrubs and the flowers were an affront to her grief. She sought refuge in the shade of the house, and once indoors, to avoid thinking about all that had happened, she cried and cried.

She was beginning to wonder what she should do once her tears had stopped, when she heard a faint noise. She listened carefully and could hardly believe her ears: it was her grandmother calling her. "Grandmother, where are you?" "In the cupboard. Pull the bobbin and the latch will go up."* The little girl did as her grandmother told her; the cupboard door opened and they fell into each other's arms. "Ah! my dear," said the grandmother, "You very nearly found me in quite a different state." "And you me, grandmother, for my dog got away." "Little rascal, I thought that was a strange smell!"

The dog and the old scoundrel together made one wolf. This wolf remained between them. They caressed and cajoled with a new passion. And what was bound to happen did happen: in the pot, forgotten on the table, the margarine melted.

---

* *Tire la chevillette, la bobinette cherra.* This is a quotation from Charles Perrault's famous version of *Little Red Riding Hood*, published in 1697.

THE PIGEON AND THE PARAKEET

Her sorrow was great, but a child's night is vaster still. One morning she emerged. She was smiling. When she realized what had happened she was angry and reproached herself for her inconstancy. But do or say what she would, her sorrow continued to fade. She had to resign herself to being not entirely unhappy. Her name was Marie. After her father's death they had put her in a convent. Black suited her. She was blonde and a dreamer. All about her, her companions played, laughing and shouting. She felt the giddy motion of their round, but was afraid to join in and remained to one side, a blue parakeet on her left shoulder. This bird had replaced her heart. It prevented her from giving in to her age and to the pleasures of the moment. It kept her in a kind of semi-happiness, a semi-sadness.

The nuns were full of concern for this unusual child, grieved by her reserve, which at the same time endeared her to them, and they longed to see her happiness complete. One day one of them seized the parakeet, threw it outside and shut the window. "Aha!" said this nun, "now you'll be like all the rest." Marie would have liked nothing better, but the bird had other ideas. Once outside, it began flying at the window, beating its wings and beak against the panes, frantically, ceaselessly, until in the end the whole class was distracted. So, in the general interest, it was decided that Marie should be allowed her little peculiarity. She did not learn very much, but she disturbed no one. And the nuns loved her as if she had been their own daughter. When she grew up they tried to keep her with them. They asked very little, and then it was for the Lord: in return for food, shelter and salvation, the sacrifice of her hair. Marie accepted. They brought scissors and a cage.

"Why the cage?"

"To shut the bird in."

"Ouch!" cried Marie.

The parakeet was digging its claws into her shoulder. Its disapproval brought the ceremony to an end. Marie set out to discover the world. The convent was in the middle of a forest. She entered it, the parakeet trembling on her shoulder. It was the kind of rare and beautiful day that comes only once in a lifetime. The happy girl walked on until the sun went down before her, radiant portal of the night.

Now the hunter was also in the forest. He had killed nothing, and he was angry. Suddenly, through the branches and the green mist, he caught sight of a blue bird. He took aim, fired and ran. . . . To his great surprise he found, beside the dead bird, an unconscious girl! He took her in his arms and carried her off.

When Marie awoke next morning there was a young man beside her, who, in a few words, filled her in on what had happened. Oh! how gallant he was! Marie, ashamed that he had gone to so much trouble, apologized and tried to find words to thank him. The hunter did the same. They were embarrassed and very moved.

"Farewell," the girl said at last.

"Wait!"

The hunter was holding a pigeon.

"Take it," he said.

Marie put her hand to her shoulder.

"My parakeet!"

And she burst into tears. In his few words the hunter had not told all. He admitted the rest: the blue parakeet was dead; he had killed it; he was desperately sorry. To make amends he was offering her his pigeon.

"Take it, please."

The girl looked at the bird through her tears.

"How ugly it is!" she cried.

"It's all I've got."

The hunter looked so crestfallen she felt sorry for him. She took the pigeon and went. The day was different now. A new forest opened up before her. The path gradually widened. She came to the edge of a field. She saw a house and heard a baby cry. She felt drawn to all this. But she was unable to go on; the pigeon had flown off. She ran after it; it brought her back to her starting point. The hunter was waiting.

"You're wicked and a liar," she told him, "I hate you."

Wicked he was, that he owned, but a liar – it was the first he knew of it.

"Whose pigeon is this?" she asked.

"Yours. I gave it to you."

"Liar! You didn't give it to me. The proof is that it's come back to you."

Night was falling. Marie and the hunter were reconciled. The next morning the girl set out again, with the pigeon on her shoulder. The hunter was whistling with satisfaction. He was sure she would be back. But soon the day grew long. . . .

The pigeon returned alone. Marie had not followed it. The young man's heart sank. He imagined monsters in the night and the girl at their mercy. He set out to look for her. "Marie! Marie!" he called. There was no answer. Suddenly he saw her sitting at the foot of a tree.

"Why didn't you answer me?"

"You don't love me."

"I adore you."

"I've lost everything. You're still free."

"That's true," said the hunter.

He stood up, took aim and shot the pigeon, which was fluttering above his head.

"I may have given you nothing," he went on, "but at least I've kept nothing myself."

The young woman held out her arms to him. A storm broke. They were shivering and unhappy. They emerged from the forest like our first ancestors. The world began anew. God took pity on them. They had a great many children, and the birds came back again.

THE ROPE AND THE HEIFER

F ather Godfrey did not stir, curled up in a ball, snug in
the belly of the night. It was the servant who had to
rouse him. In she rushed, her great bony hand like a
spider at the end of her arm, clutched his shoulder, wouldn't
let go. He struggled; she held on. Then he had no choice but
to pull himself up as far as his eyes, reassemble ears, nose and
mouth, and putting his hand to his chin, his face still awry,
say: "What is it, Marguerite?"

"The bell, *Monsieur le curé!*"

"Uh, go see who's there."

"No, the bell in the belfry."

The bell in the belfry – but that was for the Lord! He,
poor priest, had quite enough trouble as it was, already
obliged to get up in the night, dress, and go out whenever, to
his misfortune, someone came to his door. "It's the wind,
Marguerite, it's the wind." And he let himself sink back down.

"*Monsieur le curé! Monsieur le curé!*"

"Eh? What?"

"There is no wind."

So he was obliged to sit himself up, this time with more dignity, his face now all of a piece, and announce that he knew, since it wasn't the wind . . . "Are you sure of that, Marguerite?" "Sure as I'm a Christian" . . . just what it was about. He knew above all that a priest has to have an answer for everything: "Ah, yes, it's the souls in purgatory." "God a mercy!" said the servant. Whereupon he pronounced a few words in Latin, finishing off with three amens, which old Marguerite repeated before tiptoeing out.

The next morning the angelus bell was late. From his window the priest saw the verger go by with a stepladder on his shoulder. Shortly afterwards the bell rang out. The morning was radiant. At the sound of the angelus the most pious fishermen bowed their heads in prayerful contemplation; the others said to themselves, more trivially, that the time was now six o'clock, and as a just punishment for their lack of faith they were a full ten minutes out. The grass had collapsed under the dew. On the thin mist that covered the sea the boats were set out like dishes on a tablecloth. The priest emerged from the presbytery and, as usual, began to recite his breviary while waiting for mass. The sun, full and round over the mountain tops, gazed down in wonder at the familiar landscape. The day was called morning and longed to keep its name.

Then it was Marguerite's turn to come out. With her shrill voice she called to her hens and put an end to all this complacency. The hens came running, their eyes fixed to their beaks, empty-headed as hunger. The sun remembered its own appetite and set to work; it drank the dew, even ate the tablecloth, then climbed high in the sky to digest this frugal breakfast. The magic of the morning evaporated. The fishermen had jumped from their porcelain vessels into old wooden boats. The wind gusted in from all quarters and gathered

around the steeple to ask the weathercock the way. The cock
spun three times in one direction, then three times in the
other, and made up its mind: "That-a-way!" But the seagulls
came wheeling in and disagreed. The weathercock creaked,
they squealed. They would never have settled the matter if
Father Godfrey had not lifted his head, one hand on his
biretta, and reminded the wind that it alone had the right to
decide what its course should be.

"Just go whichever way you like!"

Then the cock turned to face the gulls, who let themselves be carried away, and it stopped still. Meanwhile, old
Marguerite the servant, dark and gnarled, scattered her grain
with a cautious hand for fear it would fall into the sea. When
she had finished, she counted her flock: all were there. She
also counted the boats: one was missing. Far out at sea, over
seven miles from shore, just beyond the reach of the law,
Captain Bove's schooner, favoured by the weather, was lying
undisturbed in the spot it had occupied for a full week now.
Old Marguerite turned away; she preferred not to think of her
nephew Wellie, whose boat was missing, and who might at
that very moment be anchored off the smuggler's ship, with
no protection but that of the great Saint Pierre of Miquelon.
She went back inside. Noises from the kitchen alerted Father
Godfrey that it was time to say his mass.

He was approaching the sacristy when at the far end of
the building he spied a rare parishioner, not known for his
piety during the week, diving into the church. Curiosity got the
better of his hunger. He changed course and veered away from
the sacristy. This parishioner was Bezeau the merchant, his nose
to the wind like a frantic hound, who, not finding what he was
looking for, headed straight for the verger now, and – what the
deuce? – was surprised to find him at the top of a ladder.

"Just looking for the end of our rope, Monsieur Bezeau."

"Has the belfry moved up?"

"No, the rope's been cut with a knife."

"A knife! That's no joke."

"There was no joke meant, Monsieur Bezeau."

Of this the merchant was well aware.

"Say, verger, you wouldn't have seen my heifer by any chance? I've lost her."

"Your heifer? Not that I know of."

"A devout little heifer, quite capable of coming to mass."

"Yes indeed, a fine reputation she had."

"And appetizing! Verger, you would have gotten a piece of her in due course."

"You're too kind, Monsieur Bezeau."

With that, Father Godfrey arrived on the scene.

"Well now, merchant Bezeau, have you come to serve my mass?"

"You can't be serious, Father Godfrey! That would take years off me and be dangerous for my salvation. You'd never stop confessing me. And you know how I hate to trouble you."

Merchant Bezeau spoke like a man who knows that his flour is every bit as useful to an isolated village as God's grace. Father Godfrey did not reply, feeling suddenly peeved. To have come out of his way just to be spoken to like this! There was nothing he could do: to him egalitarianism smacked of arrogance. But he managed not to appear ruffled. This Bezeau fellow hadn't an ounce of shame: did he even give a damn about his salvation, the old serpent? And what respect did he really have for his age, more dangerous himself than all the young lads of the village put together, an inveterate chaser of skirts, pulling them up with a rare dexterity, never missing a shot. He was worse than a Protestant, and yet he was as French Canadian as anybody, born like everyone else of parents who'd hailed from Montmagny – a cousin one could have done quite nicely without! It was simple: he even made Father Godfrey look kindly on the Jersey merchants, who never paid a cent in tithes to anyone, but at least had the decency to be foreigners.

"Monsieur Bezeau has lost his heifer," announced the verger.

Father Godfrey, surprised at hearing a stepladder speak, raised his eyes, fearing some machination. He saw his sorry-faced verger, who showed him the rope, cut off at the height of a man's arm.

"Burned by a fiery hand?"

"No, cut with a knife."

"Dear souls in purgatory! But this is a sacrilege."

"A sacrilege? That's just what I was a thinking myself."

"I think I might know who the culprit is," said Father Godfrey.

"And might you know the thief who stole my heifer too?" asked the merchant.

The priest stopped himself just in time from saying, "They're one and the same."

"Your heifer?"

"Yes, she disappeared last night."

"No idea."

"Oh, come now. Just stop and think. A fine devout creature, a regular little Child of Mary.* It wouldn't surprise me if she'd come to mass."

* Child of Mary (in French, *enfant de Marie*). A member of the international Catholic organization, or sodality, the Children of Mary (*les enfants de Marie*), which was founded in France and flourished in Quebec in the mid-twentieth century.

"Enough talk of this heifer," said the priest angrily. "Devout creature, indeed! And you? I know all about your devotions, merchant Bezeau!"

He knew all about them, for sure, but small good it had done him, since he'd learned everything at the confessional.

"The flesh is weak, Father Godfrey. I don't mind telling you, she made my mouth water, that creature of God – well fed, appetizing."

"Monsieur Bezeau would have given us a cut."

"A piece of the tail?"

"No, the rump of your choice."

"That would have been something new: I've never had anything from you but your leftovers, merchant Bezeau."

Merchant Bezeau was not a man to let an opportunity pass; chasing the ladies had at least taught him that. He retorted at once:

"You have to admit, Father Godfrey, that there are some mighty juicy scraps in those leftovers of mine, and you'd have a hard time getting by without them."

The verger, high on his perch, decided that the meeting had gone on long enough. It was not in his interests to let things become acrimonious. Indebted, like everyone else, to God and to the devil, he intended to stay on good terms with their representatives.

"With your permission, *Monsieur le curé,* we'll ring the bell so that merchant Bezeau can get his heifer back."

The priest muttered a response in Latin, or perhaps it was in Hebrew, but in any case the verger hadn't bothered to wait: the bell was already ringing. The merchant left the church and set off again for his store. A great rustling of cassock swept in the opposite direction, filling the nave. The priest entered the sacristy all black and re-emerged all white and gold. Mass began.

On his way, Bezeau, still sniffing the wind, came to a sudden stop, having picked up the sound of an engine that gave off something quite unlike the roar associated with a good day's catch. It came from farther out, a dull, wet, almost woozy throb. He looked out to sea to where the schooner lay, and observed a smaller boat heading in from the same spot; the closer it drew, the sharper and drier the noise became. It stopped in the midst of the fishing boats, just long enough to pull on some drums and cod, setting off again with the honest bluster of an Acadia engine leaving off work early for the day. It was old Marguerite's nephew returning home after an eventful night that was destined to go down in memory. "Confounded Wellie!" said the merchant. It was not so much that he was angry; he was doing his best to keep from laughing – after all, he had been robbed! However, his loss seemed to be more than compensated by Father Godfrey's mortification, in which he took a sincere but disproportionate delight, for he believed the priest to be nearer to God than he really was, just as the priest overestimated the extent of his own exchanges with the devil. In these troubling matters the opposing parties always edify themselves each at the other's expense and carry on a combat which, when all is said and done, is indispensable to religion.

All the same, for Father Godfrey it was a difficult mass to say, and this precisely because of God, whose anger he was unable to assuage. Canon law has all the drawbacks of colonial law. The celestial home country does not see things quite the way they are seen to be in the Gaspé. "*Seigneur*," said Father Godfrey, "our money is good; if you accept it you won't be out of pocket. Just think about it: a little piece of rope for a fine heifer, and rope is worth nothing in these parts, any fisherman can boast far more length than you, whereas a horned animal is a rare and precious commodity. Come now, *Seigneur!* If I were in your shoes, I'd just forget this whole affair." But God turned a deaf ear, a sign that he intended to stick to the letter of his law, which is quite explicit on the chapter of sacred objects – article four: to touch is to desecrate.* There was nothing to be done: canon law was against the Gaspé in general and the said Wellie in particular. He would have to denounce him from the pulpit; there would be no avoiding it. The priest returned from his mass, sullen.

He ate breakfast like an archpriest of the Church of England, receptive to bacon, closed to questions, his eyes pale, impenetrable. He was frightening to see. Under this phlegm, was divine wrath smouldering? Old Marguerite wondered. Divine wrath explodes in the pulpit on Sunday. The threat was terrible. Her nephew Wellie was in danger of being denounced before the whole parish; such a dishonour would have to be prevented. But how? By falling sick? When it came to treatment, Father Godfrey believed in the virtues of iodine and she could not bear the smell or the substance of iodine. Besides, he would be quite capable of using this sickness as an excuse to hire a helper for her; there were plenty of candidates for the job, even some who were young and shapely. Ah, sweet Jesus, that was more of a danger than iodine! Clearly, another way would have to be found.

All day long the servant thought about this business of hers. After supper she went to sit a while with her sister, Wellie's

---

* Canon law includes rules that govern the touching of liturgical objects – more specifically, holy vessels.

mother, whom prolonged widowhood and poverty and a lingering beauty had accustomed to resolving with little fuss, but sensibly, the great problems of life. The visit was helpful. She set out again, her hump lightened, tripping along like a young girl. In the gathering dusk the spiders were drawing out the first threads of the night. The western light was fading; already the church and the surrounding houses stood out against the sky like silhouettes in a shadow play. As she passed in front of the store, she gave a start. "Where are you trotting off to like this, fair Marguerite?" she heard the merchant call.

"So, you're not in bed yet, you old mackerel!"

"I was waiting for you."

She replied: "Bezeau, I'm off to put my priest to bed."

"Tell me: how is the dear fellow?"

"There's a rope in his gullet, hanging from his brains and making him gag. Are you satisfied?"

The merchant was not displeased. He raised a finger and waved her on. She continued along the road. Back at the presbytery the priest was waiting for her. He said nothing at first, and nor did she. He was sitting in his rocking chair in the kitchen. She laid the table for breakfast, then prepared to go upstairs. Father Godfrey said to her: "Where have you been, Marguerite?"

"You know very well where I've been."

"Who did you speak to on your way back?"

"You know that too, but you didn't see the man himself: quite out of sorts he was. He put me in mind of a big cow who's lost its calf."

The rocking movements had gradually become shorter. "So it was our friend Bezeau?" "It was, indeed, himself and none other." With a kick of his heel the priest set the rocking chair back in motion. Marguerite took this opportunity to come closer. Her little eyes had begun to flicker in an attempt to hide the curiosity her sharp gaze might have revealed. "Beware!" said Father Godfrey to himself. Marguerite was a housekeeper he could not manage without; he had grown too accustomed to her. Because of her age and her hump she could bring him no discredit at the bishop's palace, where purple sashes are woven.* But she had her nephew Wellie's eyes, and those eyes, especially when they began to flicker, made Father Godfrey suspicious.

"Your nephew Wellie, now . . . you have to admit!"

"What about my nephew Wellie?"

"He's going a bit too far."

"He's a sailor, Father Godfrey."

"He sails a bit too close to the schooner."

"He sails as best he can; his mother needs him."

"Where was he last night?"

"Last night, Father Godfrey, my nephew Wellie conducted himself like a true Catholic and a good *Gaspésien*."

"You don't say, Marguerite, you don't say!"

She came and stood in front of him, drawing herself up around her hump.

"And that's not all: you won't be mentioning his name in your sermon next Sunday."

The priest brought his chair to a standstill.

"A sacrilege is a sacrilege, Marguerite."

"A sacrilege! Ask merchant Bezeau what he thinks of that, or Captain Bove!"

"I don't know the Captain, but Bezeau is certainly no great theologian."

"He's the devil's henchman, and Bove . . . Bove could

---

* The purple sash of a Canon.

even be Satan himself. You don't know him – consider yourself lucky! His neck is twisted, his shoulders hunch, his head
jerks to one side, and his eyes are all shot with blood; put a
ring in his nose and you'd have a bull."

"But he has no ring and he's Captain Bove, the boss of
the schooner, a smuggler and your nephew Wellie's friend."

"His friend? For the love of Jesus! He only keeps
company with the man because it'll be him or one of his kind
who'll give him a job once his poor mother is well again."

"He could go out fishing like everyone else."

"You're forgetting that he has his engineer's diploma,
second class. On Sundays, aren't you proud to have him there
at mass in his fine uniform? He's a credit to the parish."

"But he cut my rope."

"Listen, *Monsieur le curé:* Captain Bove said to him:
'Wellie, I'm going to be needing a nice little heifer tonight.'"

"And he stole merchant Bezeau's heifer and tied her up
with the . . ."

"Do you know what that really meant, 'a nice little
heifer'? He's a bull, is Captain Bove – I warned you he was.
'Heifer' meant . . ."

"No, Marguerite, that's impossible."

"Impossible? To every monster his female. Heifers for
Captain Bove, why, they're to be found in every parish in the
Gaspé."

"But I would know."

"You don't know: you give these girls their absolution
without ever asking where it was they sinned."

"On the schooner?"

"Bove never leaves it. If he came ashore he'd be hanged."

Father Godfrey was devastated. The sea had always
been good to him. It pervaded his spirituality. He believed

that with its restless fluidity it could bring about exchanges between the eternal and the temporal, between God and his own parish. Many a time he had seen shadows glide over its surface among the morning mists or the mirages of evening and shield the arrival or the departure of a soul, the imminence of a joy or a misfortune, which he had then predicted, unfailingly. And now, on this vast magic mirror, resting against the sky and tilted toward the land, on this mirror where he had learned to read, he was being shown a hideous blot.

"Is it possible?"

"You're too good, you are. The wickedness of the world escapes you, but you couldn't help but understand my poor Wellie. Just think, *Monsieur le curé:* what a fool he must have looked when he came back to the schooner with his specimen. Think how they must have laughed at him! But he didn't care, because there had been no offence to God."

Father Godfrey remained thoughtful. He had heard a great many confessions but he realized now that there was still much he hadn't learned. There were also some gaps in his knowledge of the scriptures.

"I had better reread the Apocalypse. Perhaps he's in there in the guise of a black bull."

"You're not talking about Wellie?"

"No, Marguerite, your nephew is a true Catholic and a good *Gaspésien.* I was thinking of this Captain Bove . . . But I can't quite remember, even though it's the word of God. I'm slipping. Yes, slipping I am."

And he was overcome with dismay. Marguerite said no more; she went upstairs to bed and slept well. Father Godfrey, on the other hand, stayed awake. He went far into the night, farther than he had ever been, with the monsters of the Apocalypse for company, in an eerie calm that caused him to apprehend the trumpets and the din of the battle of Armageddon. To the raptures of the Prophet he added his own nightmares, so that by morning he was more confused than ever on the subject of Bove and the diabolical bull. He had a bad day, then a night that was better than the previous one. The following day was Saturday. Father Godfrey regained his composure. When the winds gathered around the church tower to ask their way, he didn't wait for the weathercock to creak three times or for the gulls to intervene; he shouted:

"Make for the schooner!"

With the result that before the day was out Captain Bove was obliged to weigh anchor and hightail over the horizon. "God prevails, Marguerite." "Yes, *Monsieur le curé,* especially when he is well represented." Sunday dawned as usual. It was different from other Sundays, however, because of the sermon, which was a sermon on monsters. This was a genre Father Godfrey was trying out for the very first time. He shouted loudly, and through his nose. It was always the same: when he raised his voice, it refused to come out through his mouth. "There has been in our midst a black bull. A black bull, I say. And when I say 'a black bull,' I know full well what that means. . . ."

The parishioners, for their part, hadn't the faintest idea what it meant. Everyone on the Shore knew that Captain Bove was a gentleman. Marguerite was the only one to grasp the allusion. After mass Wellie was invited to dine at the presbytery. That same evening he had supper with merchant Bezeau. Until that day people had judged him rather severely because of his drinking. But doesn't everyone have their little weaknesses? From that moment on he was seen as a true Catholic and a good *Gaspésien,* to be sure, but above all as a skilful navigator.

THE LADY FROM FERME-NEUVE

There was the river, furtive and ashamed, probably sprung from the sewers, lurking along the canal bottoms and in between the islands, making gradually for the wider reaches where water comes out into the open at last, revitalized, and conquers space; the river, unseen yet close at hand, and the sea, in the distance, it too unseen, both of them revealing their presence at the same time with the sudden appearance of the gulls. It was out in the sprawling suburb, where trains of houses shoot past at equal speed on either side of the bewildered motorist, stuck fast in his undeviating rut. There was Canon Godfrey – and myself: he, my antagonist, talking through his nose, wearing his truth high, his mouth too low; I, between nights, writing to bring myself back in touch with day. And there was that lady from Ferme-Neuve who died last year. For once the Canon and I had cooperated, and never had we wrapped things up with the old whore more smartly.

Immediately beyond the spires of Longueuil the port of Montreal rises up, with its dockyard installations; then come the skyscrapers, towering higher with each year, and behind them Mount Royal, sinking lower, in contrast, as if with age. The bridge, too, looms large. But who can say for sure, in this urban conglomerate of concrete and steel, that it really is a bridge? It could be just a giant extravaganza of metal. . . . Water is no part of the landscape, except before a storm. Then, the gulls leave the river, fly inland across Longueuil and come to circle above the suburb.

A single gull won't bring on rain, nor will the solitary frog that ventures out of the grass at night and onto the black road where twin suns sweep, lighting the advance of incredible chariots. It takes a second bird to confirm the first, and a good many frogs squashed on the asphalt to ward off a drought. The first gull might only have been an eccentric, a stray, a maverick of its species, but with the arrival of the second, followed soon by many more, you can no longer doubt the sky. . . . You become aware of something new and supple above you, something animal, alive and beautiful, dancing amid the stupid aeroplanes from the military air-field at Saint-Hubert. It is the gulls, high overhead. They come down with the rain, and then you can sense, in one hoarse cry, all the immensity of the Gulf and the Gaspé confined in that narrow bay where, more than twenty years ago, Canon Godfrey and I had embarked on our diverging careers.

The whore in this case was Death, not the lady from Ferme-Neuve, who was all gravity and restraint, with noises in her head and no joy in her soul. This lady had always found life hard and could still not get enough of it. After her husband's death she had moved to Montreal in order to be near the hospitals. She was fifty-eight years old, stiff and erect, breathing austerity, if not distress, a woman without ease or abandon, a born nun. Her mistake had been to choose the doctor as her priest. And that priest was me! A curate, quite the lowest in the hierarchy, but me all the same. I couldn't get over it, and it was too late to tell her she was wrong.

The first time she sent for me she was waiting near the window. She came out onto the front step. I had gone to her son-in-law's by mistake and was knocking on the wrong door. As I made my way over to the right address, she couldn't help noticing the blue sky and the wheeling gulls. Did she forget herself for a moment? She said, "We're certainly having a beautiful fall." But the light was dazzling her, as if it had been the Holy Ghost up there with the birds, and she shielded her eyes with her hand. We went into her house.

"The beautiful fall never lasts for long," I replied. "It's nearly over by the look of things. Did you see the gulls?"

"The white birds?"

"Some are grey."

"In Ferme-Neuve we never saw them."

"Ferme-Neuve, north of Mont-Laurier? That's understandable. They seldom go beyond the river. The rain pushes them a little farther inland."

"The rain?"

"Yes. There'll be rain tonight or tomorrow. You can be sure of that."

"Really?" she responded politely.

She had been completely medicalized.* She hadn't sent

---

* medicalized. In French, *médicalisée*, meaning, in this instance, dominated or subjugated by medicine. The term would have been something of an innovation when Ferron first published this story in 1964. He later prided himself on having anticipated by many years Ivan Illich's popularization of it in his *Medical Nemesis* (1975). Widespread though the word now is in both languages, to apply it in this way to an individual – as opposed to a condition, a realm of

for me to chat about the weather. All she required of me was a mercurial injection once a week. It was her Communion. She couldn't do without it. Her specialist, an important Bishop, had prescribed it. It was up to me, the curate, to perform the rites. And the rain began that very evening, just as I had predicted. I treated her from November 8th to December 16th exactly. It took only a moment to give the injection. Afterwards she would open her widow's trunk, take out some bills and pay me. And I would go my way. . . . A good customer! She had been well trained. It's easy to minister in such circumstances: just one quick jab and the money drops into your hands. I certainly had every reason not to want her to die. I was even a little worried, because of the mercurial – a kind of poison in her case, it seemed to me. And I was not mistaken. There's some satisfaction in that.

The bad weather had come to stay. There was a layer of clouds at every level of the sky. Some hung so low that the trees brushed through them. The gulls played hide-and-seek between the storeys. Perhaps the tides were high in the Gaspé. It was getting colder. The rain began to freeze.

Low-priced home
November in the grey suburb
Snow is falling on Ferme-Neuve
Light is falling
To flare again
With the first sun.

---

human experience, or a society usurped by or subjected to the authority of medicine – is not frequent in either French or English, and is still to push the bounds of language somewhat, just as Ferron did at the time of writing.

She had come to Montreal with her son-in-law, her daughter and their two children, who had followed her on account of her trunk. They were poor and imagined it contained a treasure. There were bills in there for sure, but how many? That was the widow's secret. They'd stopped first in Terrebonne and had suffered hell in a house where the demons had been the children. It had been too much for the grandmother. From Terrebonne they'd crossed over to Coteau-Rouge. There, they'd found a dwelling pompously called a duplex, a hovel with neither basement nor upstairs, divided into two apartments, consisting of two rooms each.

Two rooms for a widow
Who wants to be near
Our main hospitals
There is no snow here, only rain
Winter is in mourning
In mourning for the year that's gone.
She was always ill
But it's her husband
Who died
One day, just like that
She doesn't blame him
But who's to care for her now
The bottle of oil
Drips life into the fire
The dirty greasy fire
That opens its mouth
But has no tongue
Oh Holy Ghost
How far away you are.

She was not talkative. Nevertheless, with each visit I managed to glean a little more. At the convent she'd attended, she'd played the piano. Back in her village, she'd been won over by the admiration of a big, good-natured lad who thought her the embodiment of divine perfection. And they'd ended up in bed, of all places. Oh, profanation! She'd never gotten over it. Somehow, between illnesses, she had still managed to have a few children. And then her husband, not satisfied with providing for her unstintingly from his hard-earned pay, had quite simply become her nurse. The children had gotten what was left over – not much at all. The second generation was to pay for the exaggerated opinion the musician had of herself. "What will become of me?" she asked me. The answer was there in that wretched duplex, on the other side of the partition.

> So the fire won't die
> It takes the drip
> But can't digest it
> Nausea fouls the oil
> The half-burned oil
> That drips and drips
> As the water drips
> From the leaking tap
> Cold will strike in the night
> My blood will be still
> Drip by drip so the water
> Can't freeze in the pipe.
> The bare necessities
> Utter destitution
> This traveller's trunk

This bed where I no longer rest
This table where pills and potions
Take the place of fork and bread
In Ferme-Neuve the snow is falling
And the fire has flames
Long tongues lash and lick
The birch and maple
A fragrant essence
Rises from the pure white ash
What pill shall I take
What potion
The air backs up inside the bottle
I'm in the hospital
It's death they're injecting
Into my sickened fires
Rain falls on the frozen window
This hospital is only
A foretaste of the morgue
Why did I leave my home
Where is my husband gone
Where is the Holy Ghost
What will become of me
Beside this closed trunk
Pentecost is far away
How will I get there
Oh Lord, take me back
To the convent of Mont-Laurier

What words I've put in the mouth of the lady from Ferme-Neuve! We make use of the dead – it's an old rhetorical device, good for a few more or less false-sounding couplets that always meet with general approval. . . . But it's true that the bottle of oil was sickening, that it fed the fire the same way hospitals inject serum into the dying. It's true that the hut was a duplex, the widow on one side, the offspring on the other. . . . There's nothing humiliating about the bare necessities in those remote regions that are still in contact with the past. The bare necessities constituted the riches of our ancestors, but in Montreal they represent complete and utter destitution. . . . She paid me well, this widow, out of the treasure coveted by her son-in-law. In one sense I was rather relieved when she died: this money was starting to trouble my conscience. "What will become of me?" really were her last words. . . . Granted, I'm a bluffer. But can one write without artifice? There's a reason for the couplet about the fire. Only once in my life have I ever felt rich and secure. I was living in a mountain village, not very different, I suspect, from Ferme-Neuve. It was fall, and I was standing in the midst of my store of firewood. When I doubt my sense of belonging to this country, I remember that moment. It reassures me. . . . In those days we sacrificed the precious logs of maple, birch and cherry to the fire, as if it were a god. It's gone out now, that fire, replaced by a convict who heats the houses and whom we never see, who could have come up from hell, for all we know. On that subject the lady from Ferme-Neuve had quite different ideas, I'm sure. In any case she didn't torment herself with thoughts of fire or Pentecost. Did she think of returning to her village? It's quite likely. She was ending her life as a fugitive. She knew it. "What will become of me?" she asked, and there was no need for me find a reply.

It was the 16th of December. I checked the time by my watch before going in. It was ten past one in the afternoon. Through the streaming wet, half-frozen windowpane, I saw the lady get to her feet. The bed was at the back of the apartment, in the second room, which was in fact little more than an extension of the first, a kind of alcove without a curtain. I saw her get up with difficulty and move along the wall to let me in. I went and put my bag on the draining board beside the sink, where a tap was dripping. If I'd checked the time, it was because I was in a hurry. In a moment the syringe was ready. The lady stood next to me, one arm braced to take the weight of her leaning body. She was clearly not well. "What about your head noises?" She answered my question with her own, then, almost at once, stiffening down all one side of her body, while the other side abruptly gave out, she did a pirouette and fell flat on the floor, face down, with no restraint, no pity, and so quickly I hadn't time to catch her. I disliked her right then, intensely, this woman. She was severely thwarting me. Her dress was wet and her face bloodied. I stood there, over her, syringe in hand, like some kind of an assassin.

In the next apartment, on the other side of the paper partition that divided the famous duplex, they were listening. They'd heard the nasty thud, but the first rush of curiosity hadn't brought them running in. Either out of embarrassment or fear, they'd preferred to wait a while. I took my patient in my arms and placed her on the bed. I tried to clean her up a little. Blood is mucky stuff, particularly the blackish blood of the dying. "If only she'd die, her nose would stop bleeding." A good remedy, obviously. . . . The son-in-law finally appeared, a cowed young man, all deference, and too scared to speak. "Go fetch the priest," I shouted. He was only too happy to oblige, and ran off. I went on mopping up the blood. Then my prayer was granted: the lady from Ferme-Neuve became presentable again.

No sooner had she expired than Canon Godfrey came through the door in full attire, his purple stole and white surplice underneath his coat. He took off the coat and, without even bothering to ask if she was dead, launched right into his supplications. I knelt down. There was something quite professional about this priest. He even had a kind of natural talent. It's much more effective to bawl through the nose than through the mouth. It's decisive, there's no risk of a sob, you get a steady bird-like sound that drowns out all else and reduces the family's grief to a few pathetic sniffles. The son-in-law had also knelt down, by the door, timidly, like a stranger. He listened to the prayers and eyed the trunk. The family's grief was scarcely audible here. As he came back to take more holy water from the container that he'd left by my bag, the priest, who was holding the sprinkler in his right hand, twisted round and, with his left hand, pulled from the pocket on the opposite side of his cassock a yellow paper, the death certificate, which we, in our official capacity, were both required to fill in, and he held it out to me quite unashamedly, as if the handing over of this document were part of the ritual. While I wrote, he got on with his ceremony. In the meantime, the daughter had arrived with the two children; they, pale, more nervous than bright; she, a tired woman, who hadn't the strength to cry.

I went outside and looked at the time. My watch said one-thirty. The Canon joined me. I said to him: "We've established a record."

"A record? What do you mean?"

"Well, the deceased herself came and opened the door for me exactly twenty minutes ago."

"It's a record, all right. Anyone would think you'd given her the fatal jab."

"Taking care to alert Canon Godfrey beforehand, of course."

"It would certainly look that way."

"Lord! We'd have to have been in cahoots to wrap things up with the old whore so smartly!"

The Canon didn't answer. Not far from us the gulls were circling above the cemetery, an empty field where the tombstones were slow in taking hold. There were so few of them it gave the impression our little settlement hadn't yet begun its work below ground. Without the anchors that the dead provide, the suburb, however flat, had nothing to keep it in place. In the fog and rain, it seemed to float, at the mercy of each gust of wind, or even of a sudden rotation of the metropolitan boulevard – always a possibility.

"There's another one who'll go off and get buried somewhere else! . . . What exactly did she have in that trunk, by the way?"

"Not much at all. In fact, so little her heirs will probably have the impression she robbed them."

"Did she pay you well?"

"Yes. Until today, that is."

"In that case, you're probably right: she can't have left them much at all."

A gull flew very low. Right above our heads, it let out its cry. The Canon asked me: "Does that remind you of anything?" We sometimes talked about the past. I remembered I was in a hurry. I shrugged my shoulders. He did the same. And we went our separate ways.

OTHER STORIES

CHRONICLE OF ANSE SAINT-ROCH

I

Between the Madeleine lighthouse and the harbour of Mont-Louis an unmistakable line separates land and sea. Because of the height of the cliff the only access to shore is through one of four valleys, three of them visible from the water, one quite hidden from view. They are, travelling from east to west, Manche d'Epée, Gros-Morne, Anse-Pleureuse. They cut deeply into the cliff, but the coves they feed are small and exposed to wind and weather. "From Madeleine to Mont-Louis, pay no heed to what you see and sail right on," the old-timers used to say. The fourth valley, situated between Gros-Morne and Anse-Pleureuse, is not easily detected. Narrow and winding, it runs at a sharp angle into a deep and sheltered bay. It was christened the Valley of Mercy. "Don't depend on it," the sailors would say. "When you look for it you never find it, and you're sure to find it when you don't." As a result of this reputation, and also because of the fact that the larger sailing vessels could only enter it at high tide, its discreet harbour was hardly used. It was forgotten.

And though today you might hear talk of a Valley of Mercy, no one would be able to tell you where it was. It has become a legend now.

The sailor judges the coast from a distance, aware only of the rise and fall of the land. The fisherman, who sails close to it, concentrates on the shoreline and ignores all that lies beyond. Accordingly, each has his own terms to describe what he sees. Mont-Louis, Gros-Morne bear the mark of the sailor, Manche d'Epée and Anse-Pleureuse are a fisherman's names. When the Valley of Mercy was rediscovered the place was christened Anse Saint-Roch, because the fishermen who spent their summers there came down from Saint-Roch-des-Aulnaies.

In November 1840 a typhus epidemic brought over on an emigrant ship, the *Merino*, swept through the parishes of the Lower Saint Lawrence. The Abbé Toupin, the young and conscientious curate of l'Islet, was not in the least surprised, for he had long anticipated this kind of vengeance from Heaven. The epidemic lasted well into February. He had plenty of time to explain it. His preaching gained him immense popularity. People came from neighbouring parishes to hear him. However, as time went on, the Abbé Toupin's sermons grew gradually more sombre. One Sunday he rose in his pulpit, a strange expression on his face. "Dearly beloved brethren," he cried, "the end of the world is at hand!" And he fell down dead. The epidemic died out soon afterwards. But its effects were to be felt for a long time. The following spring most of the boats stayed drawn up on the shore. Fishing had lost its appeal. The spirit of adventure had worked itself out at home. From Saint-Roch, only Thomette Gingras and Jules Campion went down to the Gulf.

II

After *brecquefeste* the Reverend William Andicotte asked his wife what she felt about Canada. Intrigued, she looked down at the table, but there was nothing there to explain the question.

"William, have you had enough to eat?"

The clergyman pushed his plate aside. He was serious. He expected a reply. Canada, Canada. . . . Well, really, she hadn't the slightest idea.

"God be praised!" he cried. "Then you have nothing against my project?"

"Your project, William?"

"My mission, to be precise. I believe, dear, that Canada has need of us."

Reverend Andicotte was vicar of Liverpool Cathedral. A mournful-looking man with red hair, he could, if occasion demanded, leave off his mournful mien and laugh. Though thin, he had the appetite of a band of fat friars, and while he preached asceticism, he hardly practised it. He was a man of contrasts, unintentionally disconcerting, an eccentric and quite forbidding in his way, yet a good minister for all that, and an astute theologian. The Lord Bishop had named him his successor.

His wife loved him. He loved her in return, as much and even more. For this her love grew stronger still, and time, thanks to this steady increase, had brought them both together. As they never had been very far apart, they were now extremely close indeed. This did not prevent them from having separate worlds. He lived for his church, she for her home. They had three daughters. The eldest resembled her father, without quite managing to be ugly. The others were like their mother. All three were accomplished young ladies.

"But what about the episcopate, William?"

Reverend Andicotte had been waiting for this episcopate for ten years. The Lord Bishop had promised it to him. When the old man died it would go to him. Only for ten years now it had not been the Lord Bishop's pleasure to die. In fact he was looking fitter every year and, if things went on this way, he would soon be celebrating his centenary.

"Fie on the episcopate!"

"Let's wait a little longer."

"The old boy will bury us. No, believe me, dear, it's best we go to Canada."

She believed him, just as she had always done. Besides she was still young enough to find the fervour of mission life more appealing than episcopal decorum. It was with a deep thrill of emotion, wholesome and utterly commendable, albeit unrecognized by the Church of England, that she gave him her consent. She had once been as ignorant of marriage as she now was of Canada, and marriage had not disappointed her.

"Shall I wash the dishes?" she enquired.

"No, no. Just break them, dear."

She did not dare. After twenty years of frugal living some actions were unthinkable. In the end she washed them. It was a bad omen.

III

One month after the fateful *brecquefeste,* the minister, his wife and their three daughters boarded the *Merino.* The day before, on hearing of their departure, the Lord Bishop had died of rage. They were still laughing about it. Seagulls darted above the girls' heads with shrill cries. The Reverend himself showed more restraint. He was escorted by an old and taciturn gull, with neck drawn in and wings starched stiff, belching from time to time just to prove it had a voice. The mother followed behind, slightly dazed by all these birds.

The captain was shaving. He heard the commotion. "What's all that?" He was told it had to do with some clergyman. He rushed out of his cabin and stood in their path, one cheek pink, the other black, his razor in his hand. Against the pink, the black stood out, and the razor became a scimitar. The seagulls fell silent. The old gull, hearing the laughter fade, thought he had gone deaf. Holding back the sound he would no longer hear, he hung there, motionless, above the silence.

"Who are you?" the Reverend asked the apparition.

"And who are you?"

"I am the Reverend Andicotte."

"And I the captain of this ship."

The two men looked each other up and down, then, wheeling suddenly about, the captain disappeared again inside his cabin. Followed closely by his females, the clergyman carried on to his.

"What did you think of him, William?"

"Dear," he replied, "we'll meet with worse than that in Canada."

The *Merino*'s captain was not a church-going man. He had a strong dislike for clergymen, believing that they never laughed. And now it seemed they did. His curiosity was piqued. When he had finished shaving, he went to the Reverend's cabin. His appearance was much improved. They listened to him. He explained himself, and everyone was happy.

"But what were you laughing about?" he asked.

"About the Lord Bishop dying," explained Mary, the youngest.

The captain slapped his thighs. From now on, he decided, he would be an Anglican.

IV

The *Merino* was a former slave ship. Once the emigrants had boarded, the anchor was weighed. The emigrants forgot their woes and set their sights on the promised land. They left behind them a trail of human wreckage, of torn bellies, petrified children, demented souls and severed hands. The sails were hoisted. They were white. The ship left Liverpool, a black hulk borne on by hope.

"I'm the one who gives orders around here," the captain grumbled.

Her Majesty's regulations prevented him, at least while in England, from taking on more than two hundred passengers. Gracious Majesty, perhaps, but stupid regulations; he had already taken two thousand negroes across.

"We might as well sail with no cargo at all, just to amuse the crew."

They set sail for Hamburg. There, another three hundred emigrants embarked. The captain's mood improved: with any less than five hundred passengers on a vessel built to carry a hundred, he would have felt lonely.

"I like having souls, lots of souls, in my charge," he confided to the minister.

The minister praised his zeal, although the overcrowding it occasioned did seem to him decidedly un-Anglican. He did not wish to complain, however. It is advisable not to press a convert too hard. "Besides," he thought, "we'll meet with worse than this in Canada."

V

Jules Campion and Thomette Gingras sailed out at the beginning of May, and two weeks later they reached Mont-Louis. The next day dawned on a sea of infinite calm. It was no good hoisting the sail: it takes more than a piece of cloth at the end of a mast to get a boat on its way. The two fishermen waited for high tide before moving out of the bay, then, when they were in open water, they shipped the oars and let the ebb-tide carry them east. Below Anse-Pleureuse they came closer to shore. A few huge icicles still hung from the cliff, a sure sign that they were too early to fish for cod. They were in no hurry to get there. They got there just the same. A long bright streak, like a shadow cast by the jutting cape above, stretched before them out to sea. Here and there the swirling waters warned of submerged rocks. The tide, though ebbing, was still high. They moved in among the reefs. The hull of the boat scraped a flat rock. Campion stood at the bow and pushed with an oar. The rocks dropped suddenly out of sight beneath them, and they were in the harbour. The valley came into view. Then a single detail caught their attention: from a cabin near the shore, a pale whiff of bluish smoke rose up and disappeared without a trace into the still air.

"Christ!" shouted Thomette Gingras, "they're burning our store of hardwood!"

VI

The joy of departure lasted only as long as the departure. As soon as land was out of sight they began to be sick.

"Bah!" said the captain. "No one dies of seasickness!"

On the fifteenth day of the crossing four emigrants died. They were Poles. The captain shrugged his shoulders: they had paid their passage.

"They're not negroes. They can die when they like. After all, they're free men, aren't they?"

Besides, they had no doubt died of some Polish malady which would not affect British subjects.

VII

In her comfortable cabin on the upper deck, Mrs. Andicotte was overcome by a malaise which seemed to rise up from the hold. If she ventured out, the reeling sky descended on her with harsh, discordant cries, and she was obliged to go back inside and lie down. Elizabeth and Mary stayed with her. She wept for their youth. Jane, the eldest, accompanied her father. She put the word of God before all else and paid little heed to proprieties.

VIII

Typhus is better than the plague. It brings with it a gentle resignation. Violent shivers, with scarlet spots, grip the patient. His tongue is paralyzed. He can no longer articulate his pain, but sings it, softly, sadly, without resisting. He can be thrown overboard before he is dead.

IX

Jane learned one day that Tom, the captain's Negro slave, was dying in the hold. She went down to talk to him of God and fell into the hands of four sailors, who left her, bruised and streaked with tears and grime, alone with the Negro. He crept over to her and, with a trembling hand, wiped her face. Then Jane, observing his charity, was touched. The captain found them together.

X

The spotted shivers took hold of the minister's wife. The *Merino* had been tacking back and forth in the Gulf for a week. She died off Gros-Morne. Her body was brought out onto the deck. Above it Tom the Negro hung from a yardarm.

The captain placed a lifeboat at the disposal of the bereaved family, and the *Merino* sailed on without them to Quebec.

XI

At the sight of the smoke Thomette Gingras was seized with great indignation. He threw himself down inside the boat, rummaged about in the gear, reappeared with a loaded shotgun and shouted to his mate: "Bring 'er in, Jules!"

Jules worked the oars and the boat ran up on the beach. Gingras jumped ashore. Campion got up to follow him. A girl came out of the cabin, young, red-headed, well-built, but very scantily clad. Campion froze in the bow like a figurehead. The girl, just as taken aback as he was, stared, her mouth agape, forgetting to do up her bodice. This oversight by no means worsened things. Campion caught up with his mate.

"Don't shoot," he said. "She looks pretty tame to me."

"What'll we do?" asked Gingras, whose gun was getting him excited.

"Go take a closer look," suggested Campion.

They made as if to step forward. But at the same moment two more girls rushed suddenly out of the cabin, leaving them completely hamstrung.

Gingras, now mightily impressed, shook his gun. "Christ! I'll shoot! I'll shoot!" he yelled, so as to keep himself from shooting. Campion did his best to calm him down.

"Easy now, Thomette! Easy now!"

Just then the girls, who were clustered in front of the door, parted, and a huge figure of a man, dressed all in black, with a shock of red hair, stepped out, a Bible in his hand.

"Christ! What's that?" The figure advanced. It was coming straight for them. Gingras fired. The man opened his mouth, as if he had swallowed the bullet, then pitched forward and fell to the ground, his nose buried in his big book.

XII

At Saint-Roch-des-Aulnaies autumn came and went. The village had waited in vain for the two fishermen. They were presumed drowned. Two years later a boat from Cap Saint-Ignace brought back news that they were still alive, healthy in body but in peril of their souls, consorting with three she-devils. The following spring fishermen in great numbers sailed out from the Lower Saint Lawrence to fish the Gaspé cod. On their return they all confirmed the news: Gingras and Campion had settled in Anse Saint-Roch, each with the girl of his choice and the children born to them out of wedlock, happy, healthy, and perfectly disposed, should the opportunity arise, to take the holy vows of matrimony, and not, by any means, in peril of their souls. Their women were two magnificent creatures, with skin as white as milk and flame-red hair, distinguished ladies, who spoke English like fine society folk. As for the devilry, it was all the work of the eldest sister, a strange, thin girl, red-haired but without the milk, who spent her time reading from a big, black book, while around her hung the black child she had had by Satan before the fishermen had come.

XIII

A single bird a sea-lit day
One lone gull wheeling low
It spins and dives to skim the spray
And what you are I do not know.

Yet surely it is a sign to me
This ocean rose this stemless bloom

Showering its petals upon the sea
And your love makes my senses swoon.

A shimmering veil this dizzy flight
As tenderness reveals its fate
And a wing-tip traces in the light
Your own emerging shape.

You rise new-born from the waters' motion
Wrapped in a mantle of silent wings
Bearing the mark of the ocean
And your name my heart now sings.

Let the lone bird still spin and turn
While God trembles far above
I glimpse your body's nascent form
And know you, Goddess of Love.

XIV

Man is a wanderer. Woman holds him back. A land without
a woman, fit only for passing through, a country uninhabited
because it lacked a place to plant the stake the restless animal
is tethered to – such, for many years, was the north coast of
the Gaspé. Fishermen from Montmagny, from Cap Saint-
Ignace and l'Islet went down there every spring, but they
returned home at the end of the season. No one ever wintered
there. The adventure of Gingras and Campion marked the
end of an era. The French-Canadian woman who triumphed
over the squaw, her rival, in whose arms lay a whole new continent for the taking, was not the kind to give up her men. She
would let them go as long as she could be sure of their return;
otherwise she would go with them. And this was what the

women of the Lower Saint-Lawrence did. Since the Gaspé was no longer safe, they said farewell to the older parishes, to their serene and Catholic countryside. They came down with their men, not for one summer, not to live out some dream of late afternoons beside the sea, but, bundled up to the neck, prepared for all seasons, to give life to the country. Before long, from Méchins to Rivière-aux-Renards, every cove was settled.

XV

Under the cliff, facing out to sea, your house is not large. Your man is brave, but he is not the master. Giants hover over you at night. At dawn the wind cuts down in all its force from the cliff-tops. It passes over your roof like a thousand shrieking birds. You shiver, even in normal times, when you have nothing to fear. But when a child stirs in your womb, you are filled with dread. Why did you leave the old country, where man is master, where the houses are large and the lands small? Why did you follow the fisherman's call to this wild, forsaken bay?

XVI

Jane came to a stop on the beach. She hesitated, her own question taken up for a moment in the harsh cries of the gulls and the unsteady motion of the air. Then she recovered. She had caught sight of her son, playing with shells, surrounded by a flock of ragged and familiar crows. She had arrived here in great distress; then a child had been born and with its angry cry had reassured the whole world.

When the little black boy saw his mother, he left the shells and crows. She took him in her arms and rocked him. She was tired. She would have liked him to go to sleep, but his laughing eyes never left her. Soon afterward his uncles' boat came in. The men threw their catch up onto the shore, then climbed out themselves, happy as children. Jules Campion picked up a stone and threw it. To his surprise it hit a crow. The bird stayed where it was, its wing outstretched, its neck drawn in, its beak half open.

Jane had cried out in an attempt to stop Jules. She jumped up now, but it was too late. Misfortune had already struck. She took the bird in her hands. It stared at her fixedly. She tried to say she was sorry, but she knew that she would never be forgiven. So she let the bird go, and it hobbled off, dragging its broken wing.

Jules and Thomette laughed at her distress. Two days later the little black boy cut his foot on a shell. The cut festered, the woolly head was soaked with sweat. All night the fever raged, and at dawn the shrieking birds swept down from the cliffs to carry off his soul.

Several weeks passed and Jane did not recover from this final blow. One morning, as the sun came up, she was sitting on a log, holding in her lap the huge Bible she no longer read, when she saw the wounded crow. She got up. The bird ran off toward the path that leads to Anse-Pleureuse. She followed it. Every now and then she lost sight of it, but whenever she stopped it would reappear. The path is steep; it veers up over the mountain to avoid the jutting capes. Jane was soon exhausted; her knees gave out. She had come to a burnt clearing which stretched across the path. She looked around her and saw the entire crow nation assembled there to judge her.

XVII

The Abbé Ferland, a professor at the college of Sainte-Anne-de-la-Pocatière, a giant man with a heart of gold, spent that summer ranging up and down the north shore of the Gaspé, baptising, confessing, marrying, bringing with him the peace of God. At Madeleine, with a single stroke of an axe, he silenced the Brawler who had been terrorizing the village. When he left Anse Saint-Roch, Jules Campion and Thomette Gingras had each one taken an English girl, with skin as white as milk and flaming hair, to be his lawful wedded wife. They were the happiest men alive. And they had many more children. As for Jane Andicotte, the Abbé found her half-dead on the footpath to Anse-Pleureuse. He took her back with him. She found her final rest in the convent of the Ursulines in Quebec.

This chronicle records facts that may appear unseemly, but life itself is not always seemly. What counts is that in the end events all fall into place, and around the wild, forsaken bay, little by little, the gentle customs of the old country triumph over pagan fear, softening the cries of the birds that pass in the gusts of wind that sweep down off the land.

THE WITCH AND THE BARLEYCORN

In the Gaspé, la Mi-Carême took over from the Indians, who were becoming very tired and very old: like them, she personifies childbirth, which always disrupts a household to some extent, and she allows it to be explained to the uninitiated, or at least, to be accounted for. For example, when the children come back to the house, having been packed off to the neighbour's for the occasion, the midwife will say to them: "Don't touch your mother; la Mi-Carême has been beating her." This way of expressing things is both discreet and effective, and brings together two figures, the midwife and la Mi-Carême, the one real, the other imaginary, who complement each other and come to each other's aid, each one vouching for the existence of the other. In the same way, the folktale is intimately bound up with reality and can be seen as a form of expression that combines audacity with decency.

A witch would come after my mother at night. The witch was mute and to make herself heard she would moan and cry. My parents' room was on the ground floor between the living room and the kitchen. On holidays it served as a cloakroom and the bed would be piled high with coats. My own room was above it. If I put my ear to the floor I could hear the witch better. I had no idea what the witch wanted from her, but I still felt sorry for my mother. Nevertheless, it's wise to be suspicious of what you hear at night. You can be very wrong, and that had already happened to me once, the time my grandmother had done us the honour of coming to visit from Mont-Louis.

She had been given a room upstairs, near mine. My grandmother was a very distinguished person, with a ceremonious air and disconcerting ways. She had some strange habits, not the least of which was to always drag along with her an enormous trunk. When she'd arrived with the intention of staying a week, my father had laughed: "A week, Mother? Are you sure of that? By the looks of that trunk, I'd say you were never going to leave."

"Oh, I'll be leaving alright," my grandmother had replied. "But when I'm gone, you'll be in a sorry way. You'll be looking everywhere for *la petite Céline.* I'll have taken her with me in my big trunk."

La petite Céline was me, pressed tight against my mother, who reassured me, saying I should take no notice of my grandmother, and adding that it really was a shame, considering her age and how distinguished she was, that she should still be making such silly jokes. Even so, I remained on my guard. I wished I knew what she hid in her trunk.

"She's a real magpie," my father said. "She's been hoarding trinkets in there – odds and ends, little bits of string, any old junk that catches her eye – for half a century or maybe more. She's a wily one too, and she'd like to have us believe it's loaded with dollars and old pieces of eight, just so we'll make a great big fuss of her. But we won't; we'll give her a good spanking instead!"

Grandmother laughed. I was no further ahead, because I still didn't know what she had in her trunk, any more than my parents did. The first night, I forced myself to stay awake, and I listened. That was when I learned that it's best to distrust the noises you hear in the dark and to distrust even more the explanations you find. I had been in bed a long time when I heard my grandmother, with her cautious step, mount the stairs with her candle. She undressed, said her prayers, then opened her trunk. I listened, my heart thumping. Eventually all was silent; she had blown out her candle and lain down in bed, but without closing the trunk – of that I was almost certain.

A few minutes passed in darkest silence. I was on the point of drifting off when I gave a jump: in my grandmother's room a strange sabbath had started up, snorts alternating with whistlings. It didn't occur to me to be afraid. I was too busy trying to understand. And I understood. Or at least I thought I did. The trunk had lost its mystery. Everything was clear. I was overjoyed. I went downstairs to tell my parents of my discovery. When they heard my steps, they pretended to be asleep, he on his side of the bed, she on hers. I didn't go to my father. I never liked finding him there with my mother, in a place he'd usurped and to which I probably had more right than he. It's true, he was good to me; I liked him well enough during the day, but at night he seemed like an intruder; I even found him a little disgusting, this big hairy man, intent on playing the child. I never complained, because I was sure my mother wasn't happy about it anyway.

So I went around to the other side of the bed, and when I was next to her I stood quite still, waiting for her to speak, since I knew very well she was not asleep. There were times when, giving in to her deceit – though without holding it against her, since it was my father who put her up to it, or so it seemed to me – I would grow tired of waiting and go back upstairs to bed, without a word, and as quietly as I had come. As I was leaving I would sometimes hear my mother sigh. . . . But this time I was determined not to give in, and my mother knew it. She said, "Is that you, Céline?" How was I to answer such a stupid question? "Are you sick?" she asked. This was the second of the questions in her pathetic ritual. She only asked them to pacify the horrid intruder, lying there, jealous, in the bed, by her side.

"Mummy, I know what Grandmother has in her trunk."

"Go back to bed, Céline; you can tell me tomorrow."

"I heard everything. She opened it before she got into bed and she didn't close it. And when she was asleep they came out and started chasing each other around the room."

"What are you talking about?"

"The pig and the bird, Mummy. One snorts and the other whistles. The pig snorts and tries to catch the bird. At the last minute the bird whistles and gets away. Then they start all over again and they don't stop. Maybe they're clock-work animals. Come with me: you'll hear them too. Bring your candle – I want to see what they look like."

My father began to laugh. That was the last thing I needed. Why couldn't he have been asleep? My mother and I would have had some peace. He laughed so hard the bed shook. How crude he was! To my surprise, I thought I saw my mother's white hand in the dark; she placed it over his mouth and soon after she was laughing too, with no hint of unkindness, in that gentle way she had.

My parents' complicity alerted me: I had perhaps made a false discovery. Indeed, I was informed that the explanation for the noises lay in another of my grandmother's strange habits, which was to never sleep without snoring, snorting as she breathed in, whistling when she breathed out. As for the trunk, its mystery remained intact. As a result of this, I learned to be cautious and less inclined to trust my imagination, especially at night. It was with some lingering doubt, but based on a whole series of observations, having spent hours at a time with my ear pressed to the floor of my room listening to her groans and her cries, that I reached the conclusion that an affectionate and repugnant witch was visiting my mother and tormenting her in her sleep. I was determined not to bring this up at the wrong time. I would take care to say nothing until the moment was right. The opportunity presented itself one evening after supper when my parents seemed to have less than usual on their minds. To pass the time, they were getting me to repeat clever sayings, as if I was not smart at all, just there to keep them amused. And I told them everything. That put an end to the fun. They realized I was not their little doll. They didn't laugh this time. They gave each other embarrassed looks, then tried to deny what I had said, claiming I had dreamed it all. So I was the one who laughed. My mother cried out, appalled, "Céline!" My father said: "Poor little girl, we were hoping you would never have to know, but now you've found out, what else can I say? Yes, a witch does come sometimes to torment your mother in the night."

He heaved a sigh and added that he was doing all he could, chasing her off as soon as he caught sight of her. This gave me some satisfaction, for it meant not only that I had been right, but also that there was some reason for my father to sleep with my mother, since he was able to protect her better than I.

"But she's crafty. She keeps an eye on me. If she sees I'm exhausted, the way I often am when I've had a hard day, she'll come back and try one more time, knowing I'll have trouble waking up again."

"What is she like?"

"Horrible-looking – with crossed eyes, two holes for a nose, a drooling mouth, and three big black stumps for teeth. But it's not as though she really means any harm. She doesn't come of her own free will. Someone else sends her, and I know who it is. She's sorry your mother finds her so repulsive and she tries her best to console her. Since she doesn't know how to talk, all she can do is moan and whine. She's a pathetic creature."

I asked my father who was behind her, pushing her to come and torment my mother. He replied that it was la Mi-Carême. Madame Marie had told him so, and she knew everything.

"Wherever la Mi-Carême goes, Madame Marie goes too. They don't care for each other one little bit; yet, like it or not, they always meet. Madame Marie was in the house the day you were born, and some commotion there was! She was laughing, shouting, singing, cursing, was la Mi-Carême, with Madame Marie just leading her on, encouraging her to laugh, shout, sing and curse, coaxing her to drink. She even tried to make her dance, keeping her eye the whole time on the big sack – the one that always has a baby inside. La Mi-Carême had put it down by the door on her way in. Your poor mother was sick with fright; she was trying to stay out of sight. Then Madame Marie grabbed hold of her and threw her into the arms of la Mi-Carême: 'Dance, you two, dance!' she cried. Your mother was so brave that she managed to put on a joyful face in spite of her fear; and she danced so well that in the end la Mi-Carême had her head in a spin and thought she was going to faint. She went outside to get some air, and on her way picked up her sack. Quick, we bolted the door. Madame Marie had got her hand in the sack just in time and pulled out the most beautiful baby in the world – that was you, *ma petite Céline*. So, you see, when you want a baby, you let in la Mi-Carême, having made sure to invite Madame Marie before. And it always works, because, as everyone knows, Madame Marie – may the Lord be with her – is the canniest old woman in the whole of the Gaspé."

My father wasn't telling me anything new. I'd learned all this long ago. They'd repeated it to me again and again, at least as many times as I'd been ill. I was beginning to feel tired. My father took me on his knee, perhaps hoping to put me to sleep before we got to the part that I wanted to know. So I said to him: "If I fall asleep, wake me up," and I made him promise to. He went on to tell me how since the day I'd been born – almost five years ago now – la Mi-Carême had not set foot in the house again, always finding the door locked and the shutters closed when she came by. Sometimes she'd rattle the door and the shutters on stormy nights, but never managed to force her way in. She'd always give up and go on her way, with the wind. But as the years went by, she couldn't forget my mother and how they had danced that once, and the more she thought of her the more she longed to dance with her another time. To achieve her ends, she had sent the witch in her place.

"Where she wants to go, she goes, that one; nothing can stop her. She can slide under doors and slip through keyholes. Even if we made the whole house tight with pitch, like a boat, we wouldn't be able to block up the chimney, because then we'd be smoked out; and so, in through the chimney hole she'd come. That's why la Mi-Carême chose her. It was Madame Marie who told me. So how do you suppose we can stop this witch from coming and tormenting your mother?"

There must be a way. I turned to my mother, who was sitting next to us, listening to everything and saying nothing. What was her opinion? She raised her hand feebly to show she really didn't have one. To be sure, someone was tormenting her, but who? She couldn't tell because of the dark. A witch? It might well be, but then it might equally well be a bogeyman.

"Myself, I'd never have known," my father said, "if Madame Marie hadn't told me."

"But you described her to me, this witch! You must have seen her."

"I described her to you just the way Madame Marie described her to me. Judging by the noises I hear – and you've heard them yourself, Céline – I'd say she was not having me on."

He was right, I had to agree. My mother, however, still seemed uncertain. I slipped down off my father's knee and climbed onto her lap to comfort her.

"A witch who slides under doors and slips through keyholes is like a draft that blows; you don't need to be afraid of her."

"I'm not afraid of her; she bothers me."

"Isn't there some way to stop her?"

"Yes," said my father, "by having another baby. Only a baby's crying will keep her away. But what do we do to have another baby?"

Proud of myself, I replied: "Let la Mi-Carême into the house."

"You're a clever one, *ma petite Céline!* But you're forgetting that the reason la Mi-Carême has sent us the witch is because we don't want her here."

My mother was rocking me. I tilted my head and looked

up at her face. She was rocking herself as well as me, looking straight ahead of her at something we didn't see. I couldn't tell what she was thinking.

"Is it really that bad dancing with la Mi-Carême?"

My mother replied that it was no fun at all; she'd had enough the first time and didn't want to ever do it again.

"Then you won't have a baby and the witch will never stop tormenting you."

I don't know what she replied. My eyelids were drooping. Sleep came to the sound of my parents' whisperings. They took me up to bed. In the night the witch appeared to me, looking just as my father had said she did and just as la Mi-Carême had described her to him, affectionate and repugnant. But not once did I feel afraid of her. I felt more sorry for her than anything. I told her she should not speak.

"Give me a baby instead."

She opened her mouth; I told her not to reply.

"You only know how to moan. But you can give me a baby – I know you can."

Then the witch gave me a barleycorn and disappeared. I planted this barleycorn. From it there grew a bright red flower that swayed above me on its stalk. I told the flower I loved it.

"But it wasn't you I was expecting to see."

The flower was mute. All its petals began to part, arranging themselves in pairs to form tens of tiny mouths. Just as I thought it was about to speak, it suddenly burst open. There, in the very centre, was a baby, tinier than a thumb, and the baby dropped into my hand, as though into a cradle.*

---

* The account of the child's dream echoes a scene in Hans Christian Andersen's "Thumbelina."

The next day I woke up, happy. My father had already gone out to fish. My mother gave me my breakfast. She asked me if I had slept alright. I replied that, yes, I had. I was tempted to tell her my dream. I kept myself from doing so, because all this talk of the witch, la Mi-Carême and babies made her uncomfortable. That she was caught in a predicament will no doubt be obvious by now. But she preferred to stay in her predicament rather than talk about it. It wasn't out of resignation. She carried inside her a kind of mystery, which made her unhappy, perhaps, but also jubilant at times, and which she was above all determined to respect. It amazed me to think that one day I would be like her, that I would be a woman then, and she an old lady like my grandmother, keeping her last secrets locked away in a big trunk. She was certainly far more complicated than my father, and it was to him that I told my dream. He found it interesting.

Shortly after that they moved me to another room. They moved my bed, the bedclothes and my dolls to the one my grandmother had occupied, on the pretext that it was warmer and brighter. This room was above the living room. From that time on I never again heard moaning in the night, and this did not surprise me in the least. Hadn't I found a solution to my parents' problem? What more could I hope to contribute in an affair that really was no concern of mine? And I grew up an only child, having had no more luck with my little barleycorn than la Mi-Carême had had with her witch.

AFTERWORD*

BY BETTY BEDNARSKI

ovelist, essayist, playwright, polemicist, and, above all, master storyteller, Jacques Ferron has long been recognized as one of Quebec's foremost writers. A physician as well as a major literary figure, he is without a doubt the greatest physician-writer Canada has ever known. He completed his medical training in 1945 at Laval University and shortly afterwards went to work as a country doctor in a remote fishing village in the Gaspé. After 1948 he lived and practised in Longueuil (formerly Ville Jacques-Cartier), opposite Montreal on the south shore of the St. Lawrence River. In his essay *White Niggers of America* Pierre Vallières has paid tribute to Ferron's contribution to the lives of his working-class patients there, and the doctor showed a similar commitment to the mentally ill, working first with disturbed children at Montreal's Mont Providence and later with women patients at Saint-Jean-de-Dieu Psychiatric Hospital (now Louis-Hippolyte-Lafontaine).

---

* Adapted from the Introduction to the 1984 Anansi edition, *Selected Tales of Jacques Ferron*.

Ferron was also known as a political figure. His name was associated throughout the 1960s, 1970s, and during the early 1980s with the struggle for an independent Quebec. In 1966 he ran as a candidate for the separatist R.I.N. During the 1970 October Crisis he was chosen as a mediator between the government and the Laporte kidnappers. And he is famous as the founder of the Rhinoceros Party, which came into being in 1963 as a kind of political practical joke aimed at pointing out the futility of federal elections. In that party's pranks and antics can be seen the fantasy, the humour, and the sense of the absurd so apparent in the work of Jacques Ferron, the writer.

Even though the writer concerns us most, it is difficult to separate him from the doctor and the political figure. From his contact with the poor rural classes in the Gaspé and with his patients in Saint-Jean-de-Dieu and Ville Jacques Cartier/Longueuil, Ferron gained insight into the lives of ordinary people and deep sympathy for the quirks and foibles of humankind. Death and insanity were familiar to him, and are themes which haunt his work. As for his political involvement, it sprang first and foremost from a desire to write in a land no longer *incertain*. Ferron believed, and his work reflects this belief, that a writer must above all else be true to himself and to his origins, that a work must explore to the full the particular before it can lay claim to any universality. In his writing, the doubt and ambiguity surrounding the lives of his fellow Québécois find expression, yet are at the same time transcended. For Ferron believed too that art, in its way, can change the world, taking reality as its point of departure, then transforming it. His works, while depicting real situations, bathe them in a fresh new light, sharpening their significance and establishing a new order, a new reality.

Many critics are tempted to talk of Ferron's realism. There is in his work a down-to-earth quality, a gallic impudence, which is realism of a kind. There is realism too in the blunt frankness with which he faces death, and, above all, there is that exactness of setting in which he often seems to delight, noting, with care and a kind of loving insistence, names and place names, and names of streets, mountains, rivers. And having identified the setting, he goes on to examine many of the perplexities of modern Quebec: those of a society caught in the painful transition from rural to urban life; those of sons exiled from home, forced off the land and into "foreign" surroundings – outside of Quebec or within its cities; those of a search for identity which often ends in tragic failure, as in the case of the wretched Cadieu, who renounces his ancestral name and ends up not only without a past, but also with no hope of progeny, no future. Yet despite the semblance of realism, Ferron transports us to another world – a world of fantasy, where archangels walk the streets, where hens and dogs converse with people and even trees are capable of thought – the fabulous world of the tale.

The tale is an art we have tended to forget, relegating it as often as not to the nursery. But it has been kept alive for centuries in Quebec, where, in the guise of the folktale, its earliest and perhaps most vital form, it has been handed down by word of mouth, independent of the printed page, from father to son, from one generation of *conteurs* (storytellers) to another. These folktales fulfilled a salutary social function in the emptiness of the New World, bringing people together and providing, with the folksong and the dance, the surest rampart against the rigours and uncertainties of life in a hostile land. They were at the same time the vehicle of popular wisdom and the perfect expression of human aspirations in that rural society. For through them the inaccessible was brought near, the impossible became possible, as, momentarily, in the atmosphere of complicity generated by the tale, the *conteur* and his listeners transferred their allegiance to another world. In Ferron's own lifetime the move to the cities had already resulted in a weakening of the structures of traditional rural society. In Quebec, as in the rest of Canada, the society which took its place was a society in transition, confused and uncertain, a society in search of itself. The folktale ritual had all but disappeared.

Ferron picks up where the folktale left off. He transforms it from a spoken into a written art and broadens its relevance and its appeal. His are tales for the present, providing at the same time continuity with the past. Fantasy spreads from the country into the urban environment. The subject matter is resolutely up to date, though Ferron occasionally offers a bizarre blend of old and new, as in "Ulysses" or "Little Red Riding Hood," where he juxtaposes time-honoured traditional and legendary sequences and elements both inventive and modern, or "Mélie and the Bull," which, in spite of its contemporary setting, draws its inspiration from a folktale of international renown. Much of his material is anecdotal, often relating personal experiences; but in his treatment of it he remains true to the spirit and atmosphere of the tale. He retains many of the formal features of the oral tale: the often enigmatic opening sentence, the stereotype endings, and above all, the recurring lines, the almost ballad-like refrains, which give rhythm to the text and remind us that this is an art still close to its spoken source. However, it is no naive art; it is a highly sophisticated one, often precious, and even, at times, obscure. Ferron delights in the nuance of the written word and explores its every subtle possibility, taking us far beyond the simplicity of the popular tradition. In his hands the *conte* also happily accommodates irony and a strong didactic strain. A piece like "The Dead Cow in the Canyon," for instance, has much in common with the Voltairian *conte philosophique*. Ferron is conscious of his debt to the folktale, examples of which he heard as a child and during those years he spent in the Gaspé; but he shows great independence in his handling of it. It is a vital part of his cultural heritage and as such he has assimilated it and made it quite his own. I know of no other Quebec writer who has achieved such masterful autonomy in this form, while remaining at the same time in such close harmony with its origins. He is a *conteur* in his own right – "the last," he liked to say, "of an oral tradition, the first of the written transposition."

In his lifetime Ferron published two collections of tales – the first, *Contes du pays incertain,* which won him the Governor General's Award in 1962, the second, *Contes anglais et autres,* which dates from 1964. These were grouped together in 1968, along with several hitherto unpublished stories ("Contes inédits"), under the general title *Contes, édition intégrale.* Although from the mid-1960s onwards Ferron would publish mainly longer works, he did not abandon the *conte.* Opening with a series of autobiographical meditations, the posthumous work *La Conférence inachevée* (1987) also contained a significant cluster of stories – those Ferron himself considered as his *contes d'adieu* ("tales of farewell") and, equally poignantly, as his *contes du pays perdu* ("tales of the lost country"). But there are many more besides these. Published first in newspapers or periodicals – the majority in the predominantly physician-subscribed *Information médicale et paramédicale* – many of Ferron's stories never found their way into books. In a 1998 critical edition, Jean-Marcel Paquette has gathered together from various sources a grand total of seventy-one stories, loosely categorized as *contes*.

It is from the 1968 *Contes, édition intégrale,* now a classic in Quebec, that all of the stories in the present collection are taken. They represent the largest selection of stories by Ferron ever to be made available in English and give the reader a fine base from which to review his other, longer works, more and more of which have now appeared in translation. *Dr. Cotnoir, The Saint Elias, The Juneberry Tree, Wild Roses, Quince Jam, The Cart, The Penniless Redeemer* – all of these long works contain themes and motifs already clearly visible in the tales. The tales themselves often point the way to novels. A story like "The Bridge" marks the earliest notation, the first attempt at fusion of elements later to come together so movingly in *The Cart.* In the tales narrative voices abound: there are those that speak with the humour, the fantasy and the timeless authority of the traditional *conteur,* those that adopt the urgency of the polemicist, and those, especially in the first person stories with a contemporary setting, that announce the more personal narrator, disabused yet compassionate, who asserts himself in many of the novel-length texts. Characters, too, first come to life in the tales – doctors and derelicts, clergymen and countryfolk, men and women of the urban sprawl, the simple-minded and the mentally disturbed, and the much-loved, much-railed-at Englishman. Indeed, everything is present in the tales. All Ferron is there. They form a veritable microcosm of his work.

It has often been suggested that Ferron's works spring from the same source, that they conform to the laws of a single genre. And the significance of the tales stems above all from the importance of this genre. Critics maintain, for example, that the longer texts, the so-called novels, are in fact simply longer and more complex *contes*. The *conte* is clearly Ferron's most personal form of expression, privileged in his work as it has been in the culture of Quebec. And, what is more, rich and moving though his longer works may be, there is in the smaller units – the tales here present – a sustained magic, a perfection seldom achieved elsewhere. It is fitting that in 1972 the first book to reach the English-speaking public should have been *Tales from the Uncertain Country*, a preliminary selection of eighteen of his best known *contes*. In the present revised and expanded edition the reader will once again discover Ferron at his finest. The forty-one stories in this new collection contain the very essence of his art.

BY JACQUES FERRON

Les Confitures de coings [Quince Jam] (1972)
La Conférence inachevée [The Unfinished Lecture] (1987)
Vautour Haché [Vautour Haché] (2006)

(With Pierre L'Hérault) Par la porte d'en arrière: Entretiens
[Through the Back Door: Conversations] (1997)

LETTERS

Les Lettres aux journaux [Letters to the Editor] (1985)
(ed. Pierre Cantin, Marie Ferron, and Paul Lewis)

(With Julien Bigras) Le Désarroi [The Confusion] (1988)
(ed. Marie Ferron, Pierre Cantin, and Julien Bigras)

Une Amitié bien particulière: lettres de Jacques Ferron
à John Grube [A Special Kind of Friendship: Letters
from Jacques Ferron to John Grube] (1990)

L'Autre Ferron [The Other Ferron] (1995)
(ed. Ginette Michaud and Patrick Poirier)

Laisse courir ta plume: lettres à ses sœurs, 1933-1945
[Let Your Pen Flow: Letters to His Sisters, 1933-1945] (1998)
(ed. Lucie Joubert and Marcel Olscamp)

(With François Hébert) Vous blaguez sûrement:
correspondance (1976-1984) [You Must Be Joking:
Correspondence (1976-1984] (2000) (ed. François-Simon Labelle)

(With André Major) Nous ferons nos comptes plus tard:
correspondance 1962-1983 [We Will Make Our Reckonings Later:
Correspondence 1962-1983] (2004) (ed. Lucie Hotte)

(With Pierre Baillargeon) Tenir boutique d'esprit: correspondance
et autres textes [The Intellectual Debate Store: Correspondence
and Other Texts] (2004) (ed. Marcel Olscamp)

(With Victor-Lévy Beaulieu) Correspondances [Letters] (2005)